Ravens Rescue

By

Catherine Gruben Smith

Illustrated by

Emilie Gruben

Sola Deo Gloria

"By whom also we have access by faith into this grace wherein we stand, and rejoice in hope of the glory of God." - Romans 5:2

To Emilie:

Working with you is a deep privilege, and I am delighted with your company. Keep growing into the beautiful woman you are creating choice by choice, day by day.

Note to Readers:

Sign language is another language, not just a form of English. A signer thinks in pictures, they sign what they see, not full sentences. I have tried to portray some of the differences in the instances where Joe uses his gloves or is teaching the twins. But throughout most of the book, I translate Joe's dialogue as I would any language: making it smooth and sensible in English, just as someone would do in their mind when watching a signer.

Contents

One Month After Kallipolis...

Joe had just reached the royal kitchens when he came across the first corpse. It was a guard splayed in the entrance, acting as a doorstop. The guard had no weapons out, no laser primed; almost certainly just there to cajole a good breakfast from the staff. The body's merman suit sparkled even in the moon's light, pearly blues, pinks, purples, greens melding in a beautiful dance. But the beauty only mocked the scene. Joe's face was tight as he leapt over the guard and into the kitchens. His speed made the elegant tail of black fabric from his mask trail behind him.

He moved among the dead.

His eyes darted around the room, noting the scorch marks on the ceiling and walls, the way the corpses splayed over their work stations. *A strafing laser,* his mind automatically supplied. Death had claimed them in an instant. He stepped gently, almost reverently, over a portly woman, one arm flung over the remains of her face, a wooden spoon still in her hand.

He moved silently, quickly, efficiently. No one would have guessed how he screamed inside at the senseless death of the kitchen staff. It should have been a normal early morning for them. An ordinary day of gathering breakfast for the Atlantean nobles in the sunken castle. He stepped out of the kitchen into the hallway, slid a pair of galoshes on, and scurried up the wall like a gecko. He glanced out one of the rounded windows as he shifted toward the shadows on the ceiling and watched the green water undulate outside. Joe turned his gaze back to his task. He ran on all fours along the ceiling, his face under his mask hard and stiff.

No alarm had tripped. No one had been alive long enough to manually alert the castle. This heist was planned to perfection. Brilliant and deadly.

A voice reached the mute. He paused in the shadows of the ceiling for an instant, calculating its direction. Then he sped off, shifting onto the wall to stay in the shadows, moving automatically and silently, as if he were a shadow himself. A brighter light increased in front of him, and Joe's eyes narrowed to slits to avoid losing his night vision too quickly.

Two people stood in the doorway of the Atlantean vault. The round vault entrance shed yellow light around the traitors, like a spotlight screaming "Guilty!" A tall woman in a mer suit held out the book. The man took it.

"Be careful with that!" the woman said, her voice hard and beautiful, like an iron bar wrapped in gold.

"Having second thoughts about betraying your kingdom, Miss Athenia?" the man snorted. His white suit shifted along his middle in a way that spoke of too many meals he didn't want to confess even to himself. His blue eyes crinkled as he slid the book into the pocket of his dress coat. Neither of them noticed the soft click of Joe's camera in the shadows, cementing them together in the history of a photograph. It was amazing to take a still picture of a scene, absolute proof of a moment in time. This was a brilliant new invention!

"I'm concerned with the history and delicacy of the ancient document you just stuffed in your pocket," she snapped.

"It was tailored for this bundle, Athenia," the man said, his tone smug. "Simmons will be pleased with this night's work." Joe began to creep down the wall, closer to him.

"Simmons' boss is the one you should be worrying about," the woman said, her voice low and sultry. A certain something clung to it; longing perhaps? Joe stopped stock-still, one hand half raised, staring at her. That tone couldn't be meant to apply to Freddy...

"Freddy?" the one in the white suit asked, incredulity in his voice. The woman looked at him, pity mixing with a deep disdain on her face. She turned her back on him as she swung the vault partially closed, adjusting the dials to erase the fact the thief knew the combinations. Joe's hand moved. But he had done this type of thing so often his mind was only half on the task; he slid the book out of the man's pocket, sliding a sheaf of blank paper in its place, so smoothly the man didn't even notice a change in weight. Joe's mind was on the meaning behind the woman's words. His heartbeat began to speed as he retreated back into the shadows.

Simmons' boss, not Freddy...almost certainly the reason this woman was willing to sacrifice her loyalty, her country, her people, because that creep had promised her...what? Money, love, a new life?

The Wolf.

The Wolf was back. That's why this heist had been planned and accomplished with such easy brilliance! This had to stop. That creep killed and maimed, all for love of money and a vicious love of self. A predator lurking in the dark, planning the next lunge to kill. That's why this heist had happened tonight, the first in almost a year; the Wolf was back.

"Go," the woman said, handing the man a strafing laser. She was removing the evidence from the scene. The man stuffed it in a pocket and hurried off down the hall as the woman pulled a Ruby pistol from her pocket. She put it to her shoulder and set her jaw, her eyes closing. Joe hardly noticed. He barely registered the bright light, the gasping cry, and the smell of burnt flesh from by the vault. He slid back up the hall and dropped to the ground in an empty corridor. Joe slid his galoshes off and ran, putting all thoughts of the enemy away for now. He needed to focus. The mermaid would set off the alarm any minute. Joe had to be outside when it tripped.

The mute watched the windows as he raced soundlessly up the wide, crimson-carpeted staircases. There. Moonlight trickled faintly through that one, instead of the gunky green water of the Atlantean coast. Joe slammed a hand into the latch, his other already oiling the hinges. He pushed it open and salty, wet air slammed into his face.

A wild wailing split through the castle. It sounded like women screaming at the death of their loves. Joe cringed and vaulted feet first out the window, one hand catching it and pulling it closed, as he twisted in midair and grabbed an ornate lantern with his other hand. He hated the Atlantean alarm. It reminded him of too many times he had knelt in the shadows, watching families receive the news no one was coming home.

Half those times had come because of the Wolf. When Joe had been two steps behind, too late, or too helpless to stop it.

Joe began to climb up the side of the castle. Slimy green water undulated under him. But the castle sprawled and spread out in intricate designs. It made for easy climbing. The moon peaked out of the clouds for an instant as he climbed swiftly upward. Joe swiveled, hanging by his left hand and foot as he turned to look. The silver disc gleamed, wispy clouds crossing over her face. Joe gave her a salute. He moved off again, and the moon slid back behind her cloudy screen.

The domed top of the building was covered in the peculiar, pearly scales that glittered on the mer suits. It was beautiful, and slick. Joe slid onto the minuscule edging lying around the dome and dropped cross-legged underneath a white classical-style sculpture of a true mermaid, tail tipped and hair flowing. He pulled the book gently from where he had it tucked under his jacket and looked at it.

Its cover was yellowed with age, crinkling and ready to crumble under his touch. It depicted a man with a tattered shirt, muscles bulging, in a heroic pose with a bloodied knife, staring manfully towards a raging sea. A mermaid swooned in his arms, wearing... Joe rolled his eyes, and opened the cover. His eyes sped over the words, his fingers swiftly turning pages. Sheesh. He turned the pages a little faster, starting to move them in clumps as he skipped sections. Oh boy. Well, this explained quite a bit about the kingdom. Especially the tendency to be highly dramatic about every tiny happenstance. Joe shut the book gratefully. That was one he hoped to never crack open again.

Sunlight tinged the horizon as he flipped off the edge. Joe dangled by one hand. Concrete ground lay six stories under him, but Joe didn't seem to notice. He began to tug a window open with a flathead screwdriver. It slid open with a soft creak and the noise of the panic happening inside flowed out around him. Joe flipped through and landed in the sumptuous royal bedroom. Night clothes lay scattered carelessly in a trail toward the door. The servants had been too scared by the news of the missing book to even pick them up. He padded silently over the hardwood and sat the book gently on the gilt nightstand.

This was one country the Wolf wouldn't send into disintegration. At least not yet. The silly little Atlanteans could live to weep and laugh for another few years.

Joe climbed over the outside stonework, working his way along the darkened patches where he still blended in even with the sun coming up. He glanced in a window on the third story, where the noise seemed loudest. The nobles stood assembled, flighty, panicky, and helpless. The tall mermaid guard sat in the middle of the room. She slumped on her stool, her shoulder bandaged, the image of a hero dejected that she couldn't stop the thief and murderer. Joe wrinkled his nose. But he stayed for a moment, watching her. He knew about Ariel Athenia. He made a point of knowing about powerful people. And with her almost unlimited funds, clever brain, and iron backbone, Ariel was definitely a powerful woman. If the Wolf had her now, he wouldn't bother to keep her long. And spurning a woman like Ariel... The Raven should cultivate this contact. Joe moved down another level, scheming over the best way to open communications with her, shifting to the back of the castle and looking for his man. Ah, there he was.

A smile twitched over Joe's face as he stopped behind the upper branches of a tree to watch the man in the white suit. Ilis coat was off and flopped over the seat of his snazzy hoverer. He half lay over the oval of metal, poking at wires and coils. Let him poke. His machine wouldn't start. Joe had seen to that before he went inside after him. It should only be a matter of time now before someone came into the courtyard.

White Suit straightened. He clucked and shook his head. But he didn't look nearly worried enough. He slid his coat back on and picked up something from the backseat. It looked like a copper colored stick. Sunlight glinted off it into Joe's eye and he blinked uncomfortably. White Suit stepped away from his hoverer and did something with the thing he held.

A sharp hissing wind started from it. Darkness, a deep black, began to grow around White Suit. It whined, almost too high to register, a noise that pierced Joe's brain. The wind whipped around him, sucking and freezing. It pulled him from the wall. He flailed, just managing to tangle his limbs in the tree's branches, as they shook and bent toward where White Suit stood. Everything pulled toward him, as if a frozen tornado swirled around the black ball covering the man. Leaves, twigs, dirt, green sludgy water, it flew toward the darkness forming into a ball around White Suit. The force pulled Joe's breath, tugging at him till it seemed his joints would come apart. His teeth began to chatter at the cold. Now a solid black ball rested beside the hoverer, white zig-zags, like lightning bolts, shooting across it. The whine turned supersonic. Joe ducked his head into his arm, shaking from the cold, clinging desperately to the tree in the midst of a frozen unnatural hurricane.

The branches he clung to swung back in place, bouncing gently as sunlight and birdsong invaded. The wind was gone. The whine disappeared. The tugging non-existent. It was all gone, so suddenly it seemed unreal.

Joe fell back amidst the swaying branches, sunlight and muggy air surrounding him. No wind, no whine, the only cold what was still in his bones. He let himself drop, landing cat-like and shaking on the concrete, staring toward the place.

A hole, six feet wide, stood where White Suit had just been.

The man was gone.

The black ball was gone.

Chaos rested where he had been.

Around the whole debris littered the area. Even the asphalt was pulled up, wrinkled and warped. Joe stood, his joints shaky, his mind humming with the possibilities. What was that thing?! He needed to know more. Joe walked slowly in a circle around it, studying the scene intently, his mind racing. He needed information. This...thing was a huge gap in his knowledge of these people. The more you knew about someone, the more power you had. Knowledge *was* power. Which is why you never let people know about you. Kept them at a distance.

A door shot open just in front of Joe. The mute jerked back, eyes wide in alarm. A merman leapt on him. Fingers closed over Joe's arm, jerking him forward. The merman uniform's scales sparkled in the sunlight and his face twisted in a look of malignant smugness as he pulled the mute closer. Joe went willingly; which should have been a clue for the guard to run. The mute stepped into the man's guard and landed an elbow strike on his ribcage. It sounded like dry twigs snapping. The merman's eyes went huge as he doubled over, his breath going out of him in a sharp woosh, his face twisted with the sudden pain. Joe's knee met his face as he folded.

The sharp crack of the blow rang through the still morning.

Four people in the open doorway spun to look.

Joe turned on his heel and pounded toward the street, silently cursing all mermen and especially spies in white suits. He reached the first of the town's buildings and leapt.

Joe kicked off the wall, landed another kick higher on the opposite wall, caught the edge of the roof, and vaulted onto the tiles. He took off in a run, hunkered just enough it would be hard to get a clear shot at him. Already he could hear the hum of the mermen's hoverboards as they shot after him. The sunlight hit the colored roof tiles and sparkled, glinting into Joe's eyes and making it hard to see anything. Below him he could hear the shouts: "He's on the roof!" "Get the Mangler!" "Call for the Cat!"

Great.

Great, great, great, just what he needed this morning. Joe grimaced as he flipped over the edge and landed running on the next rooftop. Sure he was a strange person in black hang-

ing outside the castle just when their book was stolen but...
This didn't look good. The next roof glinted at him over eight
feet of roadway, hoverers rushing past, leaving steam trails to
add to the stifling humidity. Joe sped up, then arched into a
beautiful leap. His fingertips landed on wet tiles. Joe jerked
himself up without taking the time to grip the edge, and
sprang away like a deer over the next set of roofs. It was a
shame Atlantis prided itself on order, everything symmetrical
and laid out neatly. It made it hard to disappear after being
spotted.

The mute glanced into the street beside him as he slid
down a peaked roof and used his momentum to summersault
onto the next. A pod of six mermen kept up with him easily on
their hoverboards. Their uniform's fins sparked and crackled
as they moved. Their gloves were already charged, just waiting for him to fall off so they could glom him and sting him into submission.

Meow!

The sound broke through the city's noise. Everyone
paused, heads turning and eyes widening. The huge sound re-
verberated in Joe's bones. The mute gripped a peaked roof
and jerked to a stop. He crouched at the top like a new gar-
goyle, stock still except his swiveling head. Looking for the
Cat. This current one's name was "Mangler." It fit.

Mrrow!

There it came again, longer and louder. A deep throbbing purr
started into the morning air. The animal expressing her pleasure at being let free to hunt. Joe's head spun to the left and he
focused on the domed capitol of Atlantis. It sparkled with sea
greens, salmon pinks, deep purples. The inlet running over the
sunken half of the building sparkled almost as brightly, as it
stirred in the breeze. But then the sparkles were blocked to
view. A huge, furred shape set a paw on the roof of the house
beside the capital, then another, then she sprang up onto the
tiles. Sleek ginger fur glistened. Her twenty-foot tail lay behind
her, the end twitching as her green eyes focused on Joe. He

Mangler

could have laid across her skull without his feet dangling off the edge. Her collar jingled. Joe swallowed, his mouth suddenly dry despite the humidity.

Mangler crouched, her tail swishing, her eyes never leaving Joe. He didn't move, just watching the Cat, calculating. The pod of mermen surrounded the house, waiting for him to drop into the street to get out of Mangler's hunting grounds. They began to chant, laughter in their voices: "Run! Run! Run!" The Cat pounced, claws outspread.

Joe moved like a black lightning bolt, flashing by for a moment and then gone.

A huge weight thumped into the roof. Tiles scattered, someone inside screamed.

Mrrow! the Cat said, scrabbling in a circle on the roof, her tail freewheeling to help her balance. The mermen spread out, scanners running hard, trying to find where the quarry had disappeared to. The Cat's ear twitched. She spun again with a sharp hiss. Her ears slicked back and a rumbling growl started in her throat.

Joe, clinging underneath the Cat to the fur between her front legs, knew she had found him out. He wrapped the soft ginger fur tighter around his boots and left hand, took a better hold on his electric prod, and prayed.

A back paw, as wide as his back, slashed toward the mute. Five claws gleamed, ready to tear him to pieces. He struck out with his right arm, ignoring the hot feline scent clouding his senses. White sparks from the prod struck the paw. A yowl came from the Cat, anger lacing it with a deep growl. She spun in another circle, her back paw twitching and almost useless. Joe jammed his prod through the fur onto the Cat's chest and hit the button.

Mangler's hair stood on end and another, sharper yowl came from her. She sprang away, leaping over the tiled houses, heading back toward the domed capital. Prey wasn't supposed to sting like that!

Joe hung on desperately, jolting and almost sick from the

stench rolling into him. He could feel the great muscles rippling as she ran. The Cat arched over a street. For an instant, Joe felt the terrifying nothing under and around him, as if gravity itself had given up on the little mute. Then came the house-shaking boom as Mangler landed, and Joe jerked with the force.

His boots ripped free from the fur.

Joe's feet hit the roof. They dragged over tiles as he still clung to the fur with his left hand.

Claws struck out at Joe. For a fraction of a second they blurred in his vision as he saw one foot coming at him. He struck out desperately, tucking in his legs and swinging toward the Cat's ruff. Most of the charge from the prod hit empty air. And the next claw already slashed at him, as the cat furiously cut and scratched.

A sharp rip sounded on the roof. The Cat screamed, that deep growl still underlying it. The mute arched through the air, his left fist full of ginger cat fur, flailing through the humidity. Mangler leapt, one front paw striking at him as she snapped. Fetid breath, stinking of rotted meat and cat breath, hit Joe like an oven from hell. He gagged and retched. But his right hand was already moving.

He grabbed the paw coming at him.

No dodging, no screaming, no writhing. The mermen pod trailing behind in the street gasped as one man. But Joe was too busy to appreciate the sound, even if he could have heard it. He held onto the top of one claw, barely keeping it from ripping into his face, trying to ignore the way the other four flexed and scrabbled to dig into his flesh. Joe swung his legs up and locked them around the Cat's ankle joint. He shuffled over the claws, his hands a blur, and the cat yowling and shaking her paw wildly. He gripped the pinky claw and used it, twisting himself up. Mangler shrieked again, but Joe ignored it. He was on the side away from the claws.

Fetid breath hit him again. The Cat lunging forward for the kill.

Joe scrabbled up the cat leg, climbing the fur with the agility of a monkey, and a speed even Mangler didn't expect. The Cat's fangs bit down, missing Joe's leg by a fraction of an inch. But biting deep into her own paw. The Cat shrieked and jumped, landing sideways on the tiled dome of the capital. Her paws slipped, claws scrabbling for purchase. Joe raced up her neck till he balanced between her ears, a black figure knee deep in ginger fur. The Cat's back leg slid off the edge. She hissed, fright in the sound. Her other back leg slid off. Joe had time for one glance back. Two pairs of green eyes widened.

The Cat slipped off the roof. Humid, warm air swirled around them. Joe crouched, grabbing a fuzzy, stinking ear; the last thing he wanted was to freefall directly into Mangler's fangs. One hand darted into a pocket and he slipped a pair of goggles on and tucked a miniature diving lung between his teeth.

The Cat hit the water. A plume of waves spewed into the air, dyed green by chunks of algae.

"I don't know why Joe's been gone so long, Nehi," Anna shrugged. She tossed another handful of wild spinach in the salad and looked at the herbs littered over the counter. "Would rosemary be too strong of a flavor, do you think?"

"Rosemary?" Nehi asked, staring at her. "Ann, I'm talking about our safety, in our immediate situation, and you're trying to distract me with rosemary!"

"Excuse me for caring how our dinner tastes." Anna sprinkled a spoonful of thyme leaves over the spinach and turned around, her arms crossing over her chest and her chin lifting as she stared at her brother. He felt himself stiffening, knowing what was coming; that was the same look their mother got every time she told him something he needed to know but didn't want to hear. "You know you don't really believe we're in danger." Nehemiah squirmed and frowned. "We wouldn't have stayed with the Ravens if either of us actually felt it was a dangerous place to be. We could have slid into one of the towns we passed in the Kingdom of the Wise, it didn't seem too unsafe."

"Danger is everywhere out here," Nehi grumbled.

"Yes, but not in these wagon rooms, and deep down you know it. It's not the worry of danger closing in that has you upset, it's the fact you can't explain everything around you." Nehi's spine stiffened like a rod had driven into it, and Anna's hand came up, ordering him to hear her out. "I get it, Nehi. It's obvious Joe's hiding something from us, and it almost certainly has to do with the search for our book."

"Or maybe even finding Daniel!"

"Joe's probably hiding lots of things. And if he's taking the trouble to hide them, it's something we would love to know."

"Exactly!" Nehi burst in. "This is important, Anna, it might mean getting our brother back, and resurrecting our country. We can't restart the Sojourner's Kingdom without our Bible!"

"But, Nehi, Joe isn't going to tell us anything unless he wants to. We need the Ravens. We need their knowledge and their help, and you're jeopardizing that by your pushing and shoving. I... I get the feeling our little friend isn't used to having people he can trust in his life. I think, Nehi, it's going to take time, and prayer, and a lot of patience to win the trust to find out more about Joe's business."

"But I don't want to give it time," Nehemiah almost whined, and Anna hid her grin at his honesty. This wasn't something to indulge.

"Nehi, I like the Ravens. You do too. I like our life here. So do you, I see it in you every time you relax around the campfire, or laugh with Joe, or play music in the mornings. And I've seen what happens when you press Joe for answers; it hurts him too." Anna paused as Nehi's eyes darted to the floor, his shoulders slumping and his frown not just a petulant boy's. He was paying attention now. It had been a full month since Kallipolis, and in that time Nehi had managed to wake the "mad fox" in Joe again. "Both of you are miserable for days after one of the blow ups you cause, and it takes weeks to rebuild a relaxed atmosphere around our little campsite. Nehemiah, stop pushing."

"But–"

"Stop pushing, and wait for Joe."

"But–"

"You know I'm right. This is the only way you're actually going to learn what you want *and* keep Joe as a friend." Anna paused again, waiting. Nehemiah stirred a fallen spinach leaf with his toe and didn't look up. "Can I please get some kind of answer?"

"You sound just like Mom," Nehi murmured, and the words came out wet. A long sigh blew from him and he nodded, still not looking up. "All right, all right. I'll stop pushing, and digging, and just wait. But it's not going to be easy! I mean, he's been gone two full days already! What is Joe up to?"

Chapter One: The Kingdom of Gaia

"We are of God: he that knoweth God heareth us; he that is not of God heareth not us. Hereby know we the spirit of truth, and the spirit of error." 1 John 4:6

Anna leaned against Nehemiah on top of the Raven's wagon. The spring months had tripped lightly past and now, with the summer sun beating down on them, Anna felt like these wooden seats were home. Nehi chatted with Joe, perched on the bench below them, while Beau loomed beside the mute and tweaked Prissy's steering stick. The giant, hairy guinea pig snuffled the air, the leather flaps of her wind-protective helmet flopping. Anna could barely hear Prissy's squeaks; the hoverer's wind bubble was up, encapsulating the whole top of the wagon in its clear diamond-glass and creating a comfortable atmosphere during high speed travel. As they crossed the border of their first major kingdom outside their own (one of the few large enough to actually be a cog in the human machinery of the world) the road changed from rutted, dusty, and careworn to smooth and carefully tended grass. The hovering wagon evened out instead of the dipping and diving it had been doing, and Prissy emitted a happy squeak. Deeper grass ran along both sides of the road, drawing the eye to where the scrubby little bushes merged into huge oaks and hardwoods. The gnarled limbs twisted around each other like a dance frozen in time, overshadowing smaller birches until it formed a forest.

Anna's eyes drooped in the summer warmth. She had stayed up too late last night playing parlor games in the Day Room with the others, and Nehi's thick side was very comfortable. Her brother burst out laughing at something Joe signed, and Anna's eyes flew open again. She forced herself to sit up, knowing she would be asleep soon if she didn't, and listened to the conversation again.

"I guess we're going to need to refill the water reservoirs

pretty soon," Nehemiah commented. "Is there a safe place for that around here?"

"Nowhere in this world is really safe," Joe shrugged, still smiling from whatever joke had passed between them a moment ago. "Except Sojourner's Kingdom. But now that's gone. Nowhere in this world was safe. But we ought to be fine filling up at the river running along the border of Gaia, in the middle of this forest."

"Joe, if you know Sojourner's Kingdom is the only safe place," Nehemiah asked curiously, "why didn't you and Beau just settle there? A good musician could earn a pretty good upkeep, and your artwork is amazing. Why are you out banging around with flocks of satyrs, and green backs, and Guardians..." Nehemiah broke off as he saw Joe's steely blank look. He was going into his rock imitation; if Nehi insisted on an answer, it would be tomorrow morning before Joe signed anything to him. He sighed and forced himself to drop it. Joe was gradually opening up, it would just take more patience on his part.

"Forget it, little friend," Nehemiah smiled, slapping Joe's shoulder in a kindly manner. The mute looked up in surprise. "What?"

"Nothing," Joe signed quickly, though a wide smile crossed his face and a happy something shone in his green eyes. He looked away just as quickly, his gaze becoming troubled. Before Nehemiah could wonder what moved through the strange little person's mind this time, Joe grew busy with the wagon. He increased their speed and pulled up the scanner to double check the steam vents were all open. As the landscape began to blur around them and Prissy gave off her delighted squeals, Joe pulled his whistles out of one pocket. He signed it was time to learn a new song, and handed the twins a sheet of music, lyrics scrawled across it in his poor handwriting. The sounds of the whistles began to fly around the little group, in a mysterious and beautiful dance, as they traveled deeper into the forest. It was a dark, close forest, but with an ancient and settled darkness. Like a grandparents' home, where dimness and mustiness were somehow cozy and spoke of stories from years gone by.

Anna's beautiful voice began to entwine with the whistles as she caught on to the tune. Nehemiah gave a smile and started to sing along, happy and comfortable.

Ten minutes and twenty miles sped by, and Beau hit the brakes. The wagon drew to a sighing stop, and the gnarled old trees leaned over them. Joe pumped the bubble down with one hand as he pointed into the woods with his other. The clear wind protection dropped swiftly into its slit, and the musty scent of decayed plants, rich earth, and growing things filled the twins' lungs. They breathed deeply, relishing in it, as Beau hopped down and snapped the wheels on. Joe slid Prissy's wheeled shoes off the giant pig, tossing them into the cubby under the wagon seat as he vaulted back up. Beau gripped the steering stick and clicked, and Prissy shuffled off into the forest, the wagon bumping over a rough track. Nehi bit his lip and Anna felt his fingers drumming on the top of the wagon. She smiled to herself and didn't comment. After her lecture, Nehemiah had stopped digging.

His fingers kept drumming as Nehi furiously held back the questions. These Ravens knew everything, even tiny side tracks in ancient forests like this. The twins were convinced some of the fund of knowledge came from Joe's strange errands. Whenever they entered a new kingdom Joe disappeared, like that night in Kallipolis. He would always appear again several hours later (in a little mossy country called Atlantis, it was three full days, and then he showed up ravenous and covered in green goop). Joe never explained why. Sometimes he took Cobeau with him, but most often he went alone.

Running water mixed with the sound of Prissy's shuffling, the wagon's creak, and the forest's living rustle. The pig nosed a sapling aside and trundled onto a riverbank. She trilled cheerfully, then crouched to lower her thick head into the water. A little river tumbled and bubbled over mossy stones, willows and oaks leaning over it, ancient roots trailing over the banks. Anna pulled out her drawing pad and sketched the area as Cobeau unwound the hose and Nehi and Joe trotted around, opening valves. A cheerful bubbling came from the hose, filling the cylinders stored between the wagon's ceiling, floor, and walls. Joe tossed a guitar at Nehemiah and the young man dutifully jumped into the new song. It an hour time for the cylinders to compress the water to their full capacity. A good time for music practice.

Afternoon found the Ravens' wagon followed the curving roads through the forest toward the heart of Unity, the capital city of Gaia. The overgrown green of the country began to fade into naturally cut stone as buildings reared out of the forest. A moss covered house rested under a giant oak. A stone wall tumbled alongside a bubbling stream. An ivy-covered apartment house rose gently to stretch along the ground, with trees growing out of it. It was as if the rocks naturally collected and congealed to make the buildings, and Anna had to remind herself the outskirts of Unity really were deliberately fashioned. As they drew into the town, it began to look a little more like a town. The forest faded until it stood sentinel on three sides of the city, while the summer sun shone down bright and hot in the midst of the stone architecture. It was a strange, beautiful place. Moss and ivy crept in and out, creating an aura of stillness and antiquity. A few of the houses were more traditionally wooden, but even they were styled in older fashions and matched the rest of the town. Anna felt it had a restless peace, and mentioned it as they slid along the curving roads. Nehemiah said the townspeople had better clear out the ivy because it was liable to crack the stonework. Joe smiled at them and signed it was time to start drawing a crowd for a show.

Anna dropped into the wagon, walked into the night room, and reached for the bag she kept her clothes in. For a moment the memory of her closet back home, with its shelves and space to hang dresses, resurfaced. She allowed herself a sigh. But that was as far as she would drift into the melancholy memories. She rummaged for a moment and pulled out the red coat Joe had acquired for her. He had popped up one day as she was gathering wild herbs, his arms full of crimson material, informed her that her face was an asset to their concerts, and requested she wear a coat to compliment it.

Now, as Anna shook it out and the double layers flounced, she found herself smiling at how businesslike he was about it. How very different from when Daniel brought her a gift from his travels, filling her head with compliments and pointing out how nice it all looked... Where was her older brother now? Anna prayed, again, that he was alive as she slipped the vest and coat on, flipped her hair quickly into a decent position, and headed back for the wagon top. She didn't let herself dwell on it. But her usual joyful smile was absent as she hoisted herself back into the sunlight. She spotted a flash of green eyes. Spinning her head, she just caught Joe studying her with a calculating sharpness before the mute's face turned away, his expression the bland, cheerful one he usually wore. Anna chose to ignore the look.

Nehemiah stood on the top of the wagon, balancing with practiced ease as he played a tune on his guitar and Joe joined in with a merry fiddle piece. Windows opened in the apartments and houses hemming in the street. Anna took up the melody in her lovely voice and a crowd began to drift into a line behind the wagon, moving at Prissy's shuffling gait. The people here looked vague but cheerful, the twins noted with relief. That was a lot better than most of the places they had passed through. The world was dark and unnerving, and by now keeping a laser near and a wary eye open was second nature to the twins. The curving roads meandered into a large plaza, its mottled stone decorated with interlaced curving lines that tied in and out of each other. Cobeau directed the wagon into it, Prissy circled the plaza twice, giving the large crowd who had followed them a chance to get larger and draw closer, creating a natural stage for the musicians.

"Welcome, friends! Gather near, and allow your spirit to

be awed by the Ravens, musicians of a sort you have never seen or heard!" Cobeau's voice boomed out through the town. The volume he could achieve still surprised Anna. It came as a part of the change in Cobeau at each show. Offstage he was a simple, loving soul who had difficulty following a conversation and so didn't talk very much. He had become very fond of her, and when he wasn't with Joe or busy keeping them all alive, he was usually found at the table humming his tuneless hum, peeling potatoes or just sitting while Anna worked. But as announcer for the troupe, Beau suddenly became voluble and spouted off phrases and clever quips she couldn't have come up with. After the first few shows, Anna realized that Joe coached him carefully. Cobeau memorized his lines for each kingdom. If he forgot them, or needed more, there was Joe. His language was very useful for giving instructions without the audience knowing.

Anna and Joe quickly opened the rhythm makers, as Nehemiah laid their instruments out in order. They had found it necessary to expand their rhythm section to allow Joe and Nehemiah room for their duets, and occasionally trios as Anna leapt in and joined them. It was no longer feasible to lay out the rhythm section as Beau announced the show, so they had created an expansion on the side of the wagon that opened up and was let down for their marvelous creations of beats. Joe playfully tugged a curl escaping Anna's flip, then swept out of the way, making her turn the wrong direction and stare blankly over her shoulder and Nehemiah grin as he laid the whistles in their place. Cobeau grew silent on top the wagon, subtly telling the musicians the crowd had grown enough for the concert to begin. Joe signed for the twins to start with "Mountains in the Mist." He leapt into the rhythm section and stood tense, waiting. Nehi placed his violin under his chin and looked at his sister. All eyes fixed on Anna. She took a deep breath and began.

The song rolled through the square. Haunting words of mist and mountains, a shepherdess lamenting her lost love.

Anna's exquisite voice spun it around the people like a spell of beauty. The last note of the first verse hovered on the air, then dropped gently into silence.

Joe burst into his rhythm dance.

Nehi smiled as the crowd's jaws dropped and every eye opened wider. Whatever else they found in their travels, this seemed to be the universal response to Joe's dance. Anna started up again, and Nehemiah joined her on his violin, occasionally lending his voice where he felt it needed extra harmony. The song ended on a vibrant note, and the crowd erupted. Anna nodded her head graciously at the cheering crowd, wondering at their enthusiasm. They had come across people who enjoyed their music, but never quite this level of shared enthusiasm. Song followed song. Nehi and Joe faultlessly spun and danced around each other. The instruments, voices, and rhythms rose and fell, changed and spun. The crowd grew and swayed. With each additional person, greater enthusiasm filled the audience. As they finished their third encore, the cheering nearly deafened them.

Nehemiah leaned back on the wagon, sweating and shaky. This concert never ended! Wouldn't these people ever let them stop? Night crept over the world, for goodness sake! Cobeau wandered back to the wagon, his third collection bag overflowing. He looked at the drooping, sweaty twins (Joe still looked as fresh as when they had started), swung on top of the wagon, and firmly told the crowd to go home. The audience reluctantly began to file away into the town's winding streets. Anna smiled to herself as she panted and watched them go. They were an odd mix in this Kingdom of Gaia. A man walked in a tall flowing robe and pointed hat, straight and stiff, his hands tucked into voluminous sleeves. There went a lady wearing all colors of the rainbow, her brown hair flying everywhere as if it had never seen a brush. Behind her a young couple walked quietly, their hands entwined, and everything about them looking neat and serene. No, not everything. The set of the shoulders, the way their eyes shifted, that was not serene.

It was the same here as it had been everywhere else they had come so far in this dark world. Every eye lacked peace, every person looked so...so...Anna searched in her mind for the right word. She caught the gaze of a pretty middle-aged woman coming toward her in a long white skirt and a beautiful blue tunic, and found her word. Lost. They all looked so lost. Anna glanced around her, at the Ravens and her brother, busy putting away the concert things. They had chosen the name Vision Keepers for their little group; they had a vision of where they were headed, a clear sight of their real home, and were determined to keep that idea burning in front of them. Heaven waited just beyond their sojourn here on earth. God held them in the palm of His hand, and nothing could change that, and everything took on purpose and luster because of it. Anna turned back to the crowd, watching as the one in the white skirt pushed her way through the people towards the musicians.

These people didn't have that purpose, or that assurance and sight of where they were headed. And even if they didn't voice it, they must know they were missing it. That they were lost even when in their own houses. She caught the woman's eye again. She looked...searching. As if they were looking for something and couldn't find it. *"And ye shall seek Me, and find Me, when ye shall search for Me with all your heart. And I will be found of you, saith the LORD.[1]"* The verse suddenly popped into Anna's tired mind as she watched this woman making her way through the crowd. Maybe she could help at least this one person find what she was looking for.

"That was so beautiful," the woman sighed as she made it to the wagon. She folded Anna in a warm hug and rocked back and forth before letting go and pushing a strand of long blond hair out of her face. She stood beaming at Anna. "I just had to come and tell you how much you thrilled my spirit, young woman! Watching you and listening to you and your friends, I

---

[1] Jeremiah 29:13-14a

 *32*

firmly believe, set me farther up the road of enlightenment."
Anna didn't quite understand it but took it as a compliment.

"I'm very glad you enjoyed it," Anna said politely.

"Enjoyed it! I was so thrilled. I'm Lily Alman," the woman
said, holding out her hand. Anna took it with a smile, liking
this friendly, effervescent woman.

"Anna," she told Lily. Nehemiah stepped up beside her, and
Anna introduced him. Lily wrapped him in the same warm
embrace she had given his twin, and Anna giggled as she
watched surprised embarrassment flood his features. The
next instant they were trying to answer a barrage of questions
they didn't quite understand, about the spirit of their music
and what it was supposed to mean. Lily suddenly broke off to
declare the night seeped into her and she would love a cup of
tea.

"But I don't want to stop our talk, it's such a positive connection, don't you think?" she said breathlessly. "Why don't
you two come with me? You can warm up over a cup of tea. I
have blueberry, and jasmine, and..." She launched into a very
long list as she linked her arms in theirs and began to lead
them down the street.

"A par-tea sounds fabulous, thank you," Anna commented
and Nehemiah grinned at her over Lily's head.

"Satisfaction guaran-tead?" he inquired.

"Oh, I hope you like it though I'm not sure I can guarantee
it," Lily said, a bit flustered. Nehi looked away in embarrassment as his sister chuckled at his backfired pun. The twins
found happiness soaking in as this friendly person dragged
them off to tea. It felt right; that was often how things were
done in their kingdom in the old days. They had been taught
that hospitality and fellowship with whomever God put in
your life was not only a duty, but a delight. It felt homey and
nice to be welcomed so completely by this friendly stranger.
Nehemiah looked back over his shoulder at the Ravens before
Lily propelled them around the corner. Joe and Cobeau stood
watching them. They looked worried. Very worried.

"Watch what you say," Joe signed, and then he was lost to sight as Lily half led, half dragged them into the winding streets of town, chatting over music and tea and snacks. The layout of the streets was very confusing until Anna realized they formed a series of circles, all intertwined with each other and creating a pattern.

"Oh, they connect!" she burst out, and Lily blinked at her. "The roads, I mean. They all connect together."

"Yes, our roads circle and conjoin, till they connect with the large circle encompassing town," Lily smiled. "It's a beautiful picture of life, the interconnectedness of all living things, the formation of one endless being."

"It is pretty. But I prefer straight lines to circles, they get you places faster," Anna said. An awkward silence fell. Nehemiah broke it by pointing at a metal shape hanging from one of the doors they passed; a simple flower with six petals.

"I've seen those all over this country. What is it, Lily?" he asked as they walked.

"It's the flower of life, a symbol of Gaia," she answered. "Have you never heard of the wonderful ecosystem of all things, of the life flow of the earth that connects us all and is drawing us into itself?"

"Um...no. I only know of the small ecosystems God's made, and I don't think I'm particularly drawn into any of them," answered Nehemiah, beginning to feel a little uncomfortable. Lily looked at him askance, and the twins could see the troubled, searching look on her face that Anna had noticed before. It was masked by her cheerful attitude again and she pointed to a very pretty little wooden house painted in a variety of pastel colors. Herbs and flowers and vegetables ranged wild through the yard and nearly covered the walkway.

"Here we are!" Lily half sang, and the three began to push their way around the plants.

"Would you like me to clear them off for you? I used to do a lot of gardening," Anna volunteered, as she stepped carefully over a tomato vine and ducked under a rosemary plant that seemed to be trying to eat her hair. The thought pleased her. A garden wasn't something you could have in a moving musician's wagon. "If you have a pair of pruning shears it would be easy to–"

"No!" Lily cried as she opened her door and let them in. "Would you hurt the spirit of a fellow living thing? I would never prune my plants. They are part of the mother just as we are!"

"Isn't tea made from plants?" Nehemiah asked as he moved into the house, his eyes darting around the interesting rooms. They were filled with a chaotic clutter of things, antiques, art supplies, papers, felted dolls... Strange pictures of plants and animals and people hung on every wall, all twisted and intertwined in a beautiful but slightly unnerving manner. The way the objects in the pictures joined made it look as if they were all being swallowed by an invisible snake.

"Well, yes, it is," Lily answered, as she led them into her kitchen and began to pull tea boxes off the shelves and fill a kettle with water. "But these leaves are gathered after the plants have moved on to the next stage of life. I feel they wouldn't mind sharing their past bounty with us, their fellows." Anna chose not to comment. Instead she pointed to a picture of a wolf howling in violet moonlight, which merged into a skinny boy with a hand to his mouth yelling at something, and from that into a mountain that stood in cold, blue serenity.

"That's very pretty," she said. "Did you paint it?"

"Yes. I find that when I come back from a day where the friction of individuals has disturbed my spirit, it helps to be able to paint a picture of when the individual gods will be gathered together into the one. When enough little gods have gained the right degree of spirituality to catapult the rest into the new age, you know? Then all these material things we see around us will dissolve, and we will all become one great, positive, life-flow!"

"You mean you believe there will be no more individuality

at all?" Nehemiah asked.

"Yes, won't it be wonderful? No more friction, no more one creature hurting another..."

"No more personality, no more conversation, no more friendships..." Nehemiah muttered to himself. His idea of Lily's pictures, of being swallowed whole by an invisible snake, was apparently as true of her belief as it was of her pictures. Anna had latched onto something else and decided to probe it a little deeper.

"Did you say the 'little gods'? What are they?" Anna asked. Lily gave a little laugh of disbelief.

"You mean to tell me you don't even know that? What did you learn in your education? We are all gods. Just like the flowers, and the birds, and the air itself. We are all divine, living beings, evolving into a steadily higher state of consciousness. Of course, some of us are faster at it than others, but the ones farther along the path help their fellows."

"How do they help exactly?" Nehemiah asked, feeling it was probably not a pleasant thing to be "helped" in that way. Anna was still too shocked by a whole people embracing Satan's lie *"ye shall be as gods[2]"* to such a grand extent to say anything. Lily paused and considered Nehemiah's question.

"Well, they deal with the individuals who are not trying to help us into the new age, for one. That way those of us who are not as enlightened won't be scarred or held back in our path."

"They handle outside influences, like trade and immigration," Nehemiah translated, just to be sure he understood.

"Yes, and internal too, the ones who..." Lily's voice trailed off and her eyes darted to Anna and Nehemiah and shifted away in the same second. "Look, the water is hot!" she cried, and leapt up.

---

[2] Genesis 3:5

The Ravens watched the twins turn the corner and disappear amongst the winding streets, the stranger between them. The bright chatter of the crowd slowly unpacking itself and wandering away swirled around them. Neither Raven seemed to notice. They tossed the last few things in place, hopped on the wagon, and started Prissy. The pig gave a shrill little shriek as she began to roll out of town. The Ravens sat silent as they quickly slid out of the stone streets, and into the woods. No road wound here. The light darkened as they went deeper under the hanging boughs, the wagon rising and dipping erratically over the thick undergrowth. After a few minutes, Joe pulled the pig to a stop, shut off the steam, and the wagon dropped gently to the ground. The thick hum of insects and rustling of the leaves took over. A clicking came from Joe, a restless, unsettled sound.

"I don't like it."

"I think...she needs them," Beau rumbled, his big voice slow.

"Anything could happen to them out there. You know how cautious the twins are!"

"Cautious?"

"Exactly, as in 'not.' When they get around people they just talk and don't seem to even think about if the other person might be a danger." Joe clicked again, his forehead furrowed. He spun to Beau. "I'm starting up the scanner to keep an eye on the Recyclers, in case someone reports them. Then I'm going shopping. Want to come?"

"No. I'll keep watch." Beau's giant of a hand waved back toward the town. Joe hesitated for a moment. Then he nodded.

"Thank you," he signed. He reached into a pocket, pulled out a simple ear mic and handed it to his friend. The chimera took it with a beaming smile and trotted off toward the streets; he would follow the twin's scent easily. Joe watched him go, a fond smile on his face. How did Beau always know what he was thinking? The mute hadn't wanted to ask, because it really was a little paranoid of him to have the twins shadowed...but he still felt better knowing Beau would be nearby.

Joe ducked inside the wagon, trotted into the night room and dropped to his knees by the bottom bunk. He pushed a knothole and the whole bottom of the bed flew up, the mattress hitting the back wall with a soft thud. A cavity yawned under the bed, filled with gadgets and weapons. Joe rifled through the tech, idly telling himself he should learn to organize things. His hand closed over a package and he pulled out an object wrapped in black fabric. Joe let the fabric fall away. A black marble statuette of a woman in a toga glittered in the light. Joe's face softened, his expression awed and almost reverent, as he sat back on his haunches studying the exquisite beauty of the artwork. Then he snapped back to work. The fabric flew back around the statuette, he tucked it in his bag, and slipped a black folder next to it. A yellowed, ancient page in a protective sleeve stuck out the top of the folder. Joe carefully slid it back in, hiding the handwritten words scrawled over the antique document. He reached into the back of the drawer to tug out a pile of soft black leather.

Time to get dressed for a shopping spree, and deliver two very special packages to a gallery.

Chapter Two: Seek and Ye Shall Find

"And ye shall seek Me, and find Me, when ye shall search for Me with all your heart. And I will be found of you, saith the LORD:" Jeremiah 29:13-14a

Anna heaved a happy little sigh as she settled at the white kitchen table. Steam curled from her clay mug around her face, carrying the scent of cinnamon and black tea.

"This is very good," she murmured.

"You haven't even tasted it yet," Lily laughed. Anna gave a sheepish smile, but she answered.

"I meant the feeling...it's good to just sit with hot tea, not worried about anything. We've been seeing quite a bit of evil lately, and it's nice to find someone kind enough to invite two strangers in."

"Seeing what?" Lily said, her look puzzled. "Oh, you believe that there is a difference between good and evil. I had almost forgotten the word exists! My, but you are very far back on the path of spirituality, aren't you? But don't worry, with the way music flows through you two, I have no doubt you will move very quickly to a higher plane." A pause in the conversation came. They sipped their tea and looked around them. Anna's eyes went to the painting again, and she suddenly had an idea. She pulled out her leather notebook and flipped it open.

"I do a little bit of drawing myself, Lily," Anna said. She flipped through her pages, settled on one, and handed it over to her host. "When I see something that touches me, I like to draw it. They're different than yours though."

"Yes, more distinct. Not very spiritual, but beautiful," Lily murmured, smiling at the picture.

"Oh, they are spiritual," Anna said quickly, "but it's a different kind than yours. You see, we aren't creatures that will have reality dissolve and our spirits swallowed into a new age of collective nothingness. Instead we are both spirit and flesh."

"That's right," chimed in Nehemiah as Lily pulled back and

stared at her guests. "We are not gods. There's only one God, and He created spirit and flesh and holds them both. Anna's pictures look real, because reality, the world we see around us, is real and important. But they're very beautiful because we serve a beautiful, good God."

"Did you notice which picture I handed you?" Anna put in. "It's of a little boy stealing a cookie. I thought it was cute, so I drew it, but it's not really cute. It's wrong. There is a right and a wrong, and they are different. It's wrong to take someone else's things because we want them instead. But every child does it, or tries to. We are not gods, Lily, and we are not good. Every human is born evil. If you look inside yourself and are honest, you'll admit you've done things that aren't right."

"There is no difference between right and wrong," Lily muttered, her eyes wide and mouth tight. She clutched her brown clay mug to her as if to shield off these two strangers. "I have heard of these things before, of a belief that Gaia is not a oneness force contained in the earth and gathering everything into itself, but is a person."

"A Person who is not of this world," Nehemiah said quickly even though he didn't particularly like to hear God referred to as this Gaia. "But Who created it and upholds it. And Who, in His infinite love, sent His own Son, Jesus, down here. He became man. He became both God and man, in order to do what no mere man could do. He lived a perfect life. It allowed Him to die in our place to fulfill the debt."

"'Glory to God in the highest, and on earth peace, goodwill toward men![3]'" Anna burst in. "If we have faith and believe that Jesus died for us to fulfill our debt and now stands in the gap and reconciles us to God, if we believe it with our whole heart and soul, we will be saved. Saved to heaven. Not a collective oneness, but a glorious melding of all peoples in Jesus."

"Not a swallowing up," Nehemiah said, "but a uniting in a common praise to the One who has saved us and loves us."

"Christians!" Lily gasped. Her whole form shook in fear.

---

[3] Luke 2:14

"Sixty petals?" the voice was outraged, disbelieving. Joe smiled to himself as he hung onto a pipe on the ceiling. It amused him to listen to the haggling. He knew the outcome would be the stranger walking off with the Ruby laser, and paying ninety golden Gaia petals for it. Big Jim didn't take well to hagglers.

"Do you want it or not?" Big Jim growled. He shifted his hulking form as he sat behind his charging station at the front of the store. Neither man noticed a shadow drop onto the floor in the back room. Joe stole up to one of the metal shelves lining the place and began to look over the stock. He kept one ear on the conversation in the front, enjoying the stranger's wheedling. If he kept up like this, he might end up having to pay a full hundred petals. Obviously this was a new customer who didn't know Big Jim. The store lay tucked away in a basement, carefully unadvertised. You had to be a certain type of person to even know of its existence. Even then Jim had to approve you before you were allowed in the door.

Joe stood on his tiptoes and reached into a bin of smoke grenades. He flipped one in the air, testing the weight and balance, and then looked at the manufacturer. Nice. Very nice. He went on his toes again and dug into the box. Smoke grenades began tipping out, tumbling into his soft black leather bag.

"No, it *was* sixty petals." Jim's rumble had turned to a growl. Joe moved on to the next shelf, rifling through the boxes looking for his usual darts to refill his spring gun. Oh, new climbing spikes! "Now it's ninety."

"What!?"

"You're wasting my time here, man," Jim growled. "And my time is important. Got any more to say?"

Joe silently slid the lid off the box of maps, gripped the corners and flipped through them quickly. Ooh, an updated one of the Institute. Very nice. As he rolled the paper and carefully stuffed it in his bag, Joe's gaze fell on a table in the back. A

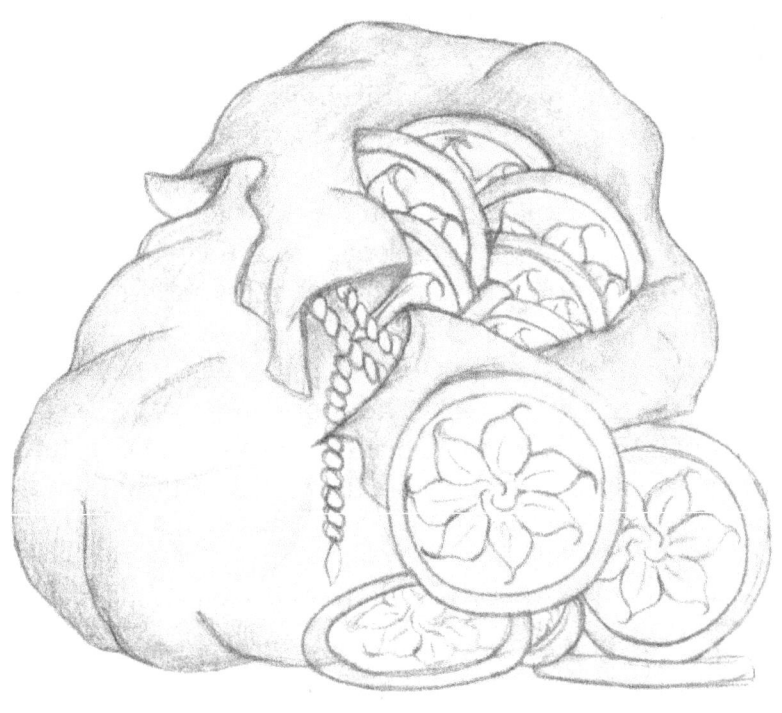

Full Gaia flower gold coins

small box rested there, uninteresting except for the white label on the front. The mute's eyes lit up. He knew that tech company, they had been trying to perfect just one thing for years. He darted over, moving in what was nearly a skip.

"Well maybe I just won't buy it then," the customer said, his voice peevish and pouty. Joe glanced through the open door. Big Jim rose, his seven-foot-bulk towering over the customer. His left hand came in view, and suddenly the bionic arm was in clear sight. The whole appendage started to glow a bright red as the fiber laser built into the arm began to prime. Joe slid his pen knife into the tape on the box, the tip of his tongue sticking out as he concentrated on making no noise. Not that either of those two would hear it with the priming laser whining; that sort of took up most of their attention right now.

"Ok, ok," the customer said his voice shaking. "I'll take it." Joe folded back the box flap and peered in. Pairs of gloves lay in a neat pile, individually wrapped in plastic. Red, white, purple, even yellow stared back at the mute. A slight frown cut over his face. That was no good. He reached in and lifted two of them to look underneath. The plastic crinkled. He winced and darted a look back at the front.

"You want that wrapped?" Jim grunted. His arm still glowed red, reflecting off the shiny metal of the krackmen lasers hanging in a rack behind the pay station. Joe risked digging a little deeper into the box. He spotted black under all the gaudy colors. A grin stretched over his face under the soft leather mask. Joe slid the gloves into his bag and looked at the itemized receipt on top the box; a fair price for selling them wholesale, let's see...

"No, no, I'll take it as is," the customer said meekly. The sound of coins clinking came to Joe as he shifted left, melding with the shadows in the back room and heading to another batch of shelves. The shoulder bag hanging from his arm began to fill as he moved along the shelves. The door to the stairs clicked closed, the bell hanging from it jingling. Joe stopped stock still, listening. Big Jim shifted off his stool. His footsteps thumped over the ground, headed toward the back. The bag's strap slid over the mute's head, drew tight across his body, and Joe scampered up the shelf. He disappeared into the shadows.

Big Jim walked into his back room, the coins clinking in his hand as he headed toward the safe. Young fool, thinking he could haggle as if he were in a fresh fish stand. He only approved that punk because he was a grandson of the legendary Barte Brengum, and the– Big Jim's eyes glittered. The new box of experimental talking gloves stood open.

The bell above the door jingled softly. Jim barreled through his store, his arm glowing red and a furious cry starting in his throat. He skidded to a halt as he neared the door. The cry strangled into a sort of hiss. A small piece of white note paper hung from the bell, oscillating gently in a circle.

As always, you keep a good stock. I left the money at the center.

Jim crossed quickly to the pay center. A pile of gold gleamed in the artificial light of the store, coins pressed into designs from all over the kingdoms. A little smile stole over him. That customer always paid. And always the right prices. Jim shook his head at the oddities of life as he sank onto his stool again and began to count the money. All he asked was one glimpse, that's all, just one glimpse of the shadow shopper! There was a lot here. Two rubies rolled out of the pile and clinked against Jim's dirty white mug. A whole lot. His eyes widened and his smile turned to a frown. He ducked suddenly, his knees hitting the ground and his stool smashing backward into the rack of lasers, making them dance and clack against each other. His hand fumbled in the recess under the pay center, his own private spot. He had made a special trip to the Underground Market last month to get...

It was gone. Jim cursed under his breath and slumped back, sitting on his ankles. His eyes went to the pile of coins,

then darted back to the opened box in his back room. A smile twitched over his face again. It suddenly turned into a laugh, loud and raucous. Oh, why not. Let the shadow shopper have it, he paid for the gadget after all, fair and square. And anyone who could raid Jim's private stash on his way out the door and still leave without even a glimpse, deserved a perk.

In the corner of the room, clinging like a gecko to the ceiling, Joe watched as Jim gathered up the payment and walked back toward his safe again. Big Jim didn't even bother counting it all. Huh. It seemed the store owner could be a trusting soul when he wanted. Joe's eyes suddenly hardened. His focus went to his ear, where the scanner still ran, steadily cycling through the calls coming in to the Recyclers. The gadget was programmed to ignore everything except certain words. Now they rolled in a rush, loud and clear, in Joe's earpiece: "two strangers," "beautiful," "dark curly hair," "Christian." Joe flipped the filters off and listened to the conversation. The caller had heard them in the streets. Others in the apartment could confirm it. The Recyclers were dispatching.

A beep came from the back room; an alert of someone turning onto the stairs from the street outside. Joe slid forward, quickly and silently, through the dark shadows on the ceiling. He lay above the door over a pipe, like a napping jaguar, as the bell jingled again to a customer's entry. Jim strode out, heading back toward his pay center. He gave a nod to Hairy Henry as he went. Joe wondered if anyone in her circle knew her full name was Henrietta. His hand darted out and slid a piece of silver felt between the door and the frame, keeping it from clicking closed. The mute lay and watched, itching to be gone, but waiting.

He had known she would come in today. Joe had timed his visit to Unity carefully. He needed to hear this conversation.

Hairy Henry sauntered toward the row of throwing knives, tossing a comment back to Jim as she went. Jim followed her with his eyes. Henry didn't seem to mind.

The conversation turned to products, then people, then

past projects. Joe lay still, tense and impatient, willing them to get to the only point he cared about. After ten minutes, Hairy moved to the throwing knives, and the subject came up.

"You still playing bodyguard?" Jim asked.

"No, I got tired of that gig. The one they wanted me to watch was an old inventor. Just tinkered away. I had nothing to do."

"I thought it was with...the unmentionable ones?" Big Jim said, one eyebrow rising. In the shadows a grim smile cut under Joe's mask. Not even Big Jim spoke aloud of the FFs. That evil group was too frightening, too shadowy, too powerful even for Jim to speak of willingly in his own shop. And somehow Nehi and Anna were involved...Joe got his mind back on the conversation with an effort. "Seems like you would have plenty to do."

"That's what I thought too," Hairy Henry said, testing a knife's edge on a leather strap. The strap fell in two. "But this old guy, Quintus Leeman, just tinkered. And I got bored really fast. Now I'm looking for a new position. You have anything?"

"I'll see," Big Jim said, shifting his bulk to head toward his hologram machine in the back room. The mute waited till Jim passed Henry, and the lady went back to her knives, still talking in a friendly way to the store proprietor; both of them facing away from the door. Joe dropped to hang upside down, his legs wrapped around the pipe. He sprayed one quick layer of ice from his CO_2 can over the bell's clapper, locking it against the side, levered the door open just enough for himself, and swarmed out to grip the duct work in the outer hall.

Joe scampered over the ceiling, neatly avoided the sensor's eye at the entryway, and dropped to the street. He unsnapped his hover board, hit the power, and dropped it. As he balanced on the board and started to rush through town, one hand shifted to his clicker while the other began to reprogram his earpiece to reach Beau. Joe leaned forward, speeding up. The wind rushed into his face, stinging his eyes till he could hardly see.

He needed to tell Beau to move in.

Nehemiah and Anna sat still, watching their host uncomfortably. Lily shook, staring unseeingly at her cup. A little moan escaped her, and the twins glanced at each other. Intense fear hadn't been a reaction they expected; what should they do next? A deep, hollow bang rang through the house. It came again, a fist rapping the door. Lily looked wildly around her as if she wished she could be swallowed into something right now and not have to deal with the situation.

"Miss Beauty, Nehi, are you there?" a deep voice rumbled from the door.

"It's Cobeau, the announcer from the concert," Anna told her host. "May I go and let him in?" Lily nodded, her eyes snapping around the room without actually looking at anything. She buried her head in her hands as Anna ran out and opened the door. Cobeau walked into the kitchen, seeming to fill the room with his bulk. He looked at Lily, rocking back and forth and moaning, her blond hair cascading around her.

"She's been like that since we told her about Jesus," Nehemiah said. Cobeau's face tightened.

"Ma'am," he rumbled as quietly as his voice could, "you know it's true. If you didn't you would have called the Recyclers." Lily looked up at the big man. Cobeau knelt beside her, sympathy and concern wrinkling his face under his black hair.

"I have to call," she said dully. Her hand shifted up toward her jaw, and Nehi noticed the tiny white scar marking a bone plant. Most people in the advanced kingdoms had them, a bone plant was the easiest way to keep in contact with friends and family, and couldn't be lost like a handheld. He and Anna had been scheduled to get theirs when they turned sixteen (that idea, of course, had been interrupted by the disintegration). So now why were his lungs constricting as she reached for hers? "I must call. You will all hold us back. We cannot go to the new age with individuals like you spreading negative influences–" Cobeau reached out and touched her cheek gently, blocking her reach for the plant.

"There is hope," he rumbled. "There is life. It's Jesus. Believe Him. Know your Creator. Serve your Creator. Be happy." Lily nodded, tears filling her pretty blue eyes.

"I believe," she gasped. "I've heard it before, and I wanted to believe, but I didn't dare. I didn't dare!" She threw her arms around the chimera and began sobbing. He enfolded her in a gentle hug, as if she were a scared child.

"There, there," he rumbled. Joe absently patted Lily's back in an encouraging way, as his eyes swept the room, looking for something. The twins and Lily jumped and she pulled back into her chair, staring wide-eyed at the mute. When had he come in?

"We have to go. Now," Joe signed.

"Why?" asked Nehemiah.

"The Recyclers," Cobeau growled. Lily froze, her eyes widening and mouth parting as fear took over her face.

"Someone heard you in the streets and guessed your beliefs," Joe signed, moving around the kitchen, his eyes darting everywhere.

"How do you know that?" Nehi blinked.

"Who are the Recyclers, and why are they important?" asked Anna, shifting away from the table as she caught Joe's restless mood. Joe ignored both questions, and kept moving, glancing in rooms and even through a few of the cupboards. Nehi saw him pocket a tooled leather bag from the drawer by the sink, and his mouth half opened in protest. But, rather to his own surprise, he closed it again.

"They are part of those on a higher plane," Lily answered. The twins translated the words in their minds: the governing class who considered they knew what was best for the rest of the country. "It is their job to remove those who insist on holding us back from the new age. We–" She paused to correct herself. "They can't have negative influences if they are to cat-

apult the rest of mankind into the new age of oneness with Gaia. So those holding humanity back are sent on to another plane of life." A loud rap sounded on the door. Everyone stopped, freezing as if they had just been bronzed. Joe kicked off a countertop and launched himself at a little string hanging from the ceiling. He swung onto it, his weight dragging part of the ceiling down, lowering him gently so his toes hung about a foot from the floor.

"Knee-High," Joe signed as he hung from the cord. Nehemiah sprang forward and held the trapdoor open. Joe unfolded a ladder from the opening. The knocking rang louder and more urgent. Cobeau motioned Anna up the ladder, shooed the horrified Lily after her, and followed. Nehemiah set his boot on the first wooden rung. A voice rang through the wooden door, and he paused, listening.

"Lily Alman! You are known to have two self-centered humans in your house. They are suspected of being followers of the Way, holding us back from the new age, and will be moved to a different vibrational plane to improve their karma." What did that mean? Nehemiah looked at Joe. The mute drew his finger quickly over his throat, rolled his eyes back, and stuck his tongue out. He recovered from his grisly pantomime and waved Nehemiah into the attic. Nehemiah found himself in a slope-ceilinged, dark attic. Boxes and dusty, unused skeletons of goods filled the place, like every other attic he had come across. It was a room where the we-might-still-use-that items went to molder and slowly decay. Joe scampered up after him, pulling the ladder and trap door closed behind him.

Heavy thumps sounded underneath them, someone hitting the front door. The thumps gave way to a resounding crash as the door caved in. Lily squeaked, and the other four shushed her. Joe pulled a fishing-line-thin wire out of his pocket. He pointed to Lily's jaw and frowned, shaking his head. She stared at him blankly. He refrained from rolling his eyes over the things he had to explain to normal people. Instead he pulled his notepad out and scribbled quickly.

They will track you through your bone plant. I need to wipe it clean. Once you're settled again, it can be reprogramed.

Lily drew in a deep breath, her heart hammering over everything that note meant; her old life wiped clean, a new one reprogramed in... She nodded, her eyes closing and mouth set in a tight line. Joe slid the wire into her jaw and hit the button on the compact control box. The quarter of the wire visible sparked white for an instant, jerking tense as it wiped the bone plant, eliminating the chance it could be tracked. The wire dropped back to a limp line and Joe swept it out, patting Lily's shoulder to tell her it was done. Her eyes fluttered open and one hand went to her jaw.

Tramping boots and heavy voices poured into the little house. Joe hopped over boxes and around crates to where the floor met the outer wall. He leaned forward, listening. Cobeau shifted to Joe's side and stared at him, bow-taut and waiting. Nehemiah glanced at the tense chimera, then back at his friend, and waited too. The sounds began to move to the back end of the house. Joe pulled a cylindrical silver thing from his pocket. It looked like a pen with about ten little copper colored balls packed into its silver fitting. Then Joe pointed it at the position where the roof met the floor and pressed a button. Darkness spread from it. A black cone where no light penetrated. An almost silent sucking wind started up at the same moment. A heavy sense of being dragged toward the darkness hit Nehi, and a sensation of cold whooshed out and stung him. His jaw dropped as he watched a perfectly circular section of the roof pull away in pieces, each one jerking apart and becoming smaller every millisecond, rushing into the darkness. The cone cut off, disappearing. Tiny bits of rubble tumbled to the floor and a perfect hole in the wall gaped at them. Joe grinned and twirled the silver stick in his hand.

"New toy," the mute signed with a brilliant grin as he saw Nehi staring at him slack-jawed, and shoved a note into his

hands.

Knew you'd be curious. It's called a PUDRE, Pulsating Ultrasonic Dark Ray Emitter. I think I'll go for simplicity and call it Dark Ray. I love it!

Dark Ray? Nehi shot a glance at the gadget again. The copper balls were Z shielding, like in Hope, his Compton laser pistol. But his Compton used gamma rays and worked hard not to create dark energy for a black hole, while this... Was that little thing actually *making* a miniature black hole, sucking things into a gravity well?! Joe stuffed his new toy in one of his large cargo pockets of his black slacks, signed Cobeau to lift the others out and Nehi to go get the girls, and slipped through the hole. Nehemiah shoved his questions away, dashed off past the piles of junk, and found Anna with an arm around Lily's shoulders. Their host knelt, one hand over her mouth as she tried not to sob. Nehemiah took her arm and pulled her to her feet, herding Lily and Anna back to Cobeau. A breeze, laced with rosemary and lavender, swirled through the gaping hole Joe had created.

"My house!" Lily gasped. Beau's hand went to his lips as the twins desperately shushed her. The voices underneath them rose up, loud and angry, and they really didn't want to be noticed.

"You have a better one in heaven now," Anna whispered to Lily. She cut it off as Cobeau took her in his arms and swung her out the hole.

Chapter Three: A Token

"Jesus answered, My kingdom is not of this world."
John 18:36a

Anna tried not to yell as her feet hit the ground with a jarring pain. Wiry fingers shot around her arm and pulled her behind an overgrown rosemary plant. Joe flashed her a grin as he dropped her arm, holding a finger to his lips for silence. He motioned her deeper into the jungle of a garden, signed for her to wait for the others, and disappeared. In a moment Lily, Nehemiah, and Cobeau joined her. Cobeau flicked a finger at the fence impatiently, and Anna began to creep toward the road. No outcry came from inside, no laser beams burned through her heart. She slid through the slats of the wooden fence and darted for the corner of an apartment building, ducking around it to get out of sight. Anna pressed against the stonework of the building, waiting for the rest to make it. As the others clustered around her she noticed they smelled of a delicious mix of herbs and vegetables.

Joe popped out of a side street and motioned them to him. They ran to follow, and he began to run too. The five of them dashed down one silent street, and then another, past the dark houses and looming trees. Anna's boots jarred against the cobblestones as she careened through the half circle street, chasing Joe's back. She could see where their street merged (no streets in this town ended, only merged) into a single circle, the city center. Joe flung out an arm, his soft leather boots digging into the rocks, stopping himself in the deep shadow cast by an overhanging apartment building. Anna careened into him. Lily slammed into Anna, her skirt tangled in the ladies' feet, and the two of them went down. Nehi twisted just in time to ram arms outstretched into the wall instead of into the pile of ladies. Beau just stopped, rocking on his toes for a moment as he sniffed the air. Lily hadn't been practicing on Joe's rhythm makers. She was gasping and reeling after their run through town, and gratefully stayed on the ground.

"Wait and watch for __." Joe signed. The twins didn't understand his last sign, but they assumed he meant danger. Joe stepped out into the light of the single lamp hanging from a pole. Something twirled around his fingers. Nehemiah snapped Hope's goggles over his eyes and blinked twice, zooming in on the thing. An intricate metal cross twirled and danced on a chain as Joe shifted it in his hand. Nehi zoomed out again to see the whole scene. A man stepped out of a doorway and came toward the mute. Nehemiah flipped the latch open on Hope's holster, his fingers hovering over her stock. The stranger held up another little metal cross, and Nehi breathed again and whipped the goggles off, clicking them back on his holster. Joe turned to the group in the shadows and motioned Lily toward him, an encouraging smile playing over his sharp face. Anna threw her arms around the former New Ager and lifted her to her feet.

"Goodbye, sister!" she said.

Lily hugged her quickly, so tight Anna's ribs ached. Then, her back straight and head high, Lily began to walk forward, running a hand through her tangled blond hair. Joe met her and pressed a silver, folk art cross into her hands.

"Is this mine?" Lily asked. Joe nodded and winked encouragingly. She glanced at his neck where his jacket collar had been crumpled and pushed down by the events of the night. "Oh, you poor thing, you're a GI!" she burst out. "Do you know what you did in your past life to become that, so that you can avoid it in your next?" Joe laughed his merry, silent laugh.

"You have a lot to learn," he signed, and then handed her the tooled leather bag he had taken from her kitchen drawer.

"This *is* mine!" Lily gaped. "My savings! How did you–" Joe cut her off with a grin and a swift motion at the stranger. He clasped hands with him quickly and warmly, and darted back to the others. The foursome watched as Lily and the man moved inside the little house. The door closed behind them. Silent darkness, almost tingling with danger, pressed in around the Vision Keepers. Cobeau sniffed.

"They're almost here," he growled.

"Where?" Joe signed.

"Everywhere."

"Wait, we're surrounded?" Nehemiah asked. "So what do we do?" Joe looked around him, sizing up their options, his green eyes bright. He pointed at an open window three flights above their heads.

"Are you serious?" Anna hissed. Joe scrambled onto Beau's shoulders, leapt to the second story windowsill, found a toe-hold in the side of the wall, climbed up to the open window, and slid inside. It took him about four seconds. Anna and Nehemiah stood gaping as he leaned out and motioned them up. Nehi caught the hiss of steam hoverers and tramping feet. He grabbed his sister and hefted Anna toward Beau. She scrambled up to the chimera's shoulders, gripped the second story windowsill and clambered onto it. Nehemiah hauled himself after her, and the two of them reached down. Beau's great hands engulfed theirs and Anna bit her lip as her fingers dug into the rough bricks of the apartment house, trembling in the effort of holding on with his tremendous weight. The chimera lodged a toe on the sill and his dragging weight left as he found a hold. All three perched on the little stone windowsill, afraid to move.

Joe clucked at them, pointing to his handhold. Anna couldn't see anything there, but she closed her eyes and reached for where he was pointing. Her fingertips found a tiny crack, and she used it to pull herself up. She gasped as Beau and Nehi pushed her and Joe pulled her into the open window. Nehemiah followed just behind her, and he and Joe began to heave Cobeau up. As they pulled him in over the sill, two hoverers whizzed into the half-circle of the street below their window. Joe's hand slammed into Cobeau's back, his big friend hit the ground, rolling into Nehemiah and Joe and taking them with him. The sharp thunk of their landing rang through the apartment house, and Nehemiah blinked away stars. A clock

ticked on the wall to the left, above a leather couch. Someone shouted an order in the street. The measured tread of marching boots rang on the stones, mingling with the sharp hiss of hoverers. The four friends waited, listening to the sounds of their pursuers pouring into the town circle below.

Light flooded the room, warm, yellow, and instantaneous. A startled squeak strangled in Anna's throat, her whole body snapping around to the doorway, her right hand automatically flattened, ready to smash into any threat. She froze, staring at the man standing in the door, his chubby finger still on the switch. It was the fat, red-haired man who had spoken up for Nehemiah the night of the disintegration. It felt so long ago. His blue eyes were round dots, enclosed in flab. It made it hard to tell what he was thinking as his gaze shifted from Anna, standing ready in a karate stance and her eyes open wide in alarm, to the pile of men on his floor underneath the window. They rested on Anna again, and he smiled.

"I think I know you, don't I?" the man said. His voice was friendly and almost flippant. Anna took heart from the tone and gave a shaky smile as she straightened.

"Yes, we met in Sojourner's Kingdom last year," she said, keeping her voice quiet. "I know this must be very strange for you–" A voice from outside the window interrupted her.

"Fredrick? Is that you up there?" the voice called. The fat man stepped toward the window.

"Excuse me," he said politely as he leaned over the three men lying underneath it. "Yes it is. Hello, Leon," he yelled back. Nehemiah and Cobeau scrambled away, deeper into the room. Joe stayed where he was. "Out on another hunt with your Recyclers?"

"Yes. Have you seen anyone?" the voice called up. "I know you don't care about these little matters, but I would appreciate any news. There were at least three of them."

"No, I've seen no one all night," Fredrick lied easily. "So sorry, my dear fellow, but I think they must have given you the slip." Person began to call to person through the streets, as the steady hiss of steam hoverers slid past. Fredrick closed the window, shutting out the sound of the Recyclers, and turned to look at his visitors.

"Thank you, sir," Nehemiah said, standing beside Anna. "It was very kind of you not to give us away to your friend."

"I like to be kind, my boy," Fredrick beamed. "I am whenever I get the chance. It will be a few minutes before you can leave; won't you sit down?" Fredrick motioned to the couch as he headed for the door. Joe came in sight as the man moved. His spring-action dart gun glinted in the light as he gripped it, his strange new PUDRE sweeping the room in his other hand. His bright eyes never left Fredrick. The fat man's steps faltered, his hand coming away from the doorknob as he stared at the mute.

"Good heavens, lad," Fredrick said. "You don't need those out. Weapons are so very nasty, don't you think? Such cruel, cold things." Joe just looked at him. A blank mask covered the mute.

"They're leaving," Cobeau rumbled, standing to the side of the window where he could see out without being seen. Joe stood up, his weapons ready in one hand, and moved toward the door. He shook Fredrick's pudgy hand gravely.

"You're welcome," Freddy said, smiling at Joe in his friendly way. Joe shooed his companions toward the door. A brief, flustered thanks stammered from the twins, and they followed him out, down the stairs, and into the night.

"Why did you let them leave, boss?" Simmons drawled. Fredrick heaved a petulant sigh and settled farther onto the leather couch.

"Because, Simmons, the little fellow held a nasty looking primitive gun and a PUDRE. You realize that interesting gadget only came on the market (a very, very select market) last month? And have you seen the price of those things? Even in the black markets under the Kingdom of the Wise the cost would give *me* pause. How did a little ugly GI get one? I didn't like the look in his eye. Besides, it might serve us just as well. You have one of your men following them?"

"Yeah, Mark. He's my best at tails," Simmons drawled. He leaned back against the doorframe, his supple form limp, his manner bored. "But I don't get it. Your trick of leaving the window open worked, it drew the runners in. Then you just let them go?"

"You idiot, we want to find the treasure the Hillsons have. Tailing them might work even better for our purposes than just capturing them, though that will do if you don't find anything. Go and join Mark. If they don't lead you to anything interesting in a day or two, persuade the two Hillson children to come back with you. I'll be thinking about a way to get that little beast out of the way so we don't have to bother with his sharp eye and disturbing new gadget, but if you could manage it around him, do so. We've got to know where they are hiding that treasure of theirs."

"You mean *you've* got to know," Simmons smirked. He spun on his heel and stalked into the night, a smile twitching over his face. He could make the hoverer ride back here with the boy and his sister last for a few hours; he would enjoy that time.

The Vision Keepers darted in and out of the shadows, staying out of sight as much as possible as they moved through Unity. Joe and Cobeau knew every street, side street, dead end, and alley. They neared the edge of town, and the mute suddenly disappeared into a tiny alcove jutting out of their alleyway. Nehi rocked to a stop, blinking at the hole in the street and wondering if he had to follow into that darkness...he didn't like dark, tight spaces...not since Abid. Joe crawled out again, his black clothes a little dusty. A bulging shoulder bag lay against his back, the strap across his body holding it tight. The mute sneezed, then darted off again before Nehi could form a question. The twins followed, winding on into the streets.

Ten more minutes and they were out of the city and moving into a dark wood. Huge hardwood trees stretched into the sky and obliterated the stars. Their branches splayed out at the forest top, interlacing, and fighting for light. Tillandsias thrived everywhere in the twisted branches. The night was black under those trees. Anna and Nehemiah expected a wood at least a little like their own at home. Instead dense undergrowth covered the ground. It caught at their feet and held on, tripping and clinging. There were plants everywhere, competing for what little could be found in the overpopulated ground, choking and starving each other. The ones that didn't survive littered the ground along with the underbrush, jutting up unexpectedly and catching at toes. After only a few feet into those woods it was too dark to see anything. The small group linked hands to keep from losing each other. Cobeau took the lead, and moved straight and true, as always. He had a marvelous sense of direction and could find a path anywhere. He found one here, even in the midst of all the dark chaos, and led them to the wagon. The four scrambled quickly on top to get away from the ugly fight covering the floor. The moon broke through the clouds and filtered through the branches to turn the world a dreamy silver.

"Who was that we left Lily with–"

"Will she be all right?"

"What bag did you grab from the alley?"

"Why did you pull your new Dark Ray on that Fredrick character?" the twins blurted breathlessly as they dropped to their seats. Joe grinned, his eyes lighting up with excitement as he held up a finger to tell them to wait. The mute swung the bag around, dug inside, pulled out a pair of black gloves, and slid them on. His hands moved swiftly, but in the night with the black gloves, the twins couldn't make out the signs. A computerized, male monotone broke through the dark.

"I go shop. Got new gloves," it said.

"Won't last long," Beau said, his big head shaking.

"I try again. Maybe gloves work better now," the monotone said, speaking Joe's signs.

"Neat," Anna commented, and she could see Joe's teeth gleam as he grinned.

"Last question first. I no trust people who lie that well. I used to lie, a lot. I no trust me then either. I find better to be slice," the gloves said. The twins blinked. Cobeau started to chortle.

"Prepared," Joe signed doggedly, and the gloves said correctly. "Better be prepared around those I no trust." He kept going before the twins could ask more. "C with a brother, a member of IDP."

"What's the IDP–" Nehi asked quickly.

"Will she be all right?" Anna interrupted.

"The International Discipleship Program," Cobeau rumbled. When Anna and Nehemiah still looked blank, Joe started to sign, the gloves speaking in their monotone.

"Being Christian illegal in most countries in world because the truth of shoulder–" Joe broke off, his lips pursing. "Truth of chest," the gloves said. Joe whipped them off, slapped them hard against the wagon top, whisked them back on, and tried again. Beau's deep chuckle wrapped around them, and Nehi fought hard to keep a grin down. "Truth of Christ almost always runs contrary to human ideas, and human ideas set up kingdoms. Of course that no stop people from following shoulder." Joe gave a huff, slid the gloves off, whistled for translation, and sped off with the chimera translating faultlessly. "No one can stop God from calling who He will. So, the Christians gather in secret. The IDP is the Way underground, a whole kingdom in secret underneath the other kingdoms. Christianity is not a territorial kingdom set up from a book. It's founded in a living person, Jesus Christ. This world needs a kingdom set apart on His word (you have no idea how much

A Token
John 18:36a

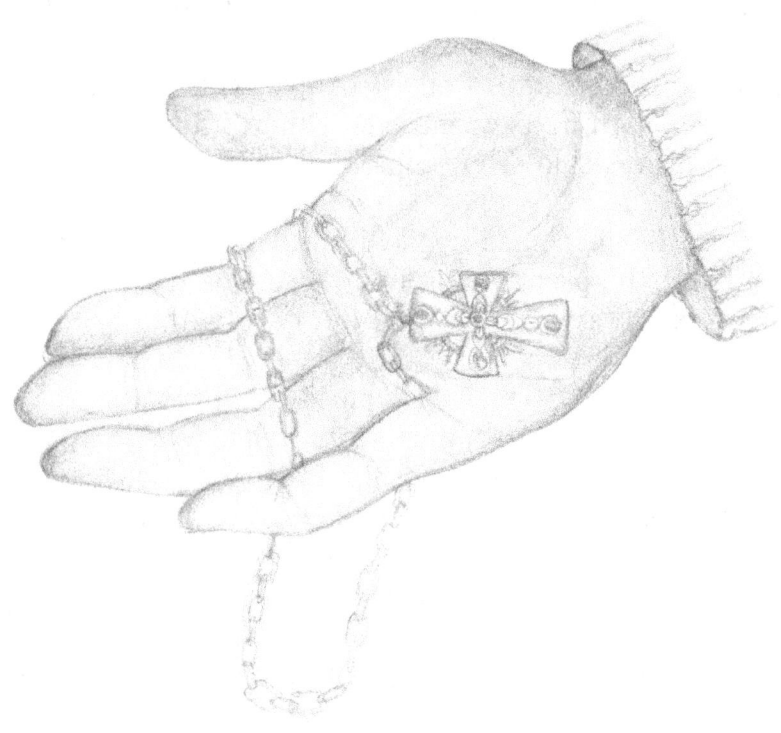

IDP Cross

we need it yet), but the country is not the Way. Jesus is the Way and everything is His territory. That man with the other cross was an IDP member."

Joe reached up to his neck and pulled a silver chain over his head. He held his hand out and the twins leaned over, looking at the piece of metal gleaming in the moonlight. A folk art design raven, cawing in mid flight, stared back at them. Joe pushed the center of the raven, the round circle of the bird's chest. The metal moved and shifted in the light, clinking musically as it changed shape, forming into a folk-art cross. Joe pushed the button again, and the raven came back into shape.

"Everyone has their own design to mask what we really wear," Joe signed, and swept the chain back over his head. "But the crosses are the same. It's an easy way to tell who is a friend and who isn't."

"So you're a part of this underground group?" Nehi asked, just to get it all clear.

"We Ravens are occasionally used as their messengers," Joe signed with a nod, and Beau rumbled. "We're some of a few who can cross through the wild lands without dying, so we take messages, and help a little back and forth between the IDP branches of the different kingdoms."

"Is that what you're doing when you disappear when we come into a new kingdom?" Anna asked.

"Sometimes," Joe signed with a facetious smile.

"Why haven't you mentioned this group to us before?" Nehemiah asked, feeling a little slighted.

"You asked about Lily," Joe signed, turning the conversation deftly to something he knew the twins desperately wanted to know. "The IDP will help her change her name and start a new life, so the Recyclers can't find her. She'll be loved and discipled, and I think she'll be very glad of the change in her lifestyle."

"Lily is better than she's ever been. She's forgiven," Cobeau said as Joe finished. There seemed little to add to that comment, and Anna and Nehemiah sat still for a few moments trying to put together everything they had just learned. As they sat still, however, they realized how tired they were. And how cold the night had become. Joe noticed too and flipped one of the seats over. It had a metal casing on the other side, and the Ravens sometimes employed it as a fire pit when they camped on the top of their wagon.

"Good idea," Anna heard Nehemiah say. She yawned and leaned against Cobeau's side. The chimera patted her head happily. She smiled as she listened to Joe and Nehemiah laughing and talking as they gathered firewood from the forest floor below. It was fun to try and guess what they were talking about from Joe's sound effects and Nehi's words. A minute and a half later, she slumped fast asleep against Beau's broad side. The others only waited to get the fire going, and then were quick to follow her example. Soon the little band lay asleep on the top of the wagon in the forest of the Kingdom of Gaia, feeling safe and content.

But even Joe and Cobeau didn't know everything about the wide world they moved in.

Moonlight broke through the forest in patches, and it lit on wild people scurrying toward the wagon. Each sap-covered hand gripped a sharp rock or club, and they swarmed through the trees. Their eyes sparkled in the light of the dying fire as they watched the group sleeping in their woods. As consistently as if the many people were one organism, only one look showed on those wild faces: livid anger.

Anna stirred in her sleep, unease seeping through the dense blackness. The feeling grew and began to include sounds that were not from her dreams. Angry voices she didn't recognize, Cobeau roaring. Nehi's hoarse shout, of pain and fury, scattered the heavy sleep. Her eyes shot open. Swirling images of color and motion filled her vision and she blinked hard, pushing herself up from the wagon top. Bother

her sluggish mind! For the hundredth time, Anna wished she could wake up like a normal person. Another blink, and she registered more. Nehemiah staggered toward her, one arm clutching his side. He stumbled to one knee as Anna shoved herself up. A ringing, wild shriek rent the air. His arm collided with her stomach, and Anna fell back on the wagon top, her brother sprawled over her.

The air left her lungs in a whoosh and she lay and blinked. A man's dirt smeared face snarled over her. Black hair flew in filthy strands around his face and only thick mud covered his chest. His grimy hand swung into her sight as he raised a gnarled tree branch over Anna's head. His nails were long and filthy, more like claws. Nehi grunted and squirmed as thuds and thumps rained. Blows. Clubs hitting her brother as he protected her with his body.

Anna woke up all the way.

Her hands shot out, latching onto the wild man's ankle. She jerked, twisting out from under Nehemiah and throwing herself backward. The man shrieked, his foot jerked from under him and his arms freewheeling. His club slammed into two more wild people, dropping them on the wagon top. Anna jabbed hard at the man's ribcage. He pitched off the wagon top, shrieking again as he scrambled to catch himself. The club tumbled from his grasp. Anna snatched the weapon as it fell and she spun on one heel, a shout lifting from her as she swung it hard, ramming it into the wild forms crowding over Nehemiah and pounding on him as he tried to get to his feet. The people fell back a few steps, snarling as they began to circle the twins. Nehi staggered up, gasping and bruised. He snatched Hope and slid beside Anna and the two of them stood back to back, rigid and staring.

Wild people were everywhere. They drooped from tree limbs like a fungus, and danced along limbs to drop onto the wagon top like a hoard of angry insects. A mass of them rolled on the undergrowth just beside the wagon; Cobeau's growls and muffled bellows drifted from under the mass. There were so many of these people!

A deep thump rang from the wagon top as Joe landed beside the twins. His jacket was still off from sleeping, and even in that moment it seemed strange to see him in the sunlight with just his sleeveless turtleneck and slacks. Blood dripped from a cut above his eyebrow, his face was paper white. But his green eyes burned. Every vestige of his humor was swallowed in a taut battle rage. But there was apology there too, as he stared at the twins. Just a glimpse of him, then he launched himself in an arching fury of blond hair and black clothes at the whirling mass of people on the chimera. Shouts and screams rent from the forest floor, but Anna barely heard it. Three wild forms charged her, screeching like birds of prey, sharpened rocks and clubs swinging. A shout ripped from Anna as she whirled her club at a knee-cap.

Nehemiah cracked his fist into a sap-smeared jaw as he swung Hope up, his mind spinning as he analyzed options. A high-pitched roar pierced the air, and he spun toward a new form racing toward him, staff raised. The laser leveled at the woman, black hair tumbling to her waist, a short dress of woven tillandsia vines curling around her. She stumbled in her mad race toward him. The fury melted off her face, color draining till she stared at him with wide, frightened black eyes. Two heartbeats pounded in Nehi as he stood, Hope leveled, calculating.

The rush paused, and Anna swept her club up, jaw squared as she stared at her attackers. The wild people stumbled, every head turning to look behind her, and she caught a glint from Hope's barrel. It was only a second, a breath, as Anna stood in the pause and prayed for wisdom for her brother. He had a choice to make.

Nehemiah's mind raced as those two-heartbeats pounded in his chest. There were too many of them. A grazing shot on this woman would hit two behind her and kill them. Death was the only option if he used his laser. He could kill fifty, maybe eighty, before they were overwhelmed. But they would

be overwhelmed. It wasn't a chance, it was just a waste of life. Hope dropped, pointing at the wagon top.

A gray blur flashed in front of Nehi's eyes for an instant. Blinding, black pain struck his head. He felt himself go limp, toppling forward, as his mind shut down. Anna's arms shot around him, and the darkness closed out everything.

Anna threw herself back, shoving her foot against the wagon's railing, muscles spasming as she forced Nehi's limp body away from the edge. Dang, he was heavy! Out of the corner of her eye she glimpsed Cobeau, roaring out of the wave of attackers, rearing up like a primal monster from a sea. Joe spun and kicked beside him, a black blur with a blond tip. Anna won the struggle and Nehemiah tipped backward toward her. She stumbled with him, gasping as she tried to cushion his fall. For an instant she glimpsed a young woman, red flowers woven into a vine dress, black hair tumbling over her shoulders. She stared at Nehemiah, her staff held in listless fingers. Her hands rose over her head and she clapped twice.

A cry, fierce and keening, poured from every throat around the four friends. Wild people swarmed Anna. The sun blotted out, crushed by the weight of people. Sweat dripped on her, the stench sent her mind reeling. Nehemiah was jerked away as hands grabbed her, too many to count. Bodies crushed into her. The weight, the smell, it overwhelmed her. Anna's consciousness spun away into a dark whirl of nightmares.

Chapter Four: Natropia

"And the LORD God took the man, and put him into the garden of Eden to dress it and to keep it." Genesis 2:15

Something hard rammed into Anna's stomach. She gasped and folded over the thing. Green leaves swam into focus as her mind began to come back. They fluttered under her. She blinked, watching the leaves as they moved. No, she was moving. And the leaves were under her. Anna closed her eyes tight, listened to her pulse pound in her head for five seconds, and opened them again.

She lay on her stomach on a large pole, her hands and feet bound below her and another vine tying her in place. The leaves fluttered all around her, layers and layers, merging into a green and brown mass. She couldn't see the ground. Anna lifted her aching head and saw more leaves. She turned to the left. Joe's small, wiry body dangled over the pole beside her, his feet and hands discolored from the vine bindings. Blood, drying slowly, covered half his face. He saw her looking at him and managed a smile and encouraging wink. The pole jerked and he winced and closed his eyes. Anna swiveled her head and saw Beau. He was bruised and cut, but pulling against his ropes, rage playing over his big face. He growled something about people that hurt his friends and a tight smile crossed Anna's face, glad to know at least one of her companions was all right. She ducked her head and looked under her arm. Nehemiah lay over the pole on Beau's other side. He lay limp, swinging with each movement of the branch. She watched him for a moment. His chest rose and fell, the breath coming in and out of his lungs. Anna's tight stomach loosened a little.

They were all here. All alive.

She turned left again and looked past Joe this time. Wild people in the trees moved the pole from hand to hand, carrying it through the treetops. As she watched, a young man (at least that's what she thought he was, it was hard to tell through all the dirt and tree sap) didn't get his grip well enough. The pole slipped down dangerously, then jerked to a stop so hard it made even Cobeau stop growling for a few seconds.

"Watch out, Nightleaf, do you want them to fall?" an older man grunted. Anna's eyebrows rose in surprise as she understood him. Which was funny because when she thought of it, there was no reason why she shouldn't. Everyone spoke the same language, all the variations in tongues had died out when humanity went on the run two hundred years ago. It just seemed that people this wild in appearance shouldn't use the same language as she did. Well, if she understood them…

"Excuse me," Anna said, as they were moved off again. Her stomach felt sick, and her chest crushed in this position. But she managed to sound fairly polite. "Excuse me?"

"What?" the older man grunted, as he helped pass the pole to twenty women standing on a branch over his head.

"Where are we? Who are you people? And where are you taking us?" Anna asked.

"Natropia, Natropians, and to Natropolis."

"Oh," Anna said, not much enlightened. She paused as the pole jerked again. "Why are we being taken to Nah…Natropolis?" One of the women answered, her voice sweet and gentle.

"For judgment, my dear. You and your friends hurt much plant life crashing through last night." Joe opened his eyes and looked at the woman. The pole jerked. He closed his eyes and carefully lowered his head again, his sharp face sharper with pain.

"Excuse me, but my friend and my brother are ill," Anna said. "Can't you please do something for them?"

"They destroyed many plants last night, burning them without mercy," a man spoke up in a harsh growl. "And judging from the weapons they both held, they've probably maimed and killed animals their whole lives. Why should we have mercy on them?"

"Now, Daylight," a plump elderly woman chided him, "we don't want to scare her, do we? We are almost to Natropolis, pretty one, now you be quiet and wait." Anna obeyed. The pole swung and shifted, always going up. Anna's head hung down, her lips pursed, as she fought the nausea from the awkward motion. The pole shifted to new hands, heaved, settled, and began to move at a steady, even pace. Anna drew in another breath and forced her head up. They were being carried over a platform made out of the intertwined, living branches of trees. Eight large men, muscles bulging, carried them along a pathway of three intertwined, thick branches. The branches connected to others, and those connected with more, making a series of interwoven pathways and platforms of tree limbs. Some of the woven circles were small, and some were larger than Anna thought possible for such a creation. Anna's neck muscles ached and she let her head dangle again.

They were moving over a thicker pathway of eight wide boughs when she began to hear the yelling. Hundreds of voices, all talking, shouting, chanting. She craned her neck again and looked forward. Three humongous trees grew close together, their smooth bark shimmering in the few rays of sunlight escaping through the higher boughs. Their branches had been carefully laced and woven together to form an intricate, beautiful platform, large enough to hold a large group of people. In fact it held a crowd. Hundreds of wild people milled between the huge trunks, animals scattered amongst the people. Most of the creatures were at home in treetops; cats, sloths, coatimundi, monkeys. But Anna noticed several dogs in the mix, and even a small deer. They reached the platform and the yelling billowed around them. Anna tensed, watching the people leaping up and down, shaking their fists at the four friends tied to the pole, the roar of their voices rattling her insides.

The men carried the pole through the crowd toward the edge of the platform, and Anna swallowed, her throat tightening as she watched. Two enormous tillandsias hung just off the platform, their twisting green limbs shooting in every direction, and their bodies at least seven feet wide.

Creepers wound in and out of the twisting shoots.

The creeper has deep green ivy-like shoots, almost black, sprouting from a bulbous body. It feeds on other lives. Its shoots sense movement and catch the lizards, birds, and whatever hapless creatures come close enough to grip. It strangles its victims and draws them into its bulbous, slimy interior to be absorbed into a part of itself. If a creeper touches you, it never lets go.

Anna's limbs were suddenly jerked back, and before she could register exactly how it happened, she was free, standing on wobbly legs, and being shoved toward one of the tillandsia cages. Two large men stepped forward, their arms covered in a thick white slime. They gripped a patch of the creeper on one of the bulbous cages and pulled it back far enough for her to fit through onto the tillandsia's body. The creepers tingled, trying to squirm away from whatever substance was smeared on the jailors. A hand shoved her, and Anna stumbled forward onto the plant.

The tillandsia shook and oscillated under her. Anna stood in the middle of the cage, her lips pursed in concentration, matching her weight to the plant's movements and forcing herself to keep her balance. If she stumbled anywhere close to the edge the creeper would grab her. And she had little doubt the screaming crowd of wild people would be delighted to see her squeezed to death by the plant. Cobeau staggered in and rammed into her. Anna gasped and grabbed his arms, trying to hold him still. The tillandsia swung wildly at the big man's weight. The chimera stood blinking, stumbling and murmuring Joe's name in a worried monotone. Anna gripped him harder, and dropped down to sit on the plant, smiling up at her big friend in an encouragement to do the same, her heartbeat pounding in her ears. He dropped to his knees. The plant shook, bouncing up and down, and Anna strangled a squeak in her throat. If they fell... Beau sat huddled beside her as the plant's movements began to slow. Anna breathed again and squinted through the creepers and twisted green shoots.

A tall, black-haired guard jerked Joe off the pole and the mute stumbled to get his feet under him. The guard rammed a hand into his chest, shoving him into the other cage; a razor-leaf tillandsia. There was hardly a surface without a knife-edge shoot sticking out of it, and the creepers were so thick Anna could only see in through brief patches as the plant moved and squirmed. Joe leapt and skipped onto the tillandsia, keeping his balance like the dancer he was.

Pain pulsed white instead of black in Nehemiah's head. Greens and browns, and a chanting, angry crowd drifted to him. For some time, other images and sensations had been drifting in and out. But just as he would begin to regain a sense of himself, his head would move, and it all swirled away into the black pain again. But this time the black didn't overtake it all. Hands grabbed him, jerking him off his sore stomach, and he could see...something. Nehi tried fuzzily to bring the world back in focus as he pitched off a wooden platform onto a razor leaf. Whip-chord taut arms shot around him, and he felt Joe cushion the fall as he smashed onto his back. Something sliced down his side and he heard a sharp hiss spill from Joe. The mute pulled him away from the sharp thing, and a loud, chanting yell pulsed around them. He felt Joe levering him to a sitting position and helped as best as he could. His best wasn't that bad, he was relieved to find. After a few seconds of sitting still, he looked around and registered where he was.

"I seem to have missed something," Nehemiah murmured, one hand pressed against his side where a thin line of blood trickled from a cut. Joe grinned in relief at hearing him speak normally, and slumped into a crouch beside him.

"Be glad you missed it," Joe signed. Nehi looked at him, forcing himself to focus through the fog around his brain. The mute's back and arms bled freely from about eight long cuts; Joe deliberately chose that in order to keep Nehi from the leaves and creepers. The mute smiled and pointed at a particularly grubby Natropian. "I am never having a pinecone war again, look what happens if you get too much sap on you!" he signed. Nehemiah laughed, and it cleared the last of the fog from his brain.

"Maybe it's something from the sap that gets drawn into the blood," Nehi answered with a painful grin.

"Seeps into the brain and corrupts," Joe signed, nodding with mock seriousness. It was a ludicrous action with the dried blood caked to him. The mute's eyes lifted, staring through the cage, and Nehi listened again. The crowd's chanting yells quieted, as if something was about to happen they didn't want to miss. Joe and Nehemiah looked out from between the vines and razor shoots. A woman walked toward them, a crown woven out of some sort of fur perched on top of her matted black hair. It was the same woman Nehemiah had held at laser point on top of the wagon. As she walked, the crowd parted around her. The wild people chanting and waving their fists caught sight of her, and slowly brought their fists to their side, stilled, and watched with a quiet deference that held both affection and respect. Silence spread with each step she took. The woman stopped in front of the two cages. Only the barking of a dog and the wind in the trees broke the stillness.

"I am Lightstep, guider of the Natropians," the woman called to the four imprisoned friends, her voice carrying, clear and sweet. She pointed at Anna and Cobeau. "You have illegally entered these lands, killing many plants in your wild run through the forest, and with your great wagon. You have harnessed a beast, enslaving her free spirit for your own ends." Lightstep pointed at Nehemiah and Joe. Even the dog quieted, and silence dropped around them, as the crowd stood still and staring.

"You are both guilty of like crimes," she pronounced, "but added to those you have taken plants from where Nature placed them and mercilessly burned them for your own use. This crime, this defamation and disturbance of the balance of

Nature, is of the worst crime you can commit. Your companion too, was guilty of this and when he was charged with his crimes, he slew many of our people with his weapon." Lightstep held up a Tolen 43. A ray of light caught the excimer laser rifle and made its black carbon stock sparkle. "He has paid for his crimes! He will lie where Nature let him fall and will return to the Nature we all spring from. It is you that we must decide what to do with now. You also had the chance to use your weapons and destroy more of Nature's children. But you chose not to. You chose life. I must consider this choice and weigh it with your crimes." Lightstep turned and spoke to the crowd. "I will be left alone with the prisoners. You have no more part in this. Go about your business, and let Nature be your guide." The crowd began to disperse, leaving only the two white-smeared jailors to guard the prisoners. Lightstep motioned them farther back, out of hearing, and stood still. A sloth dropped off a tree branch onto Lightstep's shoulders and she began to pet it absently as she stared at Nehemiah.

"Why did you spare my life?" Lightstep asked abruptly.

"I looked into your eyes and saw the likeness of my Creator." Nehemiah's voice rang out clearly, conviction strong. With a little start Anna realized it was his old voice, before their parent's death. No, that wasn't what surprised her; she heard their father ringing in his words. It was Nehemiah without the boyishness and pride. Only the truth remained, a man who knew where he stood, and lived out his convictions. "And I realized your death wouldn't help us escape your people," he added honestly.

"Creator? We are all formed randomly by Nature, she does not create," Lightstep said, her dirt-smeared brow crinkling. She stayed focused on Nehemiah as she gently pried the sloth off and helped it drop to the ground.

"No, I mean God. He created nature along with everything else. I mean Jesus, my Savior and friend." Lightstep looked interested, and a little puzzled. She ordered Nehemiah to go on. He did, willingly, and for ten uninterrupted minutes he told her of his God who created and saved. Nehemiah was just beginning to relate his words back to Natropia, explaining God had created man as keeper of the woods and creatures and not their equals, slaves, or destroyers when Lightstep held up her hand for silence.

Lightstep stood still, her head bowed and lips pursed, thinking. The movement of the creepers whispered around the tillandsias, as the vines slunk and twisted, trying to get at the living people inside. A breeze fluttered past and the thick vines creaked as the cages swung back and forth.

"I cannot let you go free," Lightstep said, her voice reluctant. "You have desecrated our laws, and the people will not let you leave." Joe gave a little whistle, and everyone looked at him. He sat cross-legged, his pale face lined. Joe smiled innocently at Lightfoot, and she looked back toward Nehemiah. But Cobeau turned and began to talk to the sloth in a low voice. The animal gave a little shudder of pleasure, every fiber focused on the chimera.

"Roll over, little one," he rumbled. The sloth happily rolled in a complete circle in its slow, methodical way. Cobeau nodded and smiled at the funny little thing. The animal shivered delightedly and gave her odd little call. Lightstep stared at Cobeau in shock.

"You are not a mere human," she murmured, awe shining on her face. "There is a part of you that connects with the great and innocent creatures. Natropians envy the animals for their closer relations to Nature, and you...you are like one of them." Cobeau said nothing, but continued to murmur to the happy sloth. A slight click came from Joe, so slight only those who knew him well could have said where the noise came from. Cobeau looked up and stared at Lightstep.

"Yes, I am chimera. There is a beautiful strand in me that connects with the natural creatures, and even to nature itself," he rumbled. His voice was the dramatic one he used when announcing their shows, and Nehemiah and Anna glanced at Joe. The mute sat signing, his movements small, secretly forming the words the chimera spoke. "Necessity drove us into your woods, for we were pursued by evil. We looked for nothing but peace and safety in Natropia. We had no other companions than what you see here. I am chimera, closer to nature than you, and I tell you we did no evil to your land. Go now and tell your people this, and release us from this unjust punishment." Lightstep hesitated, but her eyes were wide as she stared at Beau. Joe's signs became more animated, and Beau took the hint. He rose slowly to his feet, stretching up to his full height with his great shoulders squared, towering over the frightened Lightstep. "I am chimera! Would you ignore the words of one who is so much closer to nature than yourself?"

"I will go," Lightstep murmured. She darted off, leaving the four companions to pray and wonder if the sudden status of chimera friend would be able to save them. A stronger breeze stirred their hanging cages and the VK tensed and swayed with the tillandsias. The deep green creepers twisted around the great shoots. Anna's skin crawled as she watched. The breeze began to die, and the cages grew still. And then the noise of a crowd began to drift to them. The companions lifted their heads, trying to see what was coming.

Natropians poured toward them in an immense crowd. But they no longer shook their fists in anger. Now they murmured in awe. The two jailors didn't need Lightstep's order; it seemed the will of the moment ruled mainly here. They stepped forward, the creepers squirmed away from their white smeared arms, and the four friends were drawn out by many willing hands. The touch was gentle now, and careful, as they were lifted up and carried across the platform, shouts and murmurs filling the air in a senseless noise. The crowd streamed toward where a stroke of lightning had hewn a great hole out of an even greater tree. As the VK's boots thunked into the living wooden platform Lightstep swept out of the jagged hole in the tree, her eyes focused on Beau.

"What do you wish from us, chimera?" she said, respect almost dripping from her. "You have only to ask."

"I want my Joe to be better," he rumbled in his normal, simple voice. One huge, gentle hand ran down Joe's hurt face, his own big hairy one pained and troubled, as if the scalp wound and deep bruise were his. Lightstep clapped her hands and called for their healer.

"We will return you to the hairy pig and your wagon, but you must go with my people to do this," Lightstep told Beau. "They will need to know she is willing to serve you if they are to leave her in your care, chimera." Cobeau looked at Joe. The mute nodded slowly, painfully.

"I will go," Beau said reluctantly. "But watch Joe for me? Please?" Lightstep smiled at his gentle concern, and nodded. Joe turned to Anna.

"It takes two to attach Prissy's harness well," he signed. "I'm not sure I'm up to another trip through the trees just yet, Beauty, and I don't think Knee-High is either. Will you please?" Anna pursed her lips and looked at Nehemiah. He managed a weak smile. His head pounded so hard he could hear it, and any time he moved it the world spun and nausea boiled in his stomach. It made it hard to smile.

"Do you mind?" he asked quietly. Anna turned without a word (but with several unconvinced glances back at her twin) and followed the waiting group of Natropians back toward the wagon. The two boys found themselves alone with Lightstep in her tree house. They sat in silence and waited. Neither felt inclined to conversation, and Lightstep seemed to like the quiet. The rustling leaves and the steady creak of the branches around them soothed the silence. A soft knock sounded outside the tree. Nehemiah looked up to see another wild-looking man stooping to peer in. He was about thirty, and held a woven grass bag, the roots of the living grass resting in a shallow oblong of plastic filled with water. Lightstep motioned him in and pointed at the two boys. The man began to tend their hurts. He was remarkably good for someone who lived in a tree. After about twenty minutes, he repacked his bag, stood up, nodded at his patients, and walked out again. Nehi rolled his head slowly. Whatever the goop the doctor had stuffed in him and on him, it worked; he could move without everything blurring. Joe leaned over and poked Nehemiah.

"Translate, please?" the mute signed. Then he turned to Lightstep and began to sign slowly enough Nehi could follow. "You spoke of a companion. Who was it?"

"A brutal man who delighted in killing," answered Lightstep with a shudder. "He followed you into the wood and made your track a scene of carnage. It was his deeds that made my people so angry. You and your friends bruised and sometimes broke when you came through the underbrush. But he crushed and mangled on purpose, out of delight in seeing Nature's own destroyed. His end was just." Nehemiah wondered how it was just to kill a man for killing plants, but in his present position he decided not to argue it.

"You say he followed us?" Joe and Nehemiah said. Nehi tried to make Joe's words sound natural coming from his mouth, but he did a pretty poor job. He had never been good at acting.

"Yes, he came from the large town carved of rock, where you also came, a little after you arrived. Another followed him, and they stopped to speak. I crept closer through the trees to hear, for I did not like the looks of the men, and feared harm to my people."

"What did they look like, what did they say?" Nehemiah didn't need Joe's eager signs to ask quickly.

"The one who came second was tall and cruel in appearance. The one who came first (short and also cruel, but of a more brutish kind) termed him 'Simmons,'" answered Lightstep. "They spoke of judges and children, and of a treasure. The tall one went back to the place of carved stone to gather more like themselves to take the judges and children back with them." Joe began to sign again, but paused, his head tipped as he listened to something. Footsteps raced toward them. Lightstep rose to her feet, alarm beginning to cover her pretty face. A young man burst in, his chest heaving.

"You are needed. Come quickly, guide!" he gasped, his face pale under the dirt. Lightstep followed him at a run. Their footsteps faded and quiet fell again. Nehemiah and Joe looked at each other. Foreboding crept down Nehi's spine.

Chapter Five: Flight Through the Trees

"The God of my rock; in him will I trust: he is my shield, and the horn of my salvation, my high tower, and my refuge, my saviour; thou savest me from violence." 2 Samuel 22:3

Silence fell over the platform, not even a breeze rustling the leaves. Nehemiah touched his aching head gingerly, glad of the moment's peace to just sit still.

Joe grabbed Nehi's arm, his fingers biting, jerking him to his feet and away from the opening of the tree. Nehemiah turned with some heat, to tell the mute not to do that because it shook his head. But then he saw his friend's face. Joe stood rigid, his green eyes wide with horror, his breath coming in scattered short pants, his hand still biting into Nehemiah's arm. Nehi followed his horrified look, and froze.

A man walked along the platform. He looked from side to side as if he were searching leisurely for something, a little smile playing over his thick lips. Nehemiah knew that smile. It came back to him in his darkest nightmares. That man standing over him, waiting to gratify his appetite for cruelty on Nehemiah; the slave, thrown into the soundproofed room, weak, desperate, and utterly helpless to stop the torture from happening.

Simmons was near again.

Both boys shrank against the side of the tree. Simmons' firm, hated footsteps came closer. Nehemiah frantically wished these Natropians hadn't taken his laser. They could hear Simmons talking now, half to himself, half to the one he searched for.

"Come out, come out wherever you are," Simmons said, sick amusement playing under the words. "Where are you, little Hillson? You're wanted. You didn't really think you could get away from me, did you boy? You're mine. You always will be, as long as you live. And we've got to hurry or this place might just swallow us like it did poor old Mark." Simmons stopped over a pile of shining junk, the Tolen 43 glinting on the top. He clucked gently, shaking his head as he picked up the gun. Joe's grip tightened harder as he saw the laser rifle rise in Simmons' hands. "Poor old Mark. Didn't get out when he knew he should." He swung on one heel. His dark eyes fixed on the hollowed-out tree, the Tolen pointing straight into its gloom. "Didn't get out did he, boy? But what about you?" His footsteps thumped over the platform, coming nearer, and there was nowhere to go. Nehemiah quaked, paralyzed with an old fear he could not shake. That voice, that step, it cut into his strength and put him right back as the helpless slave he had been for so many months. He glanced at Joe from lowered lids, cold sweat dripping in his eyes, and saw the same terrified paralysis.

"Jesus, help!" Nehemiah whimpered, his voice not audible even in his own ears. That dreaded step outside their hiding place came nearer, bringing the laser that never wavered and made escape impossible. Nehi had no gun, no laser, no knife to throw, nothing to fend off this armed man. And he knew too well the brutal strength and speed curled in that form. Simmons stood just across from them now. All he had to do was look toward them, and they were his. Simmons stopped, his head cocked on one side as he listened to something in the distance. Nehemiah and Joe stood rigid, unable even to breathe. A harsh curse sounded from Simmons. He dropped the Tolen with a clatter, reached into a pocket of his coat, and took out a stick of copper colored metal, two feet in length. A copper ball attached to each end, about the size of Simmons' hands, and two small balls rested near the center of the wand. Nehemiah had no energy to spare on curiosity over the object; terror held his entire being.

A wailing scream ripped through the air from their left. Nehi's eyes automatically jerked toward it, though all he could see was tree bark.

A sharp whine rang through the thick air, so strange and high it pulsated through his mind more than registered in his ears. A fierce sucking wind cut through the hollowed tree, and the light darkened. Nehemiah fell to his hands and knees, scrabbling on the bark, trying not to be sucked away by the wind. A strange unearthly heaviness tugged on him, as if enormous magnets were jerking him apart from four different directions. The wind screamed at him, whipping his hair into his face.

The tugging stopped, the wind died, the keening whine left, all in an instant. Nehi fell back gasping. Dim sunlight shone around him and quiet, gentle birdsong hung in the humid air. The noise was gone. The wind was gone. Simmons was gone. And so was the place he had been standing. A circular rent in the platform glared back at Nehemiah as he stared at the place, surrounded by a wreckage of torn branches and leaves littering the area for a full yard around the hole. Shaking, Nehemiah turned toward the mute splayed on the wood beside him, hoping for some sort of explanation. Joe stared at the place Simmons had been, his mouth hanging open. Another angry scream sounded from their left, closer than the last.

"Joe, I think we should go," Nehemiah rasped. Joe stayed still with his jaw slack staring at the empty hole. "He's gone, isn't he? Isn't he?" Nehemiah's voice shrilled, one hand shoving into Joe's shoulder. The little mute came out of his shock, blinking and nodding at Nehemiah.

"He's gone," Joe signed. "Flown away somewhere with that...thing." Nehemiah's breath rattled out of him and he sagged. He didn't care how Simmons had disappeared right then, the important thing was that the horrible man was gone. Lightstep clambered onto the platform just in front of them. She looked wilder than before, if that was possible, and hardly glanced at the gaping hole in the platform.

"You have to go, now," she gasped, pressing Hope, Dark Ray, and Joe's dirk into the boys' hands. "Another stranger has been here and has done great damage. My people are convinced it was you. I have already gotten the chimera and the pretty one away. You must go now!" She darted from the tree house, with Joe on her heels. Nehemiah slid Hope in her holster and chased after his friend.

And then Lightstep proved she suited her name.

She ran along the branches and leapt to new ones as if her feet were more comfortable in the air than on anything solid. Joe followed her easily, seeming to fly through the trees, never wavering. Nehemiah didn't move so quickly among the treetops. He couldn't stop himself from looking down, at the dizzying height he had to fall if he placed his foot wrong once. Gravity seemed suddenly to sit on his shoulders with a physical weight that made his legs tremble.

A flying form caught him around the waist. Nehemiah fell heavily onto a thick oak branch, just managing to twist to one side. Hope jolted out of her holster. Nehemiah's chest tightened as he watched her bang onto the branch and bounce off, lost among the thick leaves. Two fists pounded at him as the attacker's teeth bared; the blows of a man in a fury, not a trained attack. Or... more the attack of a man trained by watching animals fight. Nehemiah squirmed to his back, his head tucked in, arms over his face. He took a second to breathe, his head spinning. Then he snapped his left arm over his attacker's, pinning the appendage to the man's side, as his left leg tucked around his enemy's leg. Nehi gave one quick roll, and he was the one on top. His arm jerked back, his eyes half slitted against the pounding in his skull, focusing with difficulty on this man's chin.

Two heavy, smelly bodies slammed into him. Nehemiah hit the branch on his side, his head bouncing on the bark. Natropians flailed blows at the young man. Nehemiah lay pinned, grunting through the abuse, trying to get an arm free to fight back, and highly annoyed with himself; he hadn't been much help on this adventure. Anna's face rose in his mind, how she had looked at him when she left with Cobeau. With a roar he jerked an arm free and struck out, judo chopping and jerking himself out from under the pile of people, with enough strength and vitality his attackers fell back. He got a few staggering, running steps ahead. A thick man rammed into him in a tackle, and Nehemiah slammed into the branch, pressed against the rough bark again. Yells and screams pulsed through his sick head, something about a murdered panther. Nehemiah kicked furiously at the man jumping on his legs, and tried to roll over to fight back. But there were too many. And he was not at home in the top of a tree. He caught a glimpse of more Natropians rushing through the branches, glaring at him as they screamed abuse, and his heart sank.

He would die as a murderer. A murderer of a panther of all things, here in these dark treetops.

A tall, snarling wild man gripped Nehemiah's shoulder, sinking his decayed teeth into the young man's leather jacket. He suddenly gave a shriek. The gripping fingers let go, and Nehi watched him tumble off the branch, only just managing to catch a limb several yards down the tree. Another stumbled backward along the limb, and Nehemiah began to struggle again. They let go of him and stepped back, fright and surprise plastered over their filthy faces. Nehemiah staggered to his feet, breathing hard, his vision fuzzing and the world sounding as if he stood in a deep well instead of a treetop. He stopped, swaying, and staring at the little figure who had run off ten grown men who fought as if they trained with wolf packs and bears.

Joe crouched on the limb between him and the Natropians. One arm held back, taut and hand flattened for a blow, legs bunched like springs, eyes burning... A large male Natropian snarled and leapt forward, the branch swaying under his movements. Joe launched toward him. The mute's leg snapped out, striking the big man in the ribs. The crack of the breaking bones rang over the snarls and shouts of the wavering Natropians. The big man paled, doubling over, his mouth open in an agonized gasp. Joe's flattened hand came down on the back of his neck as his other hand shoved into the man's spine, pushing him flat on the branch. Nehi could see the way the man jerked, fell, and lay curled after that neck strike and knew the mute had deliberately, carefully kept it from being a killing blow. Two more rushed the mute, and he spun in a beautiful circle, catching them with four different strikes and kicks before they could take a full step closer to him. They fell to the branch on top of the big man, and Joe landed in his crouch again, still, staring, waiting. A gang of five looked at each other, then darted forward as one entity, screaming in fury. Joe launched off again, perfect in his precision, a little whirlwind of lethal energy.

This was a different Joe than Nehi had yet met and he gaped as he swayed and tried to get his faculties in order. A fighter Nehi had seen in Joe, but nothing like this level of skilled training. Every movement was artfully calculated, honed to perfection, merciless in eliminating the enemy. Nothing could stand up around him. He twirled, leapt, spun, kicked, his dirk sparkling in the dying light; a dancer of lethal energy instead of peaceful music.

The Natropians fell back before him, leaping to higher branches, their wild ferocity melting before his burning determination to get Nehemiah to safety. Joe spun, grabbed Nehi around the waist, slapped Hope into the bigger boy's stomach, and began to run, guiding him through the trees as if the mute had been born here. He ran faster and faster, getting lower with every breath-snatching leap to the next limb. Nehemiah fired six shots behind them, shearing through branches and sending their nearest enemies floundering back in terror. Then he all but closed his eyes and concentrated on running; he gave up his attempts to keep the world in perfect focus, his fear of falling, and turned it all into a throbbing trust in this little friend with an arm wrapped around him. Nehemiah let Joe guide him, his feet pounding and leaping over tree branches. They ran for what felt like a year to Nehemiah, but must have only been a few minutes. Then Nehi heard Anna's shout and started paying attention again. The crowded, tangled ground of the forest floor was only about fifteen yards away, and he could see the dim light of twilight breaking through the trunks ahead. They were almost out.

Joe pointed at a thick pine branch four feet to their left and Nehemiah leapt, one hand rising to catch hold of it. The rough bark bit into his skin as he swung off the thick branch, catapulting himself forward with absolute faith in Joe's guidance. His feet landed on a bulbous tillandsia and Joe had them leaping off again as the great plant trembled and began to fall from its place suspended in the trees. The two boys landed on another great oak branch and now Nehi saw a stretch of open green grass in front of them. There was their wagon, oh that beautiful Ravens' wagon, waiting for them on the grass! They pounded over their branch, and Joe pointed to the wagon this time instead of another tree. Nehemiah put all his heart into that last mighty leap.

Empty air and clear, unfiltered sunlight rushed over him. He and Joe landed with a bone jarring thump, sprawling in a bruised heap, so hard the hovering wagon banged into the ground before rising steadily again. Cobeau leaned over them, firing an old snub nosed projectile rifle into the trees, making sure the Natropians didn't try to follow. Anna switched on the engines attached to Prissy's wheels and turned it to high. The pig gave a delighted squeal as the wind began to whip into her face. They dashed over a flat grassland, their trail of steam stretching out behind them. Nehemiah and Joe looked back as the wind bubble rose and clicked closed over them. Nehi felt Joe's breath as the mute let out a long sigh, watching the trees begin to fade away into the distance. He groaned and slumped on his back on the wagon top, his head pulsing.

"And if you ever try to tell me you're too sick to travel through a bunch of trees again," Anna continued her lecture as she smeared an arnica salve on Nehemiah's bruises in the wagon later that afternoon, "and then come leaping out of them like you have a fire on your heels, I'll...I'll punch you, that's what I'll do."

"Are you listening?" Cobeau rumbled to Joe for the thirtieth time, as he took the salve and smeared it on a dark purple bruise on Joe's cheek. Joe nodded laughingly, then winced and put a hand to his head. He looked at Nehemiah, his green eyes twinkling. Nehemiah grinned back as Anna began her lecture at the beginning again while she removed the blood soaked bandage from his torn palm and put on a new one.

"Anna," Nehemiah said, swinging her around to look at him, "I promise never to come leaping out of treetops like that again if I can help it. Does that satisfy you?"

"You missed the point completely, Nehi, it was–"

"You know, being a quack of a doctor, I have every right to duck your bill," Nehi commented with a grin. She looked at him and her wrathful gleam softened into a smile.

"Oh, I wouldn't want to get the training to be a real physician, it's all just in-doctor-nation. All right, Nehi, if that's all I'm getting from you I suppose I'll accept it. But you and Joe need to learn not to be so tough and to accept help when it's given freely. We wanted to help you!"

"Are you listening?" Cobeau rumbled at Joe. The mute signed he was, a smile still playing on his lips. His eyes met Nehi's, and Nehemiah could read the thankful look on Joe's face with ease because it sparked through him with every breath; an inexpressible gratefulness for this love and care, and the safety to rest in it. He smiled back in perfect understanding. The two boys had been reminded of dark times when they had no one, and it was awfully nice to be doctored and lectured at. Cobeau finished the salve and tossed the empty container across the room to the trash, allowing his patient to stand up. Joe moved to a cubbyhole where he kept his things for the headaches he often got. Nehemiah moved their chairs over to the wall while the mute made himself a compress. Joe used a wet cloth saturated with a delightful combination of medicinal oils, and Nehemiah breathed deeply, drinking in the spicy smell, as his friend settled in the chair next to him. Joe positioned the cloth across his forehead, laid his new black gloves on his lap, and leaned back with a little sigh. The two sat quietly watching Anna cooking dinner and Cobeau straightening the wagon from their recent race from the woods.

"So a dreadful man named Simmons and some other dreadful man were following us?" Anna asked as she caught a pancake that tried to escape her erratic flipping.

"Yes," answered Nehemiah reluctantly. He didn't want to discuss Simmons.

"And you say he was the same one who passed us in the wild land between home and Kallipolis, with the people trying to hunt us down? So, they (whoever 'they' are) were supposed to take both of us somewhere and it's important enough for them to keep at it through all these months."

"And according to Lightstep," Nehemiah added, "our guess work that day in the wild lands was right, it is about that treasure. Whatever it is."

"So it has something to do with a treasure? You didn't mention that," Anna said.

"According to Lightstep, yes," Nehi answered. He caught an escaping pancake, handed half to Joe, and began to munch.

"Considering Samuel telling us the last ransom note for our book demanded a treasure our family held, that seems significant. I wonder what happened to Samuel?" Anna said quietly as she flipped another pancake toward Nehemiah. She switched to stirring the mushrooms and eggs. "But I want to know who was following us. I suppose it's someone calling themselves the FF, if it really is the same group today and that day in the wild lands. But that's not much to go on."

"I know," Nehemiah agreed, grimacing. "It's really unnerving to be followed by something unidentified. Ann, they would have had us when the disintegration first hit if Samuel hadn't warned us to keep our last names quiet. And whoever 'they' are, they're obviously evil to have Simmons as one of theirs. Come to think of it, if Abid hadn't obliterated my real name with 'slave,' Simmons would have known it was me he was after a long time ago. I doubt I would have been around to help you get out and for the Ravens to get us both out if that had happened; I can't imagine where we might have ended up."

"I can. Not a nice place." The automated voice from the black gloves seemed harsh as it broke in. Silence dropped as the twins stared at Joe. A mushroom plopped off Anna's spoon to sizzle in the pan. His gloved hands moved again, taking no notice of their gaping. "You are right, FF is their name."

"What's the FF?" the twins said together. Joe shrugged.

"A nasty group show up more lately," the black gloves said as Joe's hands flashed. It was strange the way the gloves translated the mute exactly as he signed, with few connecting words and little sense of time. "I think you right, FF after you for a while, even at disintegration beginning. I not know much about them. I think they involved with our book come over come over." Joe swept the gloves off, slammed them into the side of the wagon, and slid them on again in the same second. "Book quest." He slid a hand out of one again, his eyes on Anna's cooking.

"Oh, and you're just now telling us, after we've nearly been in despair from finding no news for months about our book or Daniel?" Anna snapped, bringing her wooden spoon down on his hand a little harder than necessary as he reached toward her pan of cooking mushrooms. "I suppose you won't tell us anything else? Like what they're trying to do? Or how you know about them, or why they want us?" Joe shrugged and rubbed his hand, his blankness beginning to cover his features. He closed his eyes and leaned against the wagon, completely ignoring Nehi and Anna as they pleaded for an answer. A tense silence fell in the little wagon as the mushrooms sizzled.

"You know, Joe, you are ridiculously close," Nehemiah sighed. Joe shrugged again, his eyes still closed and his position unchanged.

Raven Wagon

"I'm still alive," he signed slowly, letting his gloves rest in his lap.

"Is that all you want to be? Alive?" Anna asked. Joe's eyes flew open; he blinked and looked thoughtful for a moment.

"Point taken," he signed, and snatched a pancake out of the air. He held it up as his usual self came back. "These are the best I have ever eaten!"

"Taken, but not applied," Anna muttered. She moved her pan off the stove, picked up the flashlight lying on the shelf, and spun, clicking in on as she moved. The beam caught Joe in the eyes and he stirred uncomfortably, waving his hand as if he could swat it away. Anna stared down the beam of light.

"As I thought, you Joe, have a better concussion than Nehi. You are addled of the brain, which is why we have been getting these lovely confessions from you. I'm glad your subconscious is comfortable enough with us to tell things, even if you aren't when you're normal. Now stop moving and stay still for the rest of the day. You're going to bed after we eat."

She sat the flashlight back on the stove and poured more batter in her pan. Joe sat still for a moment, blinking at nothing, as if he were trying to process what Anna had just told him. He shrugged and tossed part of the pancake to Cobeau.

"How on earth did we survive with my cooking?" Joe asked, adding Cobeau's sign: he put his hand at the level of his mouth and repeatedly clipped his thumb and first finger together as he drew his hand to the side.

"I've been meaning to ask you," Anna said, "what's that sign supposed to mean, Beau's sign?"

"It means I stick too close," Cobeau answered for his little friend. Joe punched him playfully in the arm, slid his gloves on, and signed.

"No, means he is glue that holds me together. Stickiness that puts me back again when I fall apart. Common sense that holds me to earth when I get over my head in abstracts. He is my Glue."

"You answered that question," Anna said. "That shows improvement. Maybe." She plunked a plate of hot pancakes (the few that hadn't escaped) on the table next to the mushrooms and eggs. Joe's face lit up and he swept the gloves off again as he moved quickly to the table.

"You're starting to understand most of what I sign, that's improvement too," Joe signed slowly as the group settled down to eat. The prayer before the meal was heartfelt and grateful, but all four were ravenous and talk was sparse. It wasn't until they began the job of washing up that Anna opened the conversation again.

"So, where do we go from here?" she asked. Nehemiah was facing Joe (putting the plates in the cabinet as Anna dried them) and glimpsed the real Joe's response to the question before the masked Joe answered it. The mute froze for an instant, his face strained, eyes crinkled in worry, a sharp frown drawing lines on his tight face. He covered it almost immediately by his usual easy attitude as he went back to leaning against the wall.

"KAM," he signed. Beau looked at Joe and his jaw dropped.

"Why there, Master?" the chimera rumbled, a look on the verge of terror crossing his simple features. Joe frowned at him and shook his finger, but the chimera ignored it. "Do you have to go back?" Joe's eyes darted away for an instant, but he smiled at his Glue as he signed something swiftly in response. It was too fast for the twins to catch much.

"KAM as in, the Kingdom of Autonomous Man, right?" Nehemiah asked. "And did I see something about the Kingdom of the Prophet's Peace in that last bit? I hope the answer is no."

"Yes to both, Knee-High," Joe signed, slowing down. "Prophet's Peace is on the way to KAM and I have some business there. We need to stop for a little while, unfortunately."

"What business, Joe?" Anna asked, turning on him, her trim hands going to her hips and her chin lifting. "I know we don't make enough money to support us with our sporadic concerts–"

"Exactly," Nehemiah interrupted, "what do you really do?"

Joe regarded the twins blankly for a few seconds, a sure sign he was thinking behind his mask. He made up his mind and slid his gloves on again as he dropped back in his chair, his eyes closing and head going back to rest against the wooden wall.

"I am an informant."

"What's that mean?" Anna asked eagerly. Joe smiled at his friends' bright curiosity and his hands flew. The gloves stumbled over the words as they tried to keep up with the mute. The phrases came out incoherent, and drifted into a jerky computerized, "A-a-a-a-a-a." Joe whipped them off with a little sigh, whistled for Beau, and started again.

"It's not that interesting," Joe signed and Beau rumbled. "I just tell the government in one kingdom what the government in another kingdom is up to. Sometimes I accept other commissions, but usually that's all I do."

"'All you do,'" Nehemiah said teasingly. Delight and excitement coursed through him; they had gotten an answer! But it was better not to spook Joe, and he kept the conversation on the same cheerful, even tone. "I wonder how much danger and trouble it takes you to get the information you give–"

"We know how much danger it is to go through the wild lands between your commissions," Anna interrupted. "I'm glad you're paid well. And I'm very glad you told us. Thank you."

"You're welcome," Joe signed with a grin, and Beau said, still translating automatically. Joe laughed at him and signed he could stop. Cobeau translated the sentence three times before he understood it was directed to him. The chimera stared at his little friend with the same worried look on his face. He took Joe's shoulder gently, engulfing it in his large hand.

"Joe, why do we have to go to KAM?" he rumbled.

"I'm a little more worried about Prophet's Peace," Joe signed back at Beau, obviously trying to get his mind onto another track. Beau stared at him. It wasn't working. Joe sighed and his hands sped off on his answer. Nehi's brows drew together as he concentrated, and he managed to follow the signs.

"You know I have to talk to P, we need to find out about his partner L-E-E-M-A-N and his gadget. We've been in and out several times since then. Remember, Glue? We can do it again."

"The whole time we're there I can't breathe because I'm afraid they'll find you, Master. Ow," Cobeau interjected as Joe stomped on his foot. "I mean Joe. Isn't there another way to learn–" Joe shushed him quickly and Beau went back to his straightening, worry still plastered over his face. Nehemiah and Anna glanced at each other. They had made progress; but they still had a long way to go to be trusted.

Chapter Six: The Prophet's Peace

"There is neither Jew nor Greek, there is neither bond nor free, there is neither male nor female: for ye are all one in Christ Jesus." Galatians 3:28

> ## KINGDOM OF THE
> ## PROPHET'S PEACE
>
> "MUHAMMAD IS THE APOSTLE OF GOD; AND HIS COMRADES ARE VEHEMENT AGAINST THE INFIDELS, BUT FULL OF TENDERNESS AMONG THEMSELVES."
> -QUARAN 48:29

Nehemiah shuddered as the wagon slid past the sign marking the beginning of the kingdom. Cold pressed into his skin and seeped into his bones, and he wondered if it was only him. He glanced at the others through lowered lids, his skin prickling as if his master hovered nearby again. Anna sat watching him. Nehemiah did his best to smile at her. Anna smirked and shook her head.

"You're as bad an actor as Joe says, Nehi," she commented. Anna scooted next to him and slipped her arm through her brother's. "It's all right, Nehi. I don't think the Ravens would have brought us here if they didn't know they could bring us out again. Don't worry, we'll be fine. We're already eternally fine, secure in Christ. Nothing can keep us from Him, and we will make it to heaven in the end. Sometimes going over the verses Mom and Dad made us learn from Revelations, I can almost see our eternal home. It's a beautiful vision." Nehemiah stopped shivering and Anna tried again. "I like our group name of the Vision Keepers, but I think it needs a motto. Maybe something like Dad's." She lowered her voice and went on in a tone very like their father's. "'Depart from evil and do good; seek peace and pursue it.[4]'"

"But you have to point to heaven while you do it, Ann, or it just isn't the same and Dad won't recognize you," Nehemiah smiled. He found he could look up without fear and thanked God again for giving him this sweet, strong sister. Anna glanced at him and smiled. It was working. She kept up the conversation.

"It's a pretty country, at least. I like the hills. And the forest," she said, and Nehemiah looked around, noticing the landscape for the first time since they had slowed down enough to see anything besides a colored blur. It was pretty. The road wound through sandy hills with tall trees sticking up here and there. To their right, the trees converged to form a forest, dark and beautiful, and actually tended for once.

"It's very quiet," Nehemiah said. "Is it always this quiet?"

"At the edge," Cobeau answered easily.

"Are we going to do a concert when we come to a town, Joe?" Anna asked. "We haven't practiced in a few days, but if we need to–" Joe interrupted with a shake of his head.

"We don't play music here," he signed.

"Why not?" Anna asked, her eyebrows rising.

"I thought that was just a preference of Hadi Abid," Nehemiah put in curiously. "Is it really a part of the viewpoint?" Joe gave a little shrug, holding up a hand and shaking it back and forth a little. "What?" Nehemiah said.

"Some __ say yes, some say no," Joe signed. "There is music here, I'm not sure humans can live without some form of song. But the experts on their book can't decide if it should really be

---

[4] Psalm 34:14

allowed, and if so what sort of music is all right. Hope is so slim here they err on the side of mild, pretty bland stuff. Just in case. Some towns ban it completely."

"What's that first sign, Beau?" Anna asked.

"Muslims," Cobeau answered, a growl underlying the word.

"Muslims aren't sure if music is forbidden or not, so they're extra careful about what's allowed?" Nehemiah clarified.

"I hear years ago, when the kingdom first started," Joe signed swiftly and Beau rumbled, "there were Muslims who were not so strict, who were willing to look on some things in their books as...guidelines, I guess. Or at least they interpreted some of the passages differently. But they were put down, and the Muslims we know took over."

"A few of the more lenient kind showed up in Abid's rooms to take orders sometimes," Nehi shrugged. "I met some nice Muslims. They just couldn't do anything against Abid, he was in charge."

"You say hope is slim here," Anna put in, "what hope? Hope of what?"

"The Muslims believe in a god, who they call Allah," Joe signed and Beau said. "They believe we all have a soul that goes either to final judgment or to paradise. In that respect they're like the Way and not like most of the rest of the world. But the way to paradise for a Muslim is through doing more good deeds than bad, not through a savior. That's the slim hope, that you can do more to please Allah than to displease him. He's an exacting god. And the hope's not certain, even if you do all good works all your life; Allah may decide he just doesn't like you."

"That is a slim hope," Anna said. "What a fearful way to live, always wondering if you died right then if you would be accepted or not!"

"Yes, it is a religion of fear," Nehemiah said quietly. "Fear for the believer and imposed fear on the unbelieving. There is only one sure way to get to paradise for the Muslim, Anna,

Abid explained it. You die in battle fighting against the unbelievers." Anna grimaced and leaned into Nehemiah.

"Joe, why are we here?" she asked, liking this place less
and less.

"Glue and I have work to do," he signed. "But I don't want
to stay long." Beau's big head bobbed in agreement. Joe began
to sign quickly to Beau. Nehi and Anna caught glimpses of
'coins' and Anna's sign a couple of times, and Nehemiah's
once. Joe suddenly spun toward them and slowed down so the
twins could follow it. "I don't like this country, and I don't
want to leave you two alone even near it, so do you mind tagging along with Glue and me?"

"It's a little late to ask now that we're here, isn't it?" Nehemiah snapped. Joe had the grace to look apologetic. Nehi
sighed. "Yes, we'll tag along with you. I think we would have
said yes even if you had asked in time, right Anna?"

"Yes," Anna answered immediately, and Joe smiled gratefully at them.

"I'll ask next time," he signed.

"Yes, well, you did promise something quite similar in Kallipolis," Anna said, her voice tight with annoyance. Joe's hands
went up to say something, then dropped again as he blinked.
He gave a sheepish smile and whistled for Beau, speeding up.

"Sorry, I honestly didn't think about it. And you two didn't
object until now, when we're already here. Anyway, my real
reason for starting this conversation; I'd like to split up to get
more done and get out faster. I think it would be best if you
each had a Raven with you, so how about Beauty and Glue
take the..." he paused, for a moment, searching for the correct
word before going on, "...more comfortable errand. Knee-High
and I can go for the other. Okay?" Anna and Nehemiah didn't
particularly like the sound of that, but there was little choice,
and they agreed. Joe motioned the twins inside the wagon as
Beau guided Prissy deeper into the country toward the capital
city. As they dropped through the skylight the mute opened a
cubby in an aspen tree and pulled out a pile of fabric. He

handed it to Anna with an apologetic shrug.

"Sorry," he signed, "but you should probably look like the other ladies of this country to avoid notice. It's safer." Anna unfolded the material and looked at it.

"I don't mind, Joe, but I have no idea what this is or what to do with it," she said. Joe nodded and swiftly began to drape it around her.

"Why do they wear all that extra stuff?" Nehemiah asked as he watched.

"M-o-d-e-s-t-y," Joe fingerspelled, gave his sign for it quickly, and went back to work. A moment later he stepped beside Nehemiah and the two boys looked at Anna, draped in a long, loose black robe, with a thick piece of cloth pulled over her face as a veil and wrapped around her head to cover her luscious black curls.

"All I can see are her eyes," Nehemiah commented. "I don't think I like it."

"Oh, that makes me feel good about my new outfit," Anna said with a giggle. Nehemiah began to stutter something about it not being ugly and Joe punched him laughingly in the arm to make him stop and slid his gloves on.

"You look fine, Beauty," he signed and the gloves droned. "Just remember ladies and men stay apart in public, you no look carefree, and no get indignant with rude men. Knee-High, no quote anything here, sound Muslim." Joe's hands shot up, the gloves said, "Climb," and he caught the skylight and scampered on the top of the wagon. Anna and Nehemiah followed him out into the bright sunshine, curious over his warnings. The twins dropped into their seats, and Joe's hand went to the accelerator. Anna gripped her seat as the wagon shot off, Prissy squealing in joy, the outside world a blur again.

An hour passed before Joe twisted the knob and brought their speed down. Nehi gaped at another wagon, four yards in front of them. A few more seconds of the high speed, and it would have been a collision. Ten more minutes and they found themselves passing other wagons, hoverers, cars, people everywhere, and they understood Joe's words. The majority of the women's eyes (all they could see of the ladies here) looked sad and worn while the men were generally serious and hard. There were exceptions, quite a few of them. It relieved the twins to see some couples walking arm in arm, or chatting like normal. The children seemed happy. The pretty painted wagon and giant pig drew many stares, and children laughed and clapped their hands, calling boisterous silly comments to the travelers, or racing along behind them. Half the population seemed to be children.

A large city came into sight, and the twins studied it with interest. They saw white buildings and lots of people. Soon a busy hum surrounded them, the clean smell of grass and dirt eclipsed by hot steam and asphalt, garbage and restaurants. An active, packed city; it seemed prosperous, mostly well kept, and even cheerful. Only a few minutes in, Joe and Co pulled off the main road into a dim, dank side alley. Tall factories rose over it, blocking out the bright sunshine, and Anna found herself wrinkling her nose at the smell and leaning in toward Nehi.

The road pulled out from between the buildings, and dead ended at a rust-covered warehouse, windows boarded up, and stagnate puddles filling the potholes in the small parking lot. Beau hopped down, snapped the rusty lock off the barn-sized, corrugated steel door and heaved it open. Joe prodded Prissy forward, and musty, dust-filled dimness closed over the group. Beau pulled the door closed, and it shut with a rattling bang. The sound melded with Prissy squeaking, a piercing, keening request for release. Nehi dropped down and quickly helped Beau clear off her trappings. The pig lumbered happily off to a side room. The crunch of her steady munching drifted from the room and Nehemiah looked at Joe.

"She knew right where to go. How often have you been here?" His voice echoed in the big, empty room.

"We Ravens travel a lot," Joe signed with a blank shrug. He ducked into the wagon and came out again in a moment. The pockets of his black cargo pants bulged. He handed Cobeau a black velvet bag. It jingled musically when the chimera took it and slid it in his belt.

"Be careful and keep Beauty safe, right Glue?" he signed to him. Nehi glowed with pleasant surprise as he understood the swift signs.

"Joe, what are they doing?" he asked quickly. "I know you like playing it close, but since my sister is going along I'd like to know something about it."

"Delivering messages and things to the IDP here," Joe signed.

"IDP, the Christian underground?" Anna said to make sure she remembered right. Joe nodded and teasingly clapped for a correct answer. Anna grinned and curtsied theatrically. "Is it a large group here?" Joe's face hardened, his mouth tightening in a frown.

"Sometimes," he signed.

"What's that supposed to mean?" Anna asked, flipping the material off her face to breathe better. Joe began to sign at his blurring speed, Beau rumbling the words for the twins.

"It's a very hard country for Christians to live in, Beauty. Any non-Muslims are up for enslavement or worse by the Muslims if they're caught. But despite the trouble (or sometimes I think because of it) this IDP branch is strong and fierce for our Savior. It's very hated by the Muslims, and feared too."

"Why feared?" asked Nehemiah as he saw Joe dropping his hands to his side. Joe glanced at his watch and pursed his lips. But he answered the question.

"The IDP is feared because they hold hope. They hold the only hope, peace, joy, happiness. They hold forth the only Way. And the Muslims, just like every other lost soul, know they're missing it. Some, especially when they see our brothers and sisters enduring–" Joe suddenly broke off and looked away with a wince, as if he were seeing something in his memory he'd rather he could forget. Nehemiah could guess some of it and his face hardened. Joe looked up and finished his sentence. "When they see the unshakeable faith of those of the Way, something clicks inside them, and non-Christians know it's true. People don't hold onto false hope in the face of what goes on here, they just don't. So, some Muslims convert to Christianity. And the ones who don't grow harder on the ones who do. Which makes the IDP grow and shrink at the same time. It's a complicated and frightening thing, but as Glue keeps reminding me every time I'm here, God knows what He's doing. Now come on, Knee-High, we have business to do." Joe trotted toward a side door, but Nehemiah turned to Anna. He pulled her into a hug, his scarred arms wrapping tight around her.

"Be safe, Ann!" he said fervently. "I know God's in charge, but I really don't think I could live without you."

"Jesus is more than able to fill in for me, Nehi," Anna answered with a little laugh, but Nehemiah heard a hint of anxiety in it. "I'll be fine; I have Beau and God. You be safe with the other half of the Ravens. Won't you, Nehemiah?" Anna tucked one of his black curls behind his ear, her eyes pleading.

"I'll be just as fine as you will," Nehi said quickly, and was surprised to find he meant it. Joe gave a low whistle that obviously meant, "I'm sorry to interrupt, but please hurry."

"How does he make a whistle say so much?" Anna marveled, and Nehemiah laughed.

"I'll see you tonight probably, Anna. Bye Beau!" he called as he ran to Joe. The mute pulled the door open and the two slipped out.

"Off we go," Joe signed. His green eyes sparkled, his lips twisted with a mischievous smile, as he started to jog through the city. Nehemiah ran to catch up, wondering where he was going.

"If Anna and Beau are going to the IDP, what are we doing?" Nehemiah asked. He leaned against the alley wall, the three-story buildings rising above him keeping everything around him in deep shadow. His skin prickled at every footstep he heard outside the alley. His arms wrapped around his chest, a little shiver shaking him. It still felt cold; a part of him knew it wasn't really the outside temperature he was feeling. "I mean, besides hanging around this alleyway staring at that gigantic building with strange lines all over it, as we've been doing for the past hour."

"Half," Joe signed.

"What?"

"Only half an hour," he explained. "We're watching to see who goes in that big building. And it is a s-c-r-i-p-t, not strange lines."

"All right, script. But why?"

"Most of them mean 'Allah,' and that is pretty important to them."

"What?"

"The script," Joe answered and Nehemiah chuckled.

"Joe, you are the most impossible person. You know what I'm asking, you just don't want to answer it." Joe grinned at him and turned back to watching the entrance. "So why were we in a hurry to get here if we were just going to stare at a building, because–" Joe whapped him in the stomach and Nehemiah stopped with a grunt. The mute pointed and Nehi looked out over Joe's shaggy head. A group of soldiers marched down the street. The measured tramp of their boots on the concrete was in perfect rhythm, every piece of equipment exactly in its place, every gaze focused on their leader, a tall proud man in his late forties Nehemiah would guess.

Beside the tall one, a shorter, stouter man marched, matching the soldier stride for stride. He wore a white suit instead of the long robes of most of the men in this country. His face showed the flab of someone who liked their creature comforts. If Nehi had been asked which looked prouder of his own self-righteousness, the one in the white suit or the soldier, he would have been stumped for an answer. The procession marched past and turned into the big building. The black wrought-iron gates swung open as the gatekeepers stepped back respectfully. The soldiers marched through and disappeared inside.

"That's what we were hurrying for," Joe signed, a wily smile playing over his face. "We had to know he was here before we go in, it all ___ on whether those men are inside that building."

"I don't know..." Nehemiah said, doing his best to replicate the sign he didn't know.

"H-i-n-g-e-s," Joe fingerspelled quickly for him. He looked down at his hands and grimaced. "Glue's right, my gloves aren't that reliable. And they take forever to charge. Do you mind translating for me in here? It will offer an explanation for why you're with me."

"In where?" Nehi asked. Joe pointed to the big building across the street. "What is it?"

"Government building," Joe answered easily. "Come on." He stepped out of the alleyway and strode up to the gate. Nehemiah followed, doing his best to look as calm and easy as Joe. Two guards stepped forward and barred their way. Joe held up a small white card. One of the guards stepped forward and took it, looking from the card to Joe in suspicion.

"You cannot be the informant this card speaks of," he scoffed, a grin spreading over him. "You are hardly taller than my ten-year-old son!" Joe's eyes raked the guard. Nehemiah almost didn't recognize the stern, annoyed man that stood where his friend had been a minute ago. Joe's green eyes turned to Nehemiah, his nose in the air. He snapped at Nehi for translation. The sound made Abid's face flicker past Nehi's defensive wall of prayers and verses he had playing in his mind; in that instant, his heart pounded so hard it pierced his chest with pain. But he told himself it was fine and obeyed Joe's snap.

"I am who that card says, and I have business inside today," Joe signed and Nehemiah said. The guards still hesitated.

Joe glared at them. He reached up and pushed his jacket collar down, showing the mark on his neck. The eyes of the guards grew large. The one who had spoken swallowed visibly. Joe replaced the collar and his hands moved, slowly enough for Nehi to follow.

"Let us in now," Nehemiah translated. The guards swung open the gates and stood aside. The one who had spoken before began to stutter.

"Forgive us for doubting, the Wazir will be pleased to see you–" Joe swept through the gate, cutting the apology short and snatching back his card. He marched up the steps and into the building, ignoring the curious glances from the small crowd moving in and out of the tall gilt doors. Nehemiah followed Joe into the white, airy entry, his eyes drawn automatically to the sparkling gold of the dome stories above him. But the beauty of the place was lost on him. His heartbeat was erratic as it pounded in his chest, and he couldn't control the thoughts that flew through his mind. The Wazir, the ruler of all the Prophet's Peace! Joe was welcomed by him?!

Beau ducked through an alley in the pretty neighborhood and stopped behind a brick house. He grabbed Anna around the waist, gripped the top of the seven-foot rock wall surrounding the back yard, and vaulted over. He plopped Anna in the grass beside him and looked around the empty yard. Beau glanced at his watch and leaned against the wall.

"Are we early?" Anna panted. Cobeau nodded. He patted the wall next to him and Anna leaned obediently against the stones beside Beau, wondering what Nehemiah was doing. Beau hummed tunelessly, idly watching a foot-long caterpillar inch across the immaculate grass. At the end of ten minutes the strange humming started to grate on Anna's nerves.

The gate to the yard swung open and Anna jumped as she spun toward it. A tall, blond young man stalked in, his smooth features carved into a frown. His restless gaze landed on Anna and Cobeau. Blue eyes widened and his lips parted as he stared at them.

"Cobeau," Cobeau said, and he held out an intricate cross like the one Joe had twirled in his finger in Gaia. It looked ridiculously small in Beau's hand. The metal rearranged with a musical tinkling as it lay on the chimera's palm, changing shape into a flying bird. "A Raven. Bringing greetings." The man's gaze darted from the necklace to Beau, suspicion and fear marking him.

"Layth, what are you doing. Can't I come in?" a woman's voice said from behind the man. He hesitated a moment, then took a step forward. A young woman slid past him, plumper than Anna, with nice eyes, large and brown and friendly. It was all Anna could see of her through the veil and bulky draping robe.

"Hello," Anna said, not sure what else to say.

"Where's Naadar?" Beau rumbled. "He's supposed to be here."

"You know much to know that," the young man growled.

"I know Naadar," Cobeau said. "Where is he?"

"He's with my father," the young woman said, and Layth turned on her.

"Elizabeth, we don't know who these people are, or what they're doing here!" he hissed.

"They have the IDP token, they know Naadar's supposed to be here, I've heard stories of the Ravens, and besides, does the young lady smiling and greeting you behind her veil seem Islamic, Layth?"

"That was a lovely compliment," Anna grinned. "May I say the same about you?" Elizabeth laughed and an instant liking sprang into Anna. The gate swung open with a squeak of hinges, and two men came in. One was tall and blond like Layth, the other short and stout and going bald. They looked at the towering chimera and surprised pleasure lit up their faces.

"Cobeau!" the short one cried, his arms opening wide. The

tall one just nodded, but he smiled with it. Beau grinned and swept the two of them into one of his bone-crushing hugs. The short one reeled back with a gasp, laughing breathlessly as an arm snaked around his ribs. The tall one shoved out of the grip, grunting and straightening his white tunic.

"Come, inside before someone sees us all on the lawn and becomes suspicious," he said, his keys clinking as he stalked toward a potting shed. He opened the door, flipped a switch, and yellow light blazed on a metal staircase leading into a gray tunnel. Elizabeth took the balding man's arm, then reached out and took Anna's.

"This is my father, Adam Bight," she introduced as she drew Anna inside with her. "I'm Elizabeth Bight, and aren't these veils dreadful?" Anna grinned at her.

"Anna. At least mine lets me breathe, yours looks as if it's smothering you!" The two girls and Mr. Bight chatted easily as Cobeau and Layth followed behind, both awkwardly silent, moving steadily down the staircase. Yellow light spilled from hanging bulbs that sputtered and hummed. Anna learned the Bights lived in KAM but Adam was a preacher in the IDP and when possible traveled to other branches to encourage and teach. Elizabeth, his only child, had come along this time to keep him company.

"And what are you doing here, Anna?" Elizabeth asked over the noise of their footsteps clanging on the stairs.

"My brother and I are refugees from Sojourner's Kingdom," Anna answered, wondering how long they were going to go down and where they were going. "We were rescued by the Ravens and have been traveling with them. Joe and Beau had some errands they needed to do here. You know them, Mr. Bight?"

"Well..." Adam glanced behind him at the cheerful, simple face of Cobeau and smiled. "I'm not sure I've ever met anyone that could say they know the Ravens. I know a little of them, and my personal opinion is that they are a wonderful gift God has given to His people. They've helped our branch of the IDP out of several tight spots. Very brave, very competent, and very...unexplained. They never stay long, they never say where they've been or where they're going. Of course, that could just be because Joe's...well, a Genetic Incomplete, and Cobeau as a chimera is a bit...you know."

"Yes, I do," Anna said cheerfully, slipping her arm through Beau's and receiving a beaming, blank smile in return.

"A GI, really Daddy?" Elizabeth said in surprise. "And you've been traveling with them? I'm not sure I could do that, an incomplete..." Anna's eyes snapped dangerously and Adam quickly interposed as the stairs finally ended and they stepped into a little entryway.

"It's different when you meet them in person, my dear."

Naadar fitted a key into a simple wooden door and swung it open. Anna followed the others through the door at the stair's end and found herself in a large, comfortable room with couches and pillows everywhere, all facing a small lectern. A kitchenette stood on the other side of the room with a delightful scent of coffee drifting from it, and beautiful tapestries covering the walls.

"You can take off your veil down here, Anna," Elizabeth said. Anna spun back to her and saw her companion had already done it. A round, pretty, freckled face smiled at her and Anna found she liked her even better now that she could see Elizabeth Bight. Anna whipped her veil off, her black curls bouncing as they were suddenly freed, and successfully ignored the stares of the three men who hadn't seen her before. She had gotten used to that response over the last year. Naadar snapped his mouth closed and turned to Cobeau.

"Now that we are safely in our church, what are you here for? And where is the little one, Joe?" Naadar asked.

"Joe's busy. I've brought a gift. From several other branches," Beau rumbled as he handed over the black bag. Naadar took it curiously and pulled open the string. He glanced inside, gasped, and sat down suddenly on a chair.

"How did they manage so much?" Naadar asked, his voice

quiet, trembling. Beau shrugged.

"It's enough for what you need. Otherwise God would have made more come," he said simply. Naadar smiled at him, and Anna saw tears hovering in his eyes. Naadar's light coloring and chiseled features looked very nice when he wasn't so stern.

"It is still far from as much as we need, brother, but your faith is appreciated," he said quietly.

"More will come then," Beau said confidently. Naadar looked at him for a moment, as if trying to understand the confidence in the big chimera. His eyes darted back to the bag, he pulled out a handful of coins, and handed them to Layth.

"Go and buy her back, brother," he murmured.

Chapter Seven: The Wazir's Council

"God is our refuge and strength, a very present help in trouble." Psalm 46:1

Nehi's mind raced. Who was this person he was following? What if he was a two-face traitor, an IDP on one side and a Muslim on the other? What if he had brought them all the way here just to hand them over personally to the Wazir? Back in Islamic hands! He saw Abids all around him, his master's face plastered where he knew it couldn't be. He couldn't go back to that darkness, the terror, the pain, he couldn't! The hopeless, black despair flooded him again. For a dark minute, pain flared down his back, under the scar tissue. Doubts and curses filled the young man till even God became a monster. The old panic overcame every other faculty. His feet moved, but he didn't notice, it was just blind obedience that kept him after Joe, as his soul and mind cowered and yelled at a God Who let the evil happen.

Joe stopped suddenly and Nehi walked into him and staggered back a step. It broke him out of his panicked, dark thoughts enough to look around. He was in a wide hallway, empty except for beautiful tapestries. Joe stood by a tall black door, his hand on the knob, staring at him. Nehemiah's panicking eyes met Joe's and understanding flashed between them. The mute let go of the door and swung to face him.

"It's all right, Knee-High," Joe signed, his green eyes holding Nehi's. "I won't let them have you again. Ever. Trust me. It's okay."

"Joe, I... How could He? How could *God*?" Nehi gasped, his voice thick and fast.

"God didn't, Knee-High, man did," Joe signed steadily. "You know that. And we can't see what He can. Rest, stop fighting it."

"What?" Nehemiah choked.

"Stop fighting it. Throw yourself on Christ, again, and let it

 *108*

be."

Nehemiah just stared at him. But inside he stopped trying to fight the doubts and find a reason. He just curled in a ball at the foot of the cross, again. Clinging to a God Who went through torture and death because He chose to love. A breath drew into Nehi's tight lungs. Then another, and it was easier. His lungs loosened and the full panic attack was gone.

A quick encouraging wink and slap on the shoulder from Joe and the mute disappeared around the door. Nehemiah took another deep breath and followed. It would be all right. Joe wasn't going to let them be taken. And even if they were… God was still God, and still good, no matter how he doubted it. It would be all right. Nehemiah put it behind him and focused on his surroundings.

He found himself walking into a large room, a gilded dome sparkling high overhead, and pretty mosaic designs along the walls. Nehemiah caught up with Joe. He stood still, facing a group of stern men seated on sumptuous couches in the center of the large room. The tall, proud soldier who had marched past their alleyway was one of them, Nehi noticed, and the white-suited one sat beside him. The man's face was impassive, but something about the way his eyes focused on Joe…as if he suddenly forgot everything else around him… It made Nehi wonder. Nehemiah's eyes involuntarily sought his toes before he noticed any more.

"Little Raven," a deep, strong voice resonated from the group of men. "You have been long in coming, informant. Do you bring us news yet, or have you failed? And where is your large chimera. Why do you bring this scared rabbit instead?" Nehi felt hot embarrassment rush to his face, and he lifted his head, looking for the speaker. The voice came from a shriveled old man in a long black robe. Nehi was surprised. The voice did not fit the man. A snap echoed in the hall and his gaze darted to Joe. The mute's hands moved in swift elegant signs, and Nehi translated for him.

"Who I bring with me and who I do not is none of your

business or concern, Allah's Wazir," Joe signed and Nehemiah said firmly, a bit awed that his friend dared to talk to this man like that. "I have taken as long as the business took, and I have not failed." All eyes focused on Joe. The little old man in the black robe stiffened, an excited spark showing on his wrinkled face.

"You can identify the spy in our midst?" the Wazir said slowly. Joe nodded. He reached into a pocket and pulled out a stack of folded papers. Nehi was pretty sure he saw a photograph tucked among them. Joe waved them quickly, then put them back in his pocket.

"It's right here. The name and the evidence," he signed and Nehemiah said.

"Give it to me," the Wazir said eagerly, holding out his hand.

"Where's my fee?" Joe signed inflexibly. (Nehemiah had a bit of difficulty with 'fee,' not knowing that sign, but Joe realized it in time and fingerspelled it before anyone noticed.) The Wazir's lips twitched and a look of disgust came over his face, as if a foul smell had just rolled in.

"I forget; you care nothing of justice or truth, Raven. Only for your own stomach and pleasure," he sneered. The Wazir gave the order for someone to fetch Joe's pay and settled back on his cushion. The two boys stood in front of the group and waited. After about ten minutes of uninterrupted standing, with the group staring at them, Nehemiah felt cold sweat trickling down his neck. Joe stood whistling softly and rocking back and forth on his heels, apparently as unconcerned as if he was back in his own wagon. The doors opened finally. A servant scurried in carrying a beautifully embroidered bag that clinked with each movement. The servant made to hand it to the Wazir but was waved to Joe.

The mute whipped an unadorned black bag from a pocket. He shook the wrinkles out, handed it to Nehemiah, and began transferring the contents of one bag to the other. Nehemiah almost dropped the black bag as he saw how many precious jewels and coins Joe was transferring. A proud, cynical voice added a comment to the clink and tinkle of the transferring fee.

"Yes, it is a very great deal of money. You should ask more for your translation services, boy," Nehemiah looked up and met the gaze of the soldier he and Joe had watched come in. Amusement played over the man's face and for a moment he looked human instead of like a living statue.

"I think I will next time," Nehemiah answered with a tight smile. Joe tossed the empty embroidered bag back to the servant, drew the string tight on his own black velvet bag, and tied it quickly onto the belt at his waist; all with the fluid swiftness habitual to him. He took the papers from his pocket and handed them to the Wazir. Then Joe spun on his heel and strode off, not waiting to watch what came of his news. Nehemiah trotted after Joe and the tall black doors closed behind them. Joe's head swiveled as he glanced up and down the hall. It was still empty. His austere sternness melted into the eager, expressive Joe and Nehemiah's tight shoulders relaxed to a slump as he saw his friend again. The mute glued his ear to the doors.

"Keep an eye out, Knee-High, I want to see what happens," he signed. Nehemiah watched the hall obediently, rubbing his laser's cool, smooth metal. Four minutes ticked by as Nehi stood rigid, straining to hear any sound. The tramp of feet reached him, soft, but growing quickly. He kicked Joe in the foot, pointing down the hall. Joe shot up and ducked behind one of the beautiful hanging tapestries, jerking Nehemiah with him. The boys huddled in the darkness, waiting for something to happen.

Layth took the coins slowly, a hint of hope hovering on his face for a moment. His expression melted back to the hopeless grimness, and he handed them back.

"Tariq will not give her up, especially to me," he said, the

The Wazir's Council
Psalm 46:1

words slow and halting, as if he couldn't even speak through the depth of misery choking him. "Keep it for the next who needs it."

"Who will not give up whom?" Adam Bight asked, compassionate concern for Layth's despair getting the better of his polite silence. Layth took a deep breath, and Anna could hear it rattle through him, wet and hard, before he spoke in a flat voice.

"My wife, Mahreen, was discovered to be a Christian two days ago. She is very beautiful and was offered for a high price in the market. None that I know had enough to buy her. A wealthy brute, Tariq, bought her this morning."

"They sell those who aren't Muslims?" Elizabeth asked in shock. Color flew into her cheeks and she stammered something, obviously not having meant to say that out loud.

"Yes, young Miss Bight," Naadar answered. "If they will make a good slave to someone. It is that, or they are tortured and killed if they will not accept the Muslim faith. Years ago it was not so. Many wazirs imposed taxes instead, especially on the unbelievers who were not of the Way. But fear, hatred, and prosperity has grown in the leaders, and for two generations now this has been the practice with Christians. As Layth says, his wife is very beautiful and the slavers were glad to find her. Tariq was pleased to add her to his other slaves."

"Slaves, as in something like Solomon's concubines?" Anna whispered to Mr. Bight. "Like Solomon?"

"Yes, I'm afraid so," he whispered back. "A Muslim man can have as many as he desires, and up to four wives. And he can marry wives temporarily, too."

"Good heavens," Anna murmured. She glanced at Layth's downcast eyes and set demeanor and wondered how he could live with the knowledge of his wife in a place like that. Anna looked up at Cobeau and saw his big, hairy face held the same compassion as she felt, and Adam Bight followed her gaze. One of his hands rose as an idea struck him.

"Cobeau, I don't suppose you might..." he started, but

stopped awkwardly. Anna glanced at him and caught the idea. There had been some remarkable feats done by the chimera since she had known him… She took his big, hairy hand.

"Beau, do you think you could help?" Anna prodded quietly. He stirred a pile of imaginary dirt with his toe, his eyes riveted on the task.

"I'm not supposed to leave you, Miss Beauty," Beau mumbled. Which meant he could help. She knew him well enough by now to understand his short, simple sentences.

"But Beau, Joe and Nehi didn't expect Layth's need. You know they would be the first to offer, and I'm among friends here," Beau just stirred the floor with his toe. "How would it be if I promise to stay right here and Naadar promises to see to my safety? What do you think of that, Beau?" Cobeau glanced at her and she could tell he desperately wanted to help the young couple. "Please, Beau?" Anna coaxed.

"What are you two talking about?" Naadar asked. A soft whine sounded in the room as Beau pulled the snub-nosed laser out of his belt, slid the safety off, and began to check it over. Everyone stared at it. The chimera's expression was steady and determined, and Anna knew she had won. She spun to Layth and smiled.

"Beau will go with you. He will see you get your wife back if it can be done," she said. Layth looked from her to the big chimera, his blue eyes wide and hope beginning to sparkle. Beau shifted through his pockets, shuffling through laser goggles, lock-picks, grenades, daggers, checking over the equipment before he left. The whining laser suddenly pointed at Naadar's stomach. The IDP leader tightened as he stared into the glowing red circle at the end of the barrel.

"You take care of Miss Beauty," Cobeau rumbled, a growl under the words. He turned to Anna. "Don't leave. Joe and Nehi will come."

"They're coming here?" Anna asked, but Beau had already turned to Layth, the safety back on, the silent laser tucked back in his belt out of sight, and his large, hairy face smiling and calm.

"Go on," he rumbled to the young man, motioning at the door. Layth stared at him for an instant. Then he grabbed the pile of coins, stuffed them into his pocket and bolted, Cobeau lumbering behind him. The heavy oak door clicked closed behind them.

"Well. That was sudden," Naadar commented. "The little one and who are supposed to come here?" he asked, turning to Anna.

"My brother, Nehemiah," she answered. "I don't know if that's what Beau meant though, he's a little unconnected in his thoughts sometimes."

"And you sent him with young Layth to the home of Tariq, one of the most strongly guarded households in this town?" Naadar asked acidly.

"You don't know Beau," Anna said with a disarming smile. "He may not be too sharp, but he's very good at some things. Rescues are one of them, from what I know of him."

"She's right, Naadar, the Ravens have done some remarkable things," Adam Bight put in. "And naturally you've heard about the gaurdogs of the People's Kingdom. Now, I don't actually know what lies in Cobeau's past, but I have surmised..."

"Surely that is just rumor. The chimeras cannot be trained to perform such feats as the guardogs are reported to achieve. And the Brotherhood has denied all knowledge of such a band of operatives existing," Naadar said.

"Well, the People's Kingdom isn't exactly known for telling the rest of the world a straight story, are they? Especially about things like rifling through other kingdoms' treasuries," Adam snorted. Naadar studied him thoughtfully for a moment. Then he turned to Anna, sighed, and stood up.

"Well, if I don't want the chimera's wrath coming on me, I had better make sure you are safe till he comes back. Adam, I could use your eyes, do you mind?" Mr. Bight hopped up, the heavy door closed behind the two men, and Anna and Elizabeth found themselves alone.

"Slaves," Elizabeth said quietly, shock and disgust in her voice. "I didn't realize it was a reality anywhere on this earth. I always thought it was a horror story from the past world. The effects must be dreadful, to be used as a piece of property!"

"It is," Anna said quietly, and Elizabeth looked at her in concern, her open face working as she tried to decide what to say. A little smile slid over Anna to show it was all right. "My brother and I were enslaved for the four months between when the disintegration hit and the Ravens rescued us. My time wasn't so bad, but Nehemiah's position was harsh, very harsh, and he still fights with the effects. And I don't know for sure but I think Joe, the other Raven, may have something similar to Nehi's story in his background. I get hints of it when he flinches at an unexpected movement, or in the way he doesn't look into people's eyes unless he knows them very well. It's...heartbreaking, honestly, to see the insecurity and fear brought on by even a short term of hard slavery."

Elizabeth could see the trouble in her new friend's face, and with the instinct of a woman knew it went deep. She was an impulsive young lady, with an outgoing kindness that often frightened people away. Today she decided not to practice tactfully overlooking things. Two arms wrapped around Anna's shoulders and drew her close in a tight hug, ignoring the way Anna stiffened in surprise.

"I won't say, 'It will all be all right,' even though I want to," Elizabeth said honestly. "But I do know Someone who can make it all right. Pray with me, for your brother." She dropped to her knees on a bright red cushion, one of Anna's hands in her own, and started praying. Anna settled slowly beside her, a warm smile stealing over her face and going all the way through her in a happy warmth of soul. It had been too, too long since she had someone other than Nehi to pray with. She steadied her thoughts, and began, letting all her heartbreak and aching desire to see Nehi strong again pour out. The words kept coming, and the two young ladies stayed on the cushion, praying.

Six miles across town and a quarter of a mile above them, Nehemiah crouched on a hot roof, and felt peace stealing into him as the girls carried him to the Healer.

The soldiers' stomping came quickly toward the boys and paused in front of the doors. The click of the door opening came and with it someone babbling terrified excuses in the room beyond. Nehemiah stiffened and looked at the blob of darkness he knew was Joe. A small, strong hand gripped his shoulder, telling him to wait and be still. The jabbering one moved off down the hall with the soldiers' tread, and other voices could be heard. The Wazir spoke to someone near their tapestry, probably watching the group of soldiers and their prisoner.

"He will confess I am sure, Tariq. But I wish you to check the little informant's facts anyway. We do not wish to execute the wrong man; Allah would not be pleased with a faithful believer dying at our hands."

"Yes, Wazir, but..." The proud voice of the soldier broke off, hesitant to speak against an order.

"What is it, Tariq, I do not have all day," the Wazir said testily.

"I have just arrested two Christians, a leader from KAM and a merchant." Joe's hand tightened and Nehemiah fought the urge to squirm as his friend's nails dug into his shoulder. "I was planning to break them to reach the heart of the dishonorable IDP, this will–"

"Your passion is admirable," the Wazir interrupted. "But justice comes before even that hoped for event, Tariq. See to the proof. These two new captives will wait, and will break easier the longer you have them in your power."

The two girls prayed and talked. They soon became Lizzy and Ann as they waited for something to happen in the underground church, surprised to so quickly feel as if they had been best friends for years. Both were young. They hadn't yet realized that the deepest friendships aren't formed from mere shared likes and dislikes, but by a sharing of the intensities of life. A good prayer together, a pouring out of hearts before heaven's throne, can form friendships that last through years.

After two hours, they started to chafe at being left alone with no news. Anna got off the couch to stretch and walk about the room. As she passed the door, she paused, listening. She heard footsteps coming down the long staircase. Elizabeth stood up quickly and headed toward the door with a smile, ready to greet the newcomers. Anna laid a hand on her arm and pulled her back, frowning.

"What is it?" Elizabeth asked, lowering her voice as she saw Anna's expression.

"Lizzy, those footsteps don't seem right. It sounds like when a new prisoner was being pushed down the stairs into the cellars for placement, a firm step, and a shuffling, fighting step. Oh, I'm probably just paranoid, but let's not be seen right away." Anna pulled Elizabeth after her as she whispered, and pushed her into a large cupboard that held spare pillows and coffee cups. Anna slid in after her and pulled the door to a crack, one eye fixed on the door to the stairs. The footsteps reached the bottom stairwell and paused.

The heavy door crashed open, rebounding with a bang. Elizabeth jumped, her hand going to her mouth. Anna's hand shot up, gripping her friend's arm, her dark eyes riveted to the tiny crack in the door of their cupboard.

Naadar stumbled into the room. His arms were pulled behind him, bound in place with a rough rope, joined to a length of rope pulled tight around his neck. Discolored bruises covered his face, his hair was disheveled, and a jagged cut ran across his forehead and dribbled blood down his ear. A tall soldier marched in behind him. His smooth features cut into a frown, his eyes hard as they darted around the room. He cradled a red Krackmen laser in one arm and the end of the rope from Naadar's neck in his other.

"I do not see the beautiful stranger, unbelieving filth," the soldier's hard tones cut through the air. Elizabeth started to tremble.

"I did not say she was here," Naadar said, his voice hoarse and low.

"You said nothing," the soldier sneered. His hand jerked and Naadar stumbled back, gagging and retching. "A fact which you will pay dearly for later. But if you speak now, some of the punishment may be alleviated. Where is the woman? I have given you a description of her; dark, handsome, young, olive skinned, black curls...she sounds worth finding." Naadar stood silent, his eyes focused on the ground and his jaw set in a determined line. "Tariq is looking for her, under orders from others, unbelieving filth. Others he serves, much more powerful than Tariq. They want her and her brother and you will find their gratitude at your silence even warmer than ours."

Naadar didn't lift his eyes. The soldier's lips curled in a tight cruel line as he studied the merchant. He dragged Naadar to a corner, wrapped the neck rope around his ankles, and left him to try and breathe. The soldier began to walk about the room, overturning couches and tables, delving into anywhere someone might hide. He was very efficient. They had seconds before he tried their cupboard. Anna gripped Elizabeth's hand in an effort to keep her trembling friend calm, and prayed fervently, her brain racing for a way out. She wasn't going to be caught by this nasty man, not while she lived.

Chapter Eight: Tariq's Dungeons

"... faith, if it hath not works, is dead, being alone."

James 2:17

T he boys waited behind the tapestry, ears strained and bodies tense. After five quiet minutes, they were sure the hall had cleared. Joe slid out and began to stride quickly from the building, Nehi tagging at his heels. Half a minute and the bright florescent lighting gave way to the brilliant sun blazing in the courtyard. Joe strode through the gates without a glance at the guards and moved out of sight into the maze of streets. He broke into a trot, his shoulders slumped, and he went back to himself. Nehi kept tagging, trotting along and not thinking, just moving. A couple turned into the top of their street and Joe spun into an alley, Nehemiah on his heels. The alley stank, the shadows deep as it wound between two apartment buildings. Joe paused at the top, where it spilled into another bright little street, holographic signal signs shimmering in the hot air. He waited till a group of laughing teenage boys strolled past, then trotted over the street into the next alley and kept going. After about a mile of ducking through little used ways, keeping out of sight as much as possible, Joe turned into a neighborhood, ducked into an alley, and disappeared.

Nehemiah swayed to a stop, his heartbeat pausing. For a horrid second his suspicions came back to him. He reached for Hope, his throat tightening as his pulse roared in his ears.

A thin nylon cord hit him in the nose. Nehi staggered back a step and focused on it. The cord kept sliding down, suspended in the air. Nehemiah's eyes followed it and he spotted Joe perched on the flat roof to his left. He breathed again, gripped the rope, hopped on a windowsill, and worked his way up to the roof. Joe's high collared, black leather jacket was long-sleeved (unlike the three-quarter sleeved one Nehi often wore) and as he gained his friend's side, for the first time Nehemiah realized why. Joe's left sleeve had a flap of material bent up, like the lid to a hidden compartment. Under it, gadgets and gizmos twinkled in the bright sunlight. As Joe swiftly wound the nylon cord back in place above his elbow, Nehi glimpsed trackers, a compass, a mini radar, something labeled 'Shorts out system,' a blowgun, case of darts, un-labeled black disks, and something he hoped wasn't cheese wire. Then the leather flap flipped closed, slipping so naturally in place there wasn't even a bulge.

Joe led the way behind a chimney where they couldn't be seen from the street and dropped cross-legged onto the roof tiles. Nehemiah settled beside him and waited, curious over the black discs, and silently wondering what else the mute might have hidden. Joe just stared at the opposite house, obviously not seeing it. His green eyes were bright and calculating, and the rest of his face remarkably blank.

Nehemiah sat and prayed. There was a burning shame in him for the thoughts that flooded him back in the midst of that panic. But a moment at God's throne, a whispered apology, and peace settled. It was a complete peace. A resting. And it wasn't from his strength, not really. Nehemiah recognized it, breathed a thank you, and just sat letting the dry breeze run over him and relishing in the quietness of his soul. He felt like himself again, himself before the disintegration. No. He had grown, a lot. But this was...there was no doubt, no anger. Just a living in Christ again. He smiled and rested in the peace.

Five minutes later the inner peace had become curiosity over what Joe could be thinking as the mute stared at the opposite chimney. Another five minutes, and it was plain boredom. A quarter of an hour after they had clambered up to the roof, Nehi couldn't stand the quiet anymore. He shoved Joe sharply in the shoulder, and the mute tipped to the side, only just saving himself from tumbling off to the street.

"What was that for?" Joe signed, shooting Nehi a confused look as his eyebrows drew together.

"You're taking forever! What's the next move?" Nehi de-

manded. A smile spread over the mute, then he glanced away, almost shyly.

"Thank you," he signed.

"What for?" asked Nehemiah in surprise.

"For not saying, 'Are you sure you're not a traitor?' or something like that." Joe stirred, spun to face Nehemiah, and began to sign. "I have a question for you. You heard what T said, he has a couple of our brothers in his hands. He's probably right about breaking the IDP here if he breaks them, and I wonder if Glue and…" Joe's eyes flitted up to Nehi's and away again, and for a moment Nehi watched worry wrinkle the mute's face. It disappeared, swallowed by business. "Right now T-a-r-i-q is off on my goose-chase (perfectly legitimate, by the way, the one they took away really is a traitor and not a nice one). Now might be the one time we're able to get them out of his dungeons. It's a risk for us, but not impossible. I have my white card from the Wazir after my last services, and it lets me in and out, and usually lets people with me in and out too."

"In and out of where?"

"Everywhere. Anywhere. It is not _"

"I don't know that last sign," Nehi broke in.

"I-n-f-a-l-l-i-b-l-e," Joe fingerspelled quickly.

"Wow, you have signs for things like infallible?" Nehemiah asked. Joe grinned at him.

"You're either not taking me seriously, not about to go with me, or not worried about the risks. Which is it?" he signed.

"The last," Nehemiah answered, feeling the steadiness his voice carried. "If there's any chance at all we should take it, even if it's just two random brothers and has nothing to do with the IDP. Reminds me of James, talking about faith and works, you have to have them both. I believe God's in charge, but we should help anyway. I would like to get back to Anna as soon as possible though, so how about hurrying and not staring at buildings anymore?" A laugh changed the lines on Joe's scarred face and sent his natural merriness twinkling in his eyes again.

"You're a remarkable man, Knee-High," he signed. "Follow my lead, translate for me if I need it, and let's go. Oh, and keep Hope ready. We might need her suddenly."

Joe moved to the edge of the house and leapt down into the street, landing lightly on his toes and moving off immediately. Nehemiah landed more heavily and it took him a minute to catch up. Joe strode through town, with no ducking in alleys or on top roofs this time. His stiff pride was back on, and the character that went with the look and the Wazir's white card was much too sure of himself to care who saw them. Joe drew to a stop on a small, dark street at the top of a hill with a large, guarded building alone at the top. It rose into the evening sky, jagged spikes from a high wall cutting through the air and looking as if they wanted to pierce a hole in anything that could feel pain. Joe leaned against a house and looked at the building.

"What is it?" Nehemiah murmured. "I don't like the look of that at all."

"T-a-r-i-q-'s Dungeons are what most call it," Joe signed and fingerspelled. "Where the malefactors, unbelievers, and other undesirables are taken. T's one of their best... persuaders." His hands dropped to his sides, and the stern look suddenly fell into the real Joe. His arms stole around his chest, hugging himself, shivering a little, his sharp face pinched and strained as he stared at the place. He was scared. But he drew in a breath and straightened his shoulders, his eyes closing for an instant. "God's got us, Knee-High."

"He does," Nehemiah agreed, conviction ringing through the quiet words. "Our hope is sure; keep that vision burning." A smile crept over the mute.

"You and Glue are a lot alike sometimes," he signed. *Yeah, and sometimes I'm a scared rabbit,* Nehemiah thought with an inward grimace. Maybe he was developing a split personality... No. He was growing out of childish things, and out of Abid's fear tactics and planted doubts, and into who the man he was supposed to be. "Put off the old man...[5]" It took work, and time to lose the old, and the scars it left were deep. But this afternoon Nehemiah had seen a ribbon of his own strength, like a little side spring flowing from the river of God's peace. It gave him hope that he could win out over the fears. And hope makes everything easier to bear and every strength stronger.

"Okay, let's go." Joe turned stiff again, his back straight and shoulders squared. He spun onto the sidewalk winding up the hill and marched toward the gate.

Anna could hear her pulse pounding as the soldier turned from the couch. His bright eyes focused on the cupboard. Anna forced herself not to jerk away, knowing he would see the movement. Silent prayers filled her, begging for him not to see her staring back. Elizabeth trembled violently, one hand clamped over her mouth and her face paper white. Anna put her hands on the inside of both the doors, waiting. The soldier stepped up to the cupboard. He reached for the door handle with one hand, the other holding his laser. Anna threw herself against the doors, diving through in a roll. Both doors hit the soldier in the face and he fell back, his head reeling. For half a second he was disoriented, and Anna used it.

She cupped the heavy laser rifle in her left arm, slamming her right down onto his arm as she levered up violently with her left. The weapon wrenched away into her grasp. Anna shoved the weapon up and the butt cracked into the soldier's chin. His head snapped up and he staggered, trying to pull his arms into a defensive position. Anna didn't give him the chance. She stepped forward quickly, sending a right hook to his temple. His eyes glazed and he toppled to the right, landing groggily on one knee. Anna brought the laser down on his

---

[5] Ephesians 4:20-24

skull, trying to ignore the heavy thump as it connected. He went down, hard. She stood breathing heavily, adrenaline singing through her, staring at him. Nothing moved, not even a finger twitched.

"I think I'm going to be sick," Elizabeth almost whimpered, her voice thick. Anna slung the rifle over her shoulder and put her finger to her lips.

"Shh, there might be more," she hissed at her friend. A sort of bleat slid from Elizabeth. But she stepped out of the cabinet and followed as Anna pulled out her pocketknife and ran to Naadar. He stared at Anna as she dropped to her knees beside him, the long laser bumping uncomfortably against her legs.

"You did not seem as if you could do that sort of thing," he wheezed around the halter. She slid her knife blade in between two ropes and started to saw.

"The Sojourner women are taught how to defend their faith like the men. But unlike our men, we aren't really expected to have to use our skills," Anna answered a little wryly. The rope snapped and he slumped, his limbs splaying on the floor. Anna cleared the ropes off him, handing them to Elizabeth. "Go tie that soldier up," she ordered, and turned back to Naadar. She slid an arm under his shoulder, and lifted, levering Naadar into a sitting position. Naadar struggled to his feet, grimacing and biting his lip, his eyes screwed partially shut. Anna glanced at her friend and saw Elizabeth standing over the twitching soldier, staring in bewilderment at the ropes in her hands. It took all Anna's self-control to keep from rolling her eyes and yelling at her to get on with it.

"We need to leave now, before someone comes to find that soldier," Naadar gasped as Anna supported him. Elizabeth turned to him, her face strained and white.

"My father," she said, her voice quavering. Anna forgave her some of her helplessness; Miss Bight had reason to be distracted and scared. "Was he with you–"

Naadar's hand shot toward the laser, jerked it from Anna's shoulder, leveled it at the center of the room, and hit the trig-

ger. A heavy whine filled the room as the stored energy burst through the lens. The dazzling white light of a laser beam flashed into life. For an instant, Anna saw the white flash in the middle of the soldier, where he had struggled to his knees, his hand clutching a throwing knife. The man was flung backwards. He fell on the cupboard, rocking it. The light disappeared, and Anna's stomach roiled at the remains. The cupboard toppled over on top of what was left. The sickening crash echoed around the room, and she flinched. Naadar stood on his own strength. He slung the laser over his shoulder and began to walk toward the far end of the room. Anna took Elizabeth's shaking hand and pulled her after him. Naadar tugged on a pretty tapestry hanging on the wall and a panel slid open beside it. He flipped on a light and Anna saw a bare concrete tunnel, winding off into the earth.

"There's nothing we can do for your father now, Elizabeth Bight. He's been taken by Tariq's men," Naadar said as he began to labor up the tunnel. "We must get you away safely." Elizabeth froze, swaying on her feet, her white face stricken.

"Come on, Lizzy," Anna said gently. She slipped an arm around her friend and led her into the tunnel. "God has worked miracles before now, pray that He will do it again for your father. Trust in Him, and whatever happens it will be all right in the end. Neither height nor depth can change that." Elizabeth nodded, tears streaming from her. Anna found she was weeping with her as they followed Naadar up the tunnel, her own parents' faces playing in her mind.

Joe flipped his white card out of his pocket and glowered at the guards standing at attention beside the massive lead and steel gate. Nehemiah followed quietly. His heartbeat steadily quickened, and he wondered how Joe looked so confident. The mute snapped his fingers at Nehemiah and inside he cringed.

"I have business inside, open up," Joe signed and Nehemiah ordered. The guards looked at him in disbelief and one laughed. Joe raised an eyebrow and his mouth curved into a humorless smile. He waved his card under the nose of the laughing guard. The man's laughter died in a choke. The gate swung open.

"Forgive our doubt," said a tall, black-haired man standing beside the gate guards. His tone was respectful as Joe came through with Nehemiah on his heels. The man's chiseled nose, bright eyes, and grimness reminded Nehemiah of a hawk. "We have heard of the Wazir's white card, but never seen one who carries it. You can understand why we–" Joe snapped at Nehemiah.

"What's your name?" he signed and Nehemiah said.

"Taban, esteemed one," answered the guard. A familiar twinkle showed in Joe's green eyes for a moment at being addressed as "esteemed one." He squashed it and signed again.

"I did not come to hear apologies. You have two new prisoners here, members of the Way waiting to be dealt with by Tariq himself. Take me to them."

"I am not sure that is allowed," Taban began, his frown deepening. A hand landed on his shoulder, from someone in a dark corner of the courtyard. Another tall figure, a man turned away from Nehi and Joe, stepped up to the hawkish one; a young, powerful figure, coattails carefully folded and buttoned in a cut that marked him as an officer.

"I'll take these two, return to your duties," the stranger ordered. A tingle ran through Nehi as he heard the voice, a memory of fear and awful hope and Abid's rooms...but then it was gone and he couldn't place why it had come to him. This building. It must be this place that brought it on, surrounded by so many like Abid.

"Come," the officer said from the shadows, and he began to stride for the massive building. Nehi walked quietly behind Joe as the mute followed the stranger. A young guard pulled a large iron door open for them as they neared the building, and the three marched into a packed, busy hallway. Every soldier they came to saluted and stepped aside for their guide.

"I think we got the right guard," Joe signed secretly to Nehemiah. Nehemiah didn't respond, unsure if they had, and concentrated on following and not paying attention to his surroundings. They were very unnerving and nasty surroundings. Nehemiah kept close to Joe and wished he could shut out the sounds as easily as he could the sights. The man walked on and on, deeper into the building, past cells, and rooms, and hallways, until Nehemiah thought they must be coming to the other end soon. Finally he turned into a short hallway lined with four simple, dark cells. But this hallway was deserted. Nehi automatically let the door swing shut behind him as he stepped through as the last of the party. It clanged shut, the echo reverberating around the concrete hall.

Their guide spun on his heel, kicked Joe's legs from under him, slammed a hand into the back of his leather coat, and flung the mute into an open cell. Metal clanged against metal, colliding with the echoes of the outer door as the cell locked. Hope whipped into Nehi's hand as a growl started in his throat.

"What do you think you're doing?" Nehi snarled, staring over Hope's leveled barrel.

"Saving you from more torment," the guide answered, and turned around. Hope sagged as Nehi gaped at the brown eyes staring back into his.

"Atif?" he muttered. His hand suddenly throbbed with the old pain. He had to resist the urge to rub it.

"I doubt you wanted to see me today. Or any day," Atif said, nervousness showing through his immaculate guise in the Islamic uniform. "But I was too overjoyed to see you alive and well to stand by when you walked in with this odious turncoat." He waved a hand at Joe, as the mute stood glaring through the bars, anger clear on his expressive face; fear ran just underneath it, almost hidden even to Nehi. Nehemiah just stared, trying to catch up with events as his insides churned.

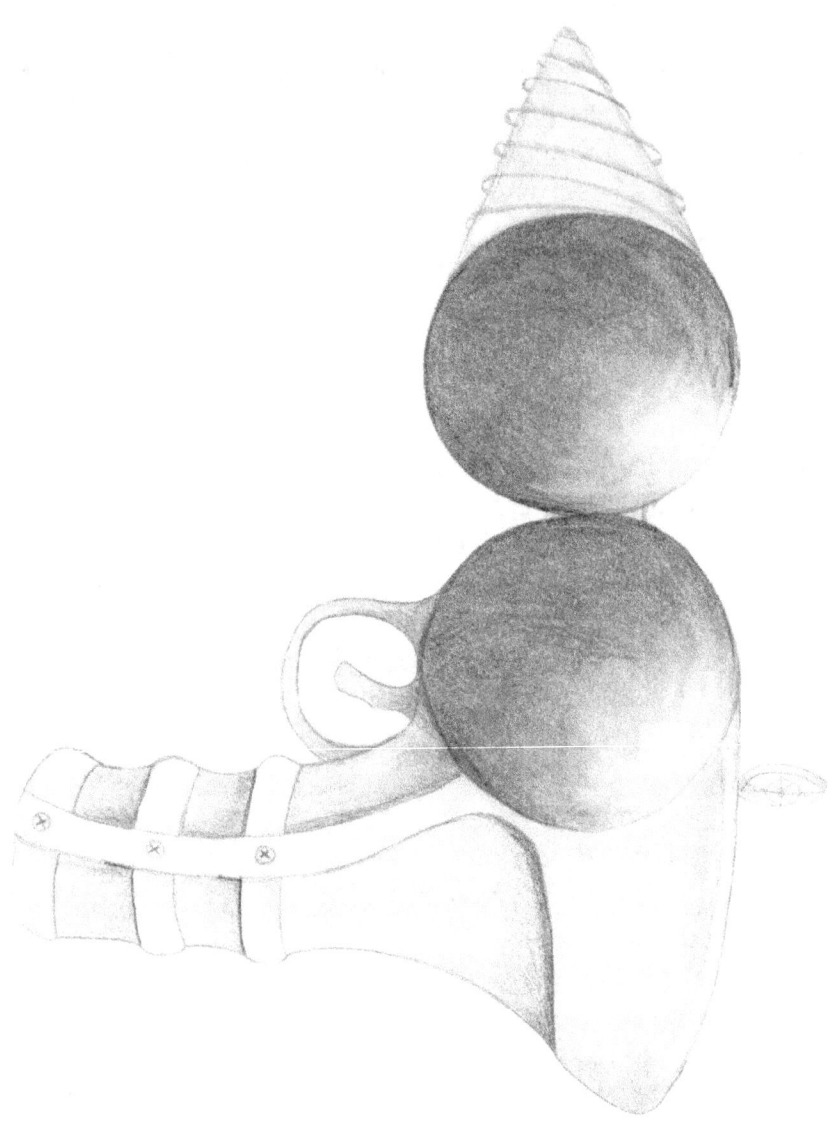

Hope

He pushed the emotions away, knowing now was not the time to sort out memories and feelings. Atif's mouth opened, then closed. Then he spoke again, quietly.

"I did go back for you. After I had reassured my superiors of my loyalty, I was able to go where I pleased. You were gone, and no one knew where. I met others searching for you, more that came to Abid's rooms and whose hearts were changed by your courage. There is a small party of us working in this jail to do what we can for our imprisoned brothers and sisters, and they will be as relieved as I am to know you live. Why you are here now, with this cretin, is a matter of great interest to me. But I will see you get out again." A sharp clicking started up from the cell as Joe switched his glare to Nehi.

"You've got it wrong," Nehi started, uncertain whether to laugh, or yell and run, at this strange turn of events. "Joe's my friend, and a brother."

"He has a white card from the Wazir himself," Atif hissed, taking a step closer to Nehi. "You cannot trust this man!"

"You have the coat of a Muslim officer," Nehi countered. Atif fell back blinking between Joe and Nehi. "We're here to get a KAM IDP leader and a merchant out."

"N-a-a-d-a-r?" Joe fingerspelled, raising an eyebrow to make it a question.

"Yes, I have heard it is Naadar who was captured," Atif answered, studying Joe. "But he has not been brought in yet." Both Joe's eyebrows rose. He whipped toward Nehi and began to sign in a rush.

"Get me out of here and take us to the one you do have! We don't have much time if that's the case." Atif hesitated, still staring at Joe. Nehi slid Hope in his holster and held out his scarred hand. Atif recoiled. Nehemiah stepped forward and gripped the man's hand in his own, clasping it hard.

"I trust you, brother," he said simply. Atif stared at their clasped hands, seeing more than the scars, his eye twitching convulsively. Nehi nodded at the cell. "Thank you for being willing to tackle an esteemed one for me. But I trust him too.

Let him out and let's get on with this business." Atif only nod-ded, his eyes down and his face tight. He reached for the keys on his belt. They weren't there. A soft clink came from the cell door and he glanced up to see the mute shoving the door open. Joe tossed the keys back and motioned up the hall. Their guide turned and began to lead the way again in silence, marching faster than before. In less than a minute they had turned out of the deserted hallway back into populated places. Another two minutes and they reached a heavily secured door at the end of a long passage. The stark gray walls of this hall were populated by fewer people, but some still moved around them as Atif began to go through the security measures.

"Where is Naadar the merchant?" Joe signed, and snapped at Nehi to translate.

"Tariq sent him with one of his own men," Atif said as a scanner ran over his thumbprint. He almost growled it.

"Why did Tariq do that?" Nehemiah said, phrasing it care-fully for the sake of any chance listeners. "It sounds like a gross breach of security to me. One man with a highly useful prisoner?"

"This is my thought also," Atif said, a heavy frown on his face as he waited for the bio scan to accept his blood sample. "But I do not think the prisoner will escape. Tariq's men are skilled." Joe snapped at Nehemiah.

"I do not like this," the mute signed, a sneering frown on his proud face. "Does Tariq do this often? You do not answer, why?" Atif studied Joe for a moment. The massive door clicked and swung open with a smooth, slow weight, and he motioned them inside. The three passed through and the door closed, leaving them standing alone in a brightly lit room. A small metal cell rested in one corner.

"The Wazir's white card allows you to come and go wher-ever you please," Atif said to Joe, with studied politeness; he still didn't trust him. "But it does not allow you into men's minds. Only if you could see into Tariq could you learn why he sends his men on these special errands. I do not know."

"I think you do," Joe signed and Nehemiah said. Joe looked at Atif searchingly for a moment. "Did he speak to you of a girl? Tall, olive skinned, black hair?" Atif looked at Joe with new respect.

"I see you do not need the card to enter men's minds," the soldier answered. "Yes, beautiful slaves are a weakness of Tariq's, the brute. He spoke to me of one most beauteous he hoped to have soon." His eyes rose to rest on Nehi. "From his description, I would say she looks a great deal like you, in feminine form." For half a second everything went black to Nehi, his stomach twisting. Anna! A foot kicked his, and Nehemiah looked up to see the two men watching him. Atif was detachedly curious, and outwardly Joe was the same. But the green eyes latched onto his for just a moment and urgently said, "Don't panic now."

"I don't like it," Joe signed and Nehemiah said steadily. The mute abruptly pointed at the single cell.

"Yes, that is where our fellow Christian is. I am glad you came, I did not know how to release him alone." He took a step toward it, but Joe whistled, motioning him back. For a moment his stiffness relaxed into something closer to the real Joe.

"This is going to cause a real stink," the mute signed and Nehi translated. "You'll be under suspicion, as well as everyone you work with. Go, get your team and get out now." Atif hesitated. It was obvious he was highly tempted. Joe softened into his normal self, seeming to whither into the small, cheerful young man he usually was. He smiled and slapped Atif's shoulder. "Go on, brother, you and your men get out and live to fight another day. I'm hopeful N-a-a-d-a-r not being here yet means he's managed a miracle and gotten himself out. Knee-High and I will bring this one with us, we'll leave through gate C after you and your men have cleared it for us on your way out."

"We can clear gate C for you," Atif nodded brightening in a grim sort of way. A clear method to help lent a more honorable air to getting out ahead of these two young brothers. "All right. We will go."

"My name's Nehemiah, by the way. I hope we meet again where we can actually have a conversation," Nehi commented, forcing a smile. Atif smiled back, tightly, opened his mouth to say something, closed it again, slapped his hand into Nehi's in a farewell, and hurried away to find his men. The door clicked closed behind him and Nehi glanced down at the small white card resting on his left palm; a simple rectangle of white paper with only a jumbled series of numbers.

He would have to figure out what it meant later, now he trotted forward to catch up to Joe, slipping the little paper in his pocket. It was time for a rescue.

Chapter Nine: Clearing Gate C

"Then all this assembly shall know that the LORD does not save with sword and spear; for the battle is the LORD's, and He will give you into our hands." 1 Samuel 17:47

Atif strode through the stark gray halls, never looking around. He stood erect and firm, assurance radiating from him; an officer on a mission. He had learned long ago pretending to be in charge usually made you in charge. And it was best to be in charge when you were surrounded by deadly enemies. General Larson passed by on his left and Atif deigned to nod. But inside, as his eye met the dark stare, heard the disdainful sniff as Larson looked him up and down, remembered the cruelties and the laughter that rang from him through the screams of his victims, Atif's skin prickled and each hair seemed to dance. It was often the way in this life he had chosen. But today, every sense was heightened and the danger pressed close. So close it was a weight constricting his chest. His fingers rhythmically tapped his palm as he walked. To those he passed, it looked like Captain Atif's absent-minded tattoo he played sometimes as he went about his business.

But in the control room, a wispy young man sat up suddenly, his fingers poised above the LED keyboard, and his green eyes tightening. He stood up, grabbed his black bag, and headed out the door; on the way to Gate C.

In the labyrinthine recesses of the mechanical workings running under the jail, Otar the Hammer stopped mid swing. His mouth hardened till every wrinkle on his wide face was accentuated. He tossed his hammer into his tool bag, grabbed it up, and began to trot toward Gate C.

Outside, at the broken south inner wall, a tall dark officer stammered mid-order and his men looked at him in surprise. Lieutenant Taban was not one to be unsure. He quickly ordered the completion of the wall, spun on his heel and walked away toward Gate C. His men glanced at each other, but didn't dare comment; Taban was not one you disobeyed.

Shareef heard the Morse call over his bone plant, vibrating in his jawbone, just like the others. But he could guess what it was about. The red-haired supplier had seen Atif walk in with two men and walk out alone. The tall young man who went in behind Atif had changed and grown, and hardly looked like the broken slave. But Shareef would never forget that face, no matter how altered. Shareef shoved his clipboard at a subordinate, mumbled something about different stock, and began to trot for Gate C. But he took the time to gather some things as he moved through the warehouse.

Atif studied the situation as he pushed through the door into the outer courtyard. The sheer concrete wall (reinforced with lead braces to discourage laser fire) rose fifteen feet into the cloudy sky, shutting out all sight of the town and freedom. The massive lead and titanium gates stood just in front of him. Fifteen feet high, two feet thick, black, solid metal. Gate C wasn't in any of his men's jurisdictions. Just being here brought them under suspicion. The gate guards stood alert and poised, aware theirs was a life and death job. If they failed Tariq, he would see their deaths were unusually harsh and cruel. Twenty guards, ten inside the gate, ten outside, each totally committed to their work. The massive black gates were bolted and locked from the inside and out.

A rectangle of light pierced through the afternoon shadows as a door shoved open. Atif recognized the silhouette in the doorway, the slouched, wispy form of Naqi his tech man. Naqi spotted his leader and headed for him. Atif waved him to the gate and began to stride for Taban. The tall officer was the strictest man working in the dungeons, but very few knew of his weapons expertise. Taban was one of the foremost experts in hand-to-hand fighting, and eighty-three percent of the weapons out on the market. Taban had told Atif that when they were first introduced, with no boasting, just fact behind it. That skill would serve well today.

The bloodstained pavement seemed to suck in the darkness of the shadows and spit it out again as the two men neared each other. Or perhaps that was only Atif's fancy. He had spent so long here, in the darkness of the dungeons, doing what good he could. Now they were getting out. And the darkness seemed to cling to him, whispering it would always keep him, always be a part of him.

"It is time?" Taban murmured.

"We must clear Gate C for an ally," Atif answered without more explanation. If they survived there would be time for that later. "Such a thing cannot be done in secret."

"So we run," Taban stated. Nothing upset his steady frown. Atif spied Otar's big head, pushed up from a duct in the ground as he surveyed the scene. "Tell me when I go in."

A sharp crack sounded from the gate. Atif spun to see the bolts draw back, so violently they slammed in place with a scrunch. In his dark shadow, Naqi's white teeth flashed in a grin. The guards spun in tight circles, scanning the area through their military helmets, their lasers coming off their shoulders and the whine of their priming filling the air. Shareef's mouth dropped open as he turned the corner into section C.

"Now," Atif ordered. Taban shot forward as though Atif had released a spring. He soared into the enemy like a bird of prey, his sharp frown cracking into a grim smile as he finally brought the war openly to the enemies. He was everywhere, smashing into bodies, jerking lasers up to fire, utilizing guards as shields and weapons. He was a blur of deadly motion. Otar rose like a demon in the old tales, his hammer held high, and slammed into the other side of the guards. He raged through them, more like a rhinoceros than an eagle, big, ferocious, and inexorable.

Atif darted into the midst of the carnage. They only had a moment before the alarm tripped, and they must be out by then. The bolts were electric, Naqi had dealt with them. But there were also the conventional locks. Atif's trained eye picked out the main guard, catching him as Taban flung him away like a used tissue. Atif grabbed the man's belt and jerked the keys with such force the belt snapped. He dashed for the gate. The horrendous sounds of slaughter roared in his ears and he could almost swear he heard Taban chuckling. He shoved the key into the lock, turned it, and Atif jerked back, straining to open the huge gates. Laser fire burst in white balls of lethal energy, striking the gate as it swung open. One lit up in a guard, dropping him with a smoking hole in his chest. Atif dragged on the key, forcing the gate open another inch, averting his face and closing his eyes to slits, silently cursing how unprepared he was for this.

Slim fingers slammed goggles over his eyes. Otar's massive hands gripped the door and Atif stepped back, moving beside Shareef as the young man flashed him a smile and expanded the two-man laser shield he held. Shareef the Supplier always had what was needed. Atif spared a glance behind him as he darted through the opening, watching Otar still tugging on the gate. Naqi ran at their heels, gagging at the carnage and clutching his gadget pack to his chest. Taban finished the last of the ten guards, spun beautifully, and sprinted to deal with the outer ten, a borrowed rifle swinging in his arms. They were all here. Ten seconds. It had taken them ten seconds to exit the gate, it was good time. But not good enough. Atif made a quick executive decision, the feel of Nehemiah's hand burning on the back of his neck. He had felt that burning sensation ever since the night he parted with the tortured slave in Abid's rooms. But tonight it shrieked at him in almost physical pain.

They had to do more than just eliminate the guards.

Atif's arm shot up, jerking Taban away from his charge. The leader of the little band gripped the laser shield with his toe and free hand and spun. A stifled exclamation came from Shareef. Taban just jerked Naqi back behind the shield as it changed positions, his frown back on.

"Otar!" Atif bellowed. He felt the weight of the lead shield shift to his arms as Shareef dropped it, and his muscles screamed. Shareef and Taban spun rhythmically around each other, ducking in and out of the shield as they provided a cover for their big friend. Otar sprinted. He wasn't a tall man, only reaching about five-foot-seven. But he weighed three hundred pounds and none of it was fat. Atif thought he could feel the ground shaking as Otar raced for the small band shuffling behind the shield. White laser beams sparked as they hit almost everywhere he looked. His heart in his mouth, Atif prayed, begging desperately for his last man to make it. What would he do if Otar was shot down? They couldn't leave him wounded, not to Tariq's mercies. But if they stayed it meant all of them would be caught.

"Oh God, make him run faster!" Atif gasped under his breath, his arms shrieking at him as he staggered another foot with the shield. White dots sparked in his eyes, and it wasn't from the beams. He was going to faint with the effort in a moment.

"Let me, boss," Otar's growl sounded, and the pressure of the shield lifted. Atif reeled and felt Naqi's thin arms around his shoulders.

"What now?" the tech man squeaked.

"Run," Atif gasped. He blinked his faculties back in order, pointed at a random alley, and sprinted off.

Behind them the alarm split through the night air. A smile almost as grim as Taban's cut across Atif's face as he led the way, carefully keeping to a pace his men could stand, and that would allow their pursuers an occasional glimpse of the quarry. Now they had done more than just clear the gate for their allies. Half the jail would empty, pouring into the streets after the traitors who had massacred the guards. And all the city's military would focus on Atif and his people, leaving other smaller things unnoticed.

Use it well, Nehemiah.

Joe trotted to the cell, his soft boots soundless on the concrete. Nehi shuffled after him, his steps reverberating with each boot fall. He stopped behind Joe, staring over the blond head as the mute stood on tiptoe to get a glimpse through the grill. Only one man was inside. He was middle-aged, balding, sitting hunched and forlorn on the hard cot. Joe tapped the iron door and gave a little whistle. The man turned a round, bruised face toward them. His eyes lit up and his mouth dropped.

"Joe!" the man gasped. The mute's face disappeared from the grill, his hand fluttered for a moment as he gave a little wave hello, then he snapped at Nehemiah. Nehi's arm shot out and his fingers clamped around Joe's neck.

"Stop with the snapping," Nehi growled, and shoved the mute away.

"Ok, ok," Joe signed, grimacing and laughing in one breath. He ran a hand over his neck dramatically then smiled with sickly sweetness. "Pretty please, will you translate, dear Knee-High?"

"Still better," Nehi muttered, his eyes rolling, and Joe grinned at him. "Don't you think this place is riddled with security?"

"Now you ask?" Joe signed, his eyes twinkling. He flipped a thin, black tablet at Nehi. It was about the size of a greeting card, the screen alive with codes flashing by in green script; scrambling every security measure, interfering with the cameras and sensors as they walked. Nehemiah looked up to tell his friend he was a genius and saw the metal door swinging open. Adam Bight stood up eagerly. He gasped and swayed, one shaking hand going to the wall, as the other went around his bruised ribs. Nehemiah slid past Joe and slipped an arm under Adam's shoulders, helping him out of the cell. The man gave him a strained smile as a thanks. Then he did a neat double take.

"I know you," he rasped. "Well, I don't know you, but I know who you are. You're Anna's brother."

"Is she all right?" Nehi almost gasped. Joe slid a rope around Adam's wrists, pulling his arms behind him and letting the rope snake out. In the same second, Joe shoved the end of the rope to Nehi, whistled for translation, and started signing.

"Sorry for the setup, A-d-a-m, it's just till we get out of this place. Think you can walk on your own?"

"Yes," Adam Bight grunted, shifting his weight away from Nehi. He met the young man's begging eyes and nodded. "She was fine when I left her with my daughter, about two hours ago. They are waiting for Cobeau to return from an errand of mercy."

"Return!" Nehi yelped. Joe prodded him in the ribs and pointed at the door out. Nehemiah spun on him, eyes wide and staring. Joe's lips pursed and his hands flashed as he signed.

"No, I didn't know Glue was leaving her, he shouldn't have. Let's get out of here, then we can find out what happened."

"But Joe–" Nehi bit it off, took a breath, and shut up. Joe was right. They had to get out first or they would be no help to anyone.

Joe dragged open the heavy door. Shouted orders, tramping feet, sobbing prisoners, a distant scream…they were back in the busy hum of business in Tariq's dungeons. Nehi followed Joe out, pushing Adam ahead of him and his hand hovering near Hope, keeping his head up and eyes straight. He couldn't hesitate. If they seemed confident no one would stop and ask their business. Joe strode on, flipping his white card absently between his knuckles as he walked. The few people who glanced their way caught the flash of white, and just kept walking.

Ten minutes slid past and Adam Bight began to stumble. Nehemiah could hear him wheezing even over the steady roar of activity around them. Things needed to change soon or their "prisoner" was going to be in trouble.

A blaring alarm cut through the hallway.

It pierced through Nehemiah's brain and shook it, drowning everything in its scream. Everywhere feet picked up to a run. People pounded through the hallways, soldiers headed to their emergency posts, guards checking on their prisoners, officers marshaling their men. Joe sped up to a trot to keep from looking suspicious as the hectic rush moved around them, and Nehemiah stepped forward, slipping an arm around Adam's laboring sides. The IDP man slumped against him and most of Adam's weight transferred to the young man. Nehi caught a flash of green eyes as Joe glanced over his shoulder. The mute slowed down. Nehi bit his tongue to keep from yelling at him to run, and tried to push their pace. Joe refused to speed up; he stayed stubbornly in front of Nehi. People dashed around them, and they plunged through the busy rush of the jail. The alarm blared on, shaking their insides with its wail. The hallways began to empty around them. Joe trotted around another corner, and suddenly no one was there but them.

Their slow pace had given the rest of the jail time to empty in the hunt for Atif and his band. Nehi glanced at his friend with new respect.

The alarm cut off. Silence tingled in their ears. Joe glanced back at them, gave an encouraging wink, and picked it up to a run. The little party sped toward a simple metal door at the end of the hall. Nehi shifted Adam to his left arm and pushed the safety off of Hope. *No goggles yet,* he told himself, *it would be too conspicuous.* He focused on forcing himself to breathe evenly through the adrenaline pumping through him. Joe's arm rammed into the door and they sped out. Shadowy twilight fell around them, swirling with dry air mixed with the scent of humanity, big city, fresh blood, and burnt flesh.

Five guards stood at Gate C. A scene of carnage splayed around them and splashed up the concrete walls. The guards spun toward the little group, tightening into formation in front of the gate. The whine of priming weapons drifted from them, and a dim red glow started from five rifles. Nehi snapped his goggles over his eyes and leveled Hope as he pounded forward. Two guards went down, a third reeled in a circle his arms flung up, and collapsed against a fourth. Joe was on the last guard before the man could tighten his finger on the trigger. As the soldier fell and Joe kicked out for the one struggling under guard number three's deadweight, he noticed guard number three was still breathing. And had no smoking holes in him. The mute's hand darted forward, snatching the keys off a belt and charging at the gate. But he took an instant to be impressed as he saw the scorch marks smoldering on the soldiers' heads and realized Nehi had just grazed his men. With a laser. That should have been impossible.

Adam gagged as Nehi pulled him through the remains to the gate. Joe gasped and tugged, his feet scrabbling on the concrete and his muscles bulging under his black jacket. The gate creaked open an inch. Nehemiah dropped Adam, hooked his fingers around the cold metal gate and heaved. A roar broke from him as every muscle pulled against his body, but the gate dragged open three feet. Joe jerked Adam through, Nehi slid past to join them, and the three raced down the hill. Their boots slammed into the asphalt streets, and they disappeared into an alley.

"Do you know where to go?" Nehemiah panted, slipping Adam's arm over his shoulder as Joe slid the rope off the IDP man's wrists. The mute nodded, slid Adam's other arm over his shoulder, and leaned into a run.

A police siren wailed to their left, and Nehemiah jumped, spinning toward the sound. Joe just kept running, pulling the other two with him. Down one alley, across a pretty street, into another rank alley filled with dumpsters and last week's rain puddles. Voices shouted orders and the tramp of soldiers' boots marched in double-time. Joe checked his course and shoved them into a tiny side street, jerked them into another alley, and kept running. Sirens wailed, men yelled, pedestrians scurried home to get out of the way. The dark of a moonless night fell over the three as they raced on, deeper into the town. The sounds of pursuit gradually drifted off to their left. Nehi sent up scattered prayers for Atif and his men as he followed Joe's lead.

The mute pulled them out of an alley, and suddenly they were surrounded by pretty, peaceful suburbia houses. He jerked them toward a single-story brick house with a high wall running around the backyard, slid his lockpick into the heavy wooden gate, and pulled them inside. A sense of relief slipped into Nehi as he kicked the gate closed behind them and the town was walled off. Adam's head lolled and the two boys carried him between them as Joe pulled the group to a potting shed. They stepped around the corner, Adam's feet dragging on the grass, and Joe froze.

A dark tunnel yawned at them behind a broken wooden door. It hung from one bottom hinge. A shrill squeal came from the hinge as a breeze hit it.

Joe took off, speeding down the stairs as if a fire burned on their heels. Nehemiah staggered after him, Adam only partially conscious between the two boys. Nehi's ankle turned and he gasped and grabbed for the railing, dragging the group to a halt. In the pause Nehemiah could hear Joe's labored breathing. It wasn't from the exertion of the night, he knew; Joe was terrified of what they would find. Or wouldn't find. Nehi let go of the rail and ran on, his mind beginning to numb as a hopeless certainty filled him.

Anna was gone.

That's what Joe was so scared about, Anna was lost. All his new-found strength dissipated like steam from a kettle.

Another broken door loomed out of the dark at the bottom of the stairs. Joe dropped Adam, slid his penlight out of his pocket, and leapt through the doorway in a professional roll. It took him deep into the room, Nehemiah could hear it as he settled Adam on the bottom step and slid up to the door, Hope sweeping the darkened area. A thin white line sped around the room as Joe took it in with his pen light, but Nehi couldn't see anything by it. The mute scurried to a wall, a click rang in the stillness, and light blazed around them.

Nothing but chaos greeted Nehemiah. No Anna. No ene-

mies. Just an overturned lectern, a cupboard lying on its side, coffee sloshed over the floor, cushions ripped and scattered... No Anna. Joe's face brightened, and he pointed at something near the cupboard. He flew across the room, leaping furniture as if they were grass blades, and flung a cushion off something. Nehi stepped into the room, Hope hanging listlessly by his side.

A charred body sprawled in front of Joe as the mute knelt, studying the scene. It used to be a young soldier. Now it was this...ruin. Everything turned to ruins.

Joe leapt off again, speeding to a corner. He jerked two sliced ropes into his hands and spun to Nehemiah, his face shining with relief.

"I think she got away," Joe signed.

"Think?" Nehemiah murmured, and winced as he heard the cynical despair in his own voice. Joe punched his shoulder, not gently, his green eyes staring into Nehemiah's. "I'm sorry," he answered with an effort. "I won't give up hope, Joe."

"Jesus, your hope, promised never to give up on you," Joe signed. Nehemiah nodded, forcing his tight shoulders to loosen. "Let's go find her."

An hour passed. Anna paced through the windowless tunnel, the only sounds their echoing footsteps, Naadar's wheezes, and Elizabeth's soft weeping. The floor had continued mostly even, but now it began to rise uphill. Naadar's breathing came in labored, painful gasps. Anna slipped her arm around him without asking if he wanted it, taking the heavy laser from his grasp. Naadar slumped, his weight landing on her, and Anna grunted, struggling to get a better hold on him. She suddenly realized he was only on his feet by strength of will. His eyes were dim and his head hung down as if he no longer cared where his feet took him.

"Naadar, where are we going?" Anna asked, realizing she

was going to be in charge soon.

"Our secondary meeting place," he wheezed.

"Where?"

"Outside town, copse of pine trees." His words came out choppy, each breath a wet rattle.

"Will the others know to look for us there? Joe and Layth?" Anna asked, voicing the worry she had kept to herself. Naadar nodded. His head slumped and more of his weight transferred to her. They walked on, and the tunnel grew steeper. By the time they reached where the tunnel stopped at a carved wooden trapdoor, Elizabeth supported Naadar's other side, his feet dragging with each step. Anna pushed open the door with an effort, struggling to keep her hold on the drooping Naadar. Fresh, pine scented air washed over them, laced with dim evening sunlight. Anna heaved again, and the three staggered out. A beautiful sunset lit up the sky in front of them, split in two by a copse of pine trees that stretched out till it grew into a real forest. Anna breathed a deep sigh and thanked God for a breath of beauty in such a disturbing day. She couldn't see anyone and Anna quickly switched the light out in the tunnel, slammed the trapdoor shut, and led her little group over the few yards of open ground into the copse of pine trees.

Naadar revived a little when they pushed through the branches into the wood. He pointed deeper into the trees. The two girls stumbled through the growing darkness, scraped by pine boughs as they supported Naadar between them. The needles scraped their skin, poking, hard, and hurting. After about five minutes of slow travel, Anna saw a sliver of brighter light to her left and pulled the group toward it. They stumbled out into a small clearing. A charred circle of ground rested in the center, a weathered box in the middle. Anna's hopes rose as she saw it.

"Here," the IDP leader muttered. He sank to the ground with a rattling sigh. Anna looked around her as she unwrapped the veil from around her waist. The pine trees grew close and thick, and they were screened from sight here. She tucked her cumbersome veil underneath Naadar's head, stepped up to the box, and hooked her fingers under it to lift it. A grunt slid from her at the weight. It took most of her strength to heave it up so it fell on its side. She smiled as she saw what she had hoped resting on the circle of charred ground; a Kilburn heater, all the connectors set up and waiting.

"Lizzy, keep an eye out here, I'm going to explore," Anna said. She stood up and slid back into the trees. It was much easier now she wasn't dragging Naadar with her, and the long needles didn't seem quite so threatening. When she pushed out of the trees, a cold breeze washed over her, teasing her hair and skirts. Anna shivered and hugged herself as she stared at the horizon. No lights twinkled in the deepening twilight. No one lived near here. Activating the heater should be safe enough in their copse, so long as they cleared out the smoky pine needles and kept that lead lined box up. *Good,* she thought with another shiver, and pushed gratefully into the shelter of the trees, making her way back to the clearing. Elizabeth knelt beside Naadar, and Anna was pleased to see she had made her own explorations and discovered a stash of fresh water and some prepacked food. She had used a container of the water to clean Naadar's face, and it helped. Just having the blood gone helped everything seem a little more normal.

Anna pulled the Krackman laser closer to the heater and laid the barrel carefully in the box, the nose close to the lead lining. Her hands moved swiftly over the rifle, removing the Pylum battery, attaching the connector in its place, and hunting for where the output plug went. She found it, attached it all, and flipped it on. A soft red glow bathed the clearing. It hummed, and began to put out heat as the laser primed, bouncing back and forth between the medium and the mirrors inside the rifle. Anna leaned the box back over the rifle, blocking most of the light, and sat on her heels to eye it. It seemed to be working fine... The Kilburn heater utilized the heat from the lasing process, and it was a smart gadget. But the lead-lined box was a necessary safety feature, as without the Pylum battery draining the heat away, sometimes a laser grew too hot, too tired of waiting, and decided to stop priming and fire. Anna preferred a decent campfire. It was prettier, smelled better, and wouldn't suddenly fill your campsite with lethal blasts from a rifle. But the Kilburn gave off very little light to be spotted by enemies, and it was smokeless. Two very important points in a situation like tonight.

"Ann, do you really think he's gone?" Elizabeth murmured. Anna sighed and looked up at the treetops, swaying in the dimming twilight. Everyone kept looking to her for strength, for hope. She didn't feel strong or very hopeful.

"I don't know, Lizzy. But God does. Why don't you come pray with me?" She knelt in front of the heater, and Elizabeth gratefully sank down beside her. The two girls began to pray again, earnestly and wholeheartedly.

A branch snapped in the woods. Anna dove for the rifle and jerked it up, knocking the box back to its side and swiveling to face the noise. The whine of the big laser filled the copse.

"Come out very slowly if you don't want to be incinerated," Anna growled into the darkness.

Chapter Ten: Tales and Travels

"As for God, His way is perfect: the word of the LORD is tried: He is a buckler to all them that trust in Him."

2 Samuel 22:31

D on't shoot, Anna! With the way you use those things you might accidentally hit us," Nehemiah called out of the woods. Anna threw the rifle back in the box, and clapped her hands in relief and joy, as she used to do when she was three. Then she felt very silly and decided to make up for it by being bossy.

"Well, don't just stand there, come on and get warm, Nehi!" she ordered. Nehemiah brushed past the last of the trees and caught her in a tight hug, lifting her off the ground in his enthusiasm. A soft sob came from him, and Anna patted Nehemiah's head gently. He plunked her on the ground, glowering at her.

"I told you to be careful, Anna Ruth," he said sharply, "and I find you've killed a soldier and run through miles of tunnel, while– who's that?" he said, pointing at Naadar. "Another victim to your bad aim?" Anna shoved him playfully.

"Don't be beastly, and I did not shoot that soldier," Anna said. "Naadar did when the enemy pulled a knife on us. I only knocked him down when–"

"Naadar, that would be–" Nehemiah interrupted.

"Where's Joe?" Anna cut in. A cheerful whistle answered her question. Joe stepped out of the trees, supporting Mr. Bight. Anna and Elizabeth both yelled, though Elizabeth's was more of a shriek. She rushed to her father and a jumble of words filled the copse as everyone spoke at once and no one could hear anyone else. Joe gave his silent laugh at the medley of voices and searched through his pockets as he moved to Naadar. When the basics of their stories were understood and the Bights and Hillsons decided they could be quiet again, they found Naadar awake, his battered face cleaned, splints and bandages wrapped around the fingers of his right hand, and a wholesome smell of medicinal oils drifting from his direction. Joe sat beside him, quietly tracing designs in the pine needle-covered ground with his finger.

"Beauty, where's Glue?" he signed as soon as he could catch Anna's eye. Anna explained, with Naadar and Adam adding in details as they settled near the heater and Elizabeth tended her father. After they were done with the story Joe sat still, watching the glow from the box. His blank look showed the twins he was thinking hard about something. Nehemiah was about to ask him what, when Elizabeth laid a hand on his arm.

"Thank you for rescuing my father," she said earnestly. "I know it was a risk you didn't have to take."

"You're welcome," Nehemiah said, "but it was Joe who thought of it, planned it, and did it. He's the one you ought to thank."

"Really?" Elizabeth said, honest surprise on her face as she glanced at Joe. He sat with his knees pulled up to his chest, his chin resting on them, not paying attention to the conversations buzzing around him. Anna had to admit he didn't look exactly brilliant; a messy-haired, scrawny mute staring blankly at the soft glow coming from under the box. But that shouldn't matter.

"Why are you surprised?" she asked, and was taken aback at the sharpness of her voice.

"Well, I mean, he's an incomplete," Elizabeth stammered.

"What's that have to do with anything?" Anna snapped. Elizabeth thought for a moment.

"I really don't know." She stood up, crossed over to Joe, and hugged the mute tight. Joe's eyes popped open in a look of such frightened shock, everyone chuckled.

"Thank you," Elizabeth said. Joe patted her arm awkwardly and Elizabeth let him go and sat down by her exhausted father on the other side of the heater. She smiled at Anna in a way that asked for peace, and Anna smiled back and granted it. Joe glanced from one to the other, gave a little shrug, and turned to Nehemiah.

"I'm going looking for Glue," he signed.

"Not on your own you're not!" Nehemiah burst out. The Bights and Naadar blinked at him, and Anna explained what Joe had signed.

"Joe, are you sure?" she added. "You're probably the most hunted man in all of the Prophet's Peace right now, from what Nehemiah's told me. You should take Nehi, though I admit it scares me to offer it."

"I really am better on my own this time," he signed at the twins. "But thanks for being __ it…makes me happy."

"What's…" Anna tried to copy the sign she didn't know and grinned good-naturedly when Joe laughed. He repeated the sign correctly and quickly fingerspelled it for her

"C-o-n-c-e-r-n-e-d."

"Well we are concerned, you shouldn't go back alone," Nehemiah said. "Two can help better than one."

"He's right," Anna said, but she couldn't help her lips tightening.

"In most cases," Joe shrugged, Nehemiah translating for the others. "But I'm a strange case. I always have been and always will be. I'll do better on my own, honest."

"How?" Nehemiah said stubbornly as Joe began to load an old projectile pistol and feel in his pockets to see what he had left. "Your white card won't do you any good, it's probably already been repealed by the Wazir."

"What white card?" Naadar asked, his voice quick and suspicious. Joe shot a glance at Nehemiah that said clearly, "Please don't answer that." But Anna was the only one who saw it. Nehemiah was already explaining. Naadar's face changed, his entire body stiffening and dark suspicion written on his battered features as he turned on Joe.

"You have a white card issued by the Wazir himself?" he said, his voice almost dripping menace. "What do you do with our esteemed leader, Joe? Perhaps tell him who is an unbeliever to fill Tariq's dungeons?" Joe just looked at Naadar and didn't answer.

"Now wait a minute–" Nehemiah started, but Joe put a finger on his lips and pointed his pistol into the woods. Everyone stiffened, listening. Someone blundered through the underbrush, they could hear it now. Joe motioned Nehi to guard the campsite and slipped into the woods. After a moment of tense quiet, the group around the campfire heard him whistle, a sharp, commanding sound.

"Joe! My Joe!" Cobeau roared. Shoulders slumped, tight breaths were let out, as everyone relaxed. A moment later a disheveled, shining Layth pushed his way into the clearing with Beau behind him. Joe perched happily on the chimera's big shoulders and a beautiful young lady lay in his strong, gentle arms. Layth held one of her hands and from the look on his face he would never let go until Jesus called him home. He turned to Anna, beaming and shining. She almost didn't recognize him.

"Thank you for sending Cobeau with me," he said earnestly. "I only have my wife back because of him." Beau set the young woman down by the heater and turned to Anna, shaking a big finger at her.

"I told you to wait there, Miss Beauty," he said in a hurt rumble.

"I know," Anna answered, trying to look penitent. "And I did, for a very long time, but we had to leave after a while. You found me again." He didn't look pacified. "I'm sorry I had to leave, Beau, and couldn't obey your order." He hesitated, then nodded. Joe laughed and flipped off his shoulders, landing on his feet in front of the big man.

"For that matter, we told you to stay with Beauty, Glue, so if there's any apologizing to do, you ought to do it," he signed quickly to him.

"I understood that!" Anna grinned. Joe smiled at her and applauded, back to his normal cheerful self now that all three of his little troupe were near.

"Should I?" Beau asked, his forehead crinkling. Joe shook his head with a little smile.

"Not this time," he signed. "But next time, make sure your charge is a little more secure before you go after another one, okay?" Beau looked blankly at him. Joe smiled, shook his head in mock despair, and whistled for translation from him. He pulled a familiar velvet bag from one of his large pockets and handed it to Naadar.

"A gift to add to your other gift," he signed and Cobeau said. "From a brother to your IDP branch."

"Now you have as much as you need," Cobeau added. Naadar took the bag warily, his gaze dark and angry as he looked at the little mute. But when he looked inside the bag his mouth dropped open as he stared, riveted.

"I think I just went unconscious again and am dreaming," he finally muttered.

"It's enough now," Beau stated.

"Enough for what we needed, and to build a new underground church too," Naadar nodded, his voice husky.

"Be careful," Joe signed at him and Beau rumbled. "You're a tagged man, show your face and they'll pick you up. Hand over your branch to a new leader as soon as you can and get out of the country."

"And why should I take counsel from you?" Naadar snarled. His tone cut, so icy the Hillsons and Bights pulled back and stared at him. Joe went blank, his mask dropping over him with a completeness that hid every vestige of emotion or thought. He just shrugged.

"I'm no traitor, Naadar of the Prophet's Peace," he signed and Beau said.

"If you hold a white card from the Wazir, it is because you aid him and he finds you very valuable," Naadar growled. Layth and his wife started, their heads whipping around as they stared at Joe. "Perhaps that is how you and Cobeau escaped Tariq's dungeons after only three days?"

"Wait, you've been in there?" Adam interrupted, looking at

Joe in amazement. "As a prisoner! And you still went after me, risking getting pulled into that...that horror again?" Joe just shrugged and tapped Cobeau on the arm.

"We're going now. Goodbye," Cobeau said with a bright smile at the group in the clearing. The twins looked at them in surprise. Joe just gave them a nod.

"All right then," Anna said. She stood up and gave Elizabeth a tight hug. "Goodbye, dear, I pray we'll meet again!"

"Anna, you and your brother don't have to go with them," Naadar said as she and Nehemiah brushed the pine needles off themselves before joining the Ravens on the edge of the trees. "If they are that close with the Wazir..." His voice trailed off as both the twins stared at him.

"We trust the Ravens," Nehemiah said in a tone that made the words a rebuke. Anna softened it with a smile as she nodded. They said quick goodbyes and began the walk back to the wagon. It was a long, dark walk, keeping to the shadowed places, darting from cover to cover to avoid people. Anna felt as if she would gladly sleep for a week by the time they reached the warehouse. In a few moments the Ravens had Prissy harnessed and the wagon zipped off, headed out of the country. Anna's head nodded and she leaned heavily against Nehemiah. He slid an arm around her to make sure she didn't topple over when she fell asleep.

"Joe, how did you know Tariq was looking for Anna?" Nehi asked. Anna woke up a little at hearing her name.

"That's right," she added, covering a yawn. "And what about that soldier? He said Tariq was working for someone that wanted me. Do you know what that was about?"

"T's an FF," Joe signed.

"My eyes are so tired, can you use your gloves?" Anna asked, and yawned.

"Recharging. It takes a long time," Joe shrugged. Anna's eyes fluttered closed; she was missing Joe's half of the conversation.

"So Tariq's an FF?" Nehi asked. "But I thought they were a

group by themselves, Tariq works for the Wazir doesn't he?"

"They are a separate group, but they have __ everywhere. They even had some in Sojourner's Kingdom."

"Some what? Do that sign again," Nehemiah said. Joe did and prodded Beau.

"Pawns," he rumbled.

"What?" said Nehemiah.

"That's the sign, pawns. Like in that game with the checks and horses where the king gets killed," Beau said and Nehemiah blinked at him.

"Chess, he means," Joe signed with a laugh.

"Oh. So the FFs have pawns everywhere, got it. They were even in my kingdom? Everywhere? Wait, that means we can be spotted anywhere we go, not to mention the danger of being followed by loose FFs." Joe nodded. "Who are these people? What are they looking for?" Joe just shrugged, his face showing nothing. "No you don't, I can understand your signs by now, and you are not hiding behind your muteness any longer. You obviously know more then you're telling me!"

Joe's green eyes locked onto his dark ones and held them, searching for something. Joe dropped his eyes and reached for a pan flute lying beside his seat. Music soared around them, the mute shutting down the conversation. Nehemiah's jaw squared. He shifted Anna to a more comfortable position and waited. For five minutes Joe played, eyes closed, pouring himself into the haunting melody, heartbroken memories colliding with hope, mixed with an underlying danger. The country whizzed by in a shadowy blur and Joe played on. The song drew to a gentle close, and Joe took a breath to start a new one.

"Who are these people, Joe?" Nehi broke in, his voice low and earnest. Joe sighed, a soft tired sound in the night.

"I don't know too much about them, honest Knee-High," Joe signed, turning reluctantly so Nehi could see his movements. "I've suspected T of being one of theirs for a while now, and when A-t-i-f talked of 'his men' that went off and did special tasks, and his using N, I risked a guess. Now I know he's an FF."

"But why were they looking for Anna?" Nehemiah prodded. Joe suddenly looked away, a troubled expression on his face. "You're worrying me. Joe?"

"I'm not sure," he signed defiantly. The mute's wall was up, his expression blank, and Nehi knew he would only make the wall higher by insisting. But he insisted anyway. After trying for ten minutes and getting Joe into his rock imitation, he found he was annoyed and exasperated, but no longer worried. Nehi gave up and moved off to put Anna to bed. She partially woke up when he dropped her through the skylight into the Day Room, muttered something about cheese supplies, crawled into a chair and went back to sleep. Nehemiah dropped down next to her, carted her to bed, and tossed a blanket over her. He stayed beside his sister for a little while, praying, thanking his King fervently for being able to put Anna into bed, knowing they were both safe and in the care of friends.

Nehi sighed and turned toward the skylight again. He didn't want to be alone tonight. But he paused in the day room and flipped on the burner for light. He reached in his pocket and drew out the little card Atif had slipped to him. It was a simple set of numbers, "783495." Nothing else. Nehi stared at it, cudgeling his brain for a meaning as he turned the card on his palm. Something brought Enoch Mickelson to mind, Nehi's old self-defense teacher and the leader of the Judge's guards. Something he had said, a lesson... Six numbers, starting with a seven... A military bone plant. The lesson returned to Nehi with almost shocking clarity; sunshine streaming into the old-barn-turned-classroom, Mickelson at the holograph-board expounding on military matters, Peter pretending to take notes in the chair beside Nehi as both boys doodled ridiculous pictures of their droning teacher. A smile flitted over Nehemiah's face at the memory, warm and melancholy as he stood alone in the darkened wagon.

He knew what the card was for.

Atif had a military bone plant. Unlike a personal plant, his would be available anywhere, and couldn't be turned off. It was a way to contact him, anywhere in the world, at anytime. Of course Nehi would have to find a frequency transmitter that connected with the chip inserted in the mandible under Atif's ear. Something like a Grady personal pad. Those weren't easy to come by. And it would be extremely dangerous for the ex-Muslim if this number were intercepted. Atif and his people would be tagged now, on the run, known as converts and traitors to the Islamic state; tagged as Christians, a dangerous thing in most countries.

Nehi stared at the simple white card. Atif had taken an enormous risk to give him this. A bone plant could be used to trace a man, even to kill him from a thousand miles away if you had the right equipment. Nehemiah studied the numbers again, quietly settling them in his mind. Then he stuck the card in the little flames licking off the gas burner. He watched as it crumbled to black ash in the trashcan. Nehi straightened up, flipped the burner off, hopped on the table, gripped the skylight, and pulled himself out on top of the wagon.

Beau sat humming his tuneless hum as he steered the wheeled pig, and Joe lounged beside him, his freckled, scarred face turned to the stars. Nehi plopped on his seat and the three rode on in silence, the wind whistling around them. After about twenty minutes the pig's wheeled shoes began to squeak. It was an annoying way to break the quiet. Joe stirred as if he were waking up, increased their speed, and pumped the wind bubble up. The soft breeze, carrying the scent of dirt and steam, cut off along with the drone of the summer bugs. Nehemiah sat in the quiet stillness under the clear bubble, letting the minutes tick on as the landscape blurred. A low whistle came from Joe and Nehi glanced up, coming out of his own thoughts with difficulty. The mute gave him a gentle smile.

"A whole band of brothers with this A-t-i-f character, Knee-High. Did you catch that?"

"I did," Nehemiah murmured huskily.

"Because of your courage. God uses even the worst in this life. Thank Him for the knowledge, and move on. Again. It's all right. You're free, and so are they. Free and heaven-bound now," Joe signed. A sniffle escaped Nehemiah.

"No one warned me growing in the faith was such a see-saw of emotions," Nehi said, trying to make it a chuckle, his voice wet. Another sniff came from him. Joe's lips twisted in a smile that didn't reach his eyes and he shrugged.

"Mourning and brutal trauma recovery tend to add their own spin to it." The mute paused, awkward shyness playing over him. Then he signed again, hesitantly, as if he couldn't decide if he should ask. "So you're feeling the growth?"

"Yes." Nehemiah's answer came quick, automatic. He stumbled out a fuller reply. "Well, I guess starting to see more of...how relying and resting on God brings peace through it all. Or how God is bringing me through it, and there's a strength to knowing that. Maybe? I don't know how to describe it. I don't think I'll try." Joe just nodded. But he smiled, and it was a happy, tired smile that said he was pleased to hear it. Beau yawned, a long, dog-like sound. The miles slid under them and the three men watched the kingdom fade to wilderness. Nehemiah stirred in his seat, stretching his long legs. His reddened eyes turned to the little scraggly mute below him.

"Joe, do you ever reach the end? I mean, does the hole ripped in my soul from Mom and Dad being...does it close? And then after, Abid and Simmons and... It would be really nice to know the haunting will eventually fade to a stop." Another shrug lifted the mute's shoulders. He kept his eyes turned away, a heavy weariness lining his scarred face.

"I'll let you know if I ever learn that answer."

Atif's heart was trying to pound its way out of his chest with a hammer as large as Otar's. Its beat blared in his ears and filled his head as his fingers gripped the last corner and spun him onto the loading dock. The massive gray transports hummed at the edge of the platform. He vaguely recognized the shimmering air was from the heat waves coming off the engines, and not just from his sparking, shaky vision. Behind him he heard Naqi spilling his guts out again; the effort of trying to keep up with this all-night madcap run had nearly killed the skinny techy.

The great gray tanks lurched, metal squealing as the drivers tested the couplings. They were leaving. Atif gripped Naqi's shirtfront and put on one last burst of speed. White dots danced in his vision and even the roar of the revving engines was lost in the sound of his own pulse. The blessed rectangle of a door inside grew smaller, spinning into itself, the metal plates slowly clamping down. Atif pushed off the dock in a mighty leap, jerking Naqi with him through the blackness. He slammed into the metal floor and rolled, banging up against a wall with a sharp clang, his head bent sideways as his feet slowly slid down the wall back toward the ground. Otar's massive weight smashed into him and Atif's neck screamed in protest as another weight slammed into Otar. Metal crashed somewhere outside the heap of bodies on him, and artificial light spurted into fitful, humming life. All was arms and legs and sweat and gasps for a few seconds. Then Atif managed to jerk himself upright, leaning heavily against the wall.

Shareef and Otar sprawled on top of Naqi, gasping out apologies and relieved laughter as they tried to gather enough strength to get up. Taban stood frowning, balanced perfectly against the shaking, vibrating motion of the hot transport. IIe was human enough to be panting at least, Atif noticed absently as he gasped in air.

They had run all night. Dodging every official the Wazir had, the entire town out for their blood. It had been one harrowing escape after another, and Atif knew it was only by their mismatched, varied skills and God's providence that they had reached these transports.

But now the doors were shut.

Atif let his eyes close in relief as he leaned against the vibrating wall and gasped in more air. They were safe. For now, at least. The transports through the wild lands made their money partially by being the only thing tough enough to make it overland through the lethal places between kingdoms. But part of their money came from never asking questions of their customers, and by clinging to the fact that once the doors were closed, anyone inside was in the neutral ground of the wild lands. No kingdom had sway here. No single thing had sway here. Atif's eyes shot open again as he realized that wasn't quite right. Money and might still held sway.

Taban stood in what seemed to be casual conversation with one of the Riders; the people employed by the transport service, who never left the cars, and always wore full tactical gear, ready for any assault on their caravan. As he watched, a clinking bag of coins slipped discretely from Taban into the Rider's black-gloved hand. Atif shifted toward a metal bench at the back of the car, letting relief play through him again. They were accepted. They were safe. He just sat, panting. No one else rode in this section. Most would be in the upper level, where a few grimy windows let in the sunlight. A few more would be on the lower levels, keeping an eye on their cargoes to see no Riders or malcontents wandered away with their goods. Gradually the bench filled around Atif, as the team pulled themselves upright and teetered over, bracing themselves against the lurching, rumbling ride. Taban settled cat-like on the edge of the bench beside his leader.

"How much?" Atif asked.

"Too much. But we are cleared to go as far as we wish," Taban answered.

"Yes, but how do we get off?" Otar growled. "We have no papers."

"My father knew a man in Kallipolis," Shareef said brightly. "I can fix that for us."

"Your father was a remarkable man," Naqi chuckled between gasps. Shareef just grinned at him. The techy sobered and looked at his boss. Inside, Atif wondered again why he was "the boss," when he was the youngest in this band. But he didn't let it show. Instead he braced himself for the question he knew would come.

"What now?" Naqi asked. Even their panting quieted as everyone waited to hear his answer. Atif sat still, his mind racing along the few words dropped by the strange little mute with Nehemiah Hillson, and Tariq's unexplained dalliances with someone besides the Wazir's men. There was something else out there, something bestial, deadly to his brothers and sisters, snaking under more than just the Prophet's Peace. This thing, this other entity, needed to be stopped. It was more dangerous to his fellow Christians even than Islam, for it stretched farther than one kingdom. From a few conversations overheard from Tariq, Atif knew it was a deadly malignity with bands wrapped around nearly the entire world. And around one despicably black heart. Images of Simmons' tall, powerful form sauntering into Abid's rooms flashed across his mind, coupled with similar images of him strolling into Tariq's private quarters as if he owned them. Tariq had allowed it. Now, Atif wondered if he had allowed it because Simmons was a part of this larger animal snaking through the world. A more important part of it than Tariq, perhaps? The last time that wicked man had come, Atif had been detailed to authorize his paperwork, and he knew where Simmons was headed as of two weeks ago.

"We are going snake hunting," Atif said. His legs slid out, his hands slipped behind his head, and he closed his eyes. His men glanced at each other and settled back to wait. Atif was thinking. They were content to wait and follow where he detailed.

Chapter Eleven: Bloodstream Day

"And the LORD God formed man of the dust of the ground, and breathed into his nostrils the breath of life: and man became a living soul." Genesis 2:7

The blue light of the hologram projector seemed weak and hard to make out in the bright sunlight streaming through the wagon's skylight. Joe shoved it over to the corner with his toe, hoping to find more shadows. The woman's eyelids sparkled even in the hologram's blue light as it projected the shape of her head into the day room.

"I don't know you, Raven," she said. Her hair flowed down her shoulders like a smooth stream, her beauty exquisite. But Joe knew her eyes were hard, and her soul harder still. "How can I be sure you won't just report my position to the Wolf for a fee?"

"I get near Wolf, I get eaten," Joe signed. Countries away, the automated voice of his gloves drifted to the woman and sounded like a sophisticated voice changer. The words spun with the shape of a raven in flight formed by the woman's hologram projector. No face, no background, nothing to be able to guess who she dealt with. "But you want to find Wolf."

"I want to rip the Wolf's heart out and watch that monster writhe," the woman spat, rage suddenly overtaking her perfect features, burning behind her shining eyes. Her words shook with it.

"I know," Joe's gloves stated. "Your sources have told you that I have been trying to eliminate Wolf for years. Let's work together and see it become a reality."

"This is the second time you've contacted me with this proposition. I still don't know you enough to trust you. And I'm going to ask you again, Raven, how can you help me?" The woman's perfectly plucked eyebrow went up, staring down her sharp nose at the projector.

"I know where Wolf is." The words hung in the air, prickling in the silence. "I know what Wolf is working on. I know how to take the monster out."

"Why haven't you destroyed Wolf then? What are you lacking that you come to me?" The voice was guarded, cautious but with an interest making it dance.

"Resources, agents, feet on the ground," Joe signed. "I can't be there to set it all up, not for the first half of the business. It will take time to do it right, and I cannot be there through the entirety of the play."

"Tell me."

"There's more. I am not sure death should be our choice, Wolf has knowledge of something that–"

"You make contact telling me how to setup Wolf's death. And now you're already backing out?" Ariel Athenia's voice dripped distain, and Joe grimaced in the wagon. For an instant he didn't know what to sign. He wanted Wolf dead. It would be so much easier to just have the monster out of the picture! But...

"I know what you treasure more than love and vengeance," Joe signed. He could almost feel the woman stiffen. "I have impatience clawing at my gut, I want Wolf gone. But–"

"I want nothing more than that Wolf's head on a platter," the woman said, every word ringing like a crowbar bashing an anvil. "Send me your plan, Raven."

The latch to the skylight snapped back as someone pulled it open from above. Joe hopped on top the hologram disc, shutting it off with his toe as he moved and covering it with his foot. His movements a blur, he pulled his gloves off, shoved them into his pocket, and snatched a pear off the counter.

As Anna dropped into the wagon she saw the mute leaning idly against the counter, looking bored, as he munched a partially eaten pear. He had stayed in the wagon an awful lot since they crossed the border into KAM yesterday.

"Toss one over for the rest of us too, please," she said, and Joe obeyed. Anna caught the pears and reached for the skylight again. "Come on, Joe, it's a beautiful day for once!" Joe obediently followed behind her, only lingering a moment to rinse off his sticky hands; Anna didn't see him shove a hologram disc under the sink with his bare foot. The mute pulled himself out of the skylight to the wagon top behind her, and Anna spun to him eagerly. He grinned, then gave a dramatic look of horror.

"I know that expression. More questions!" he signed, and pressed a hand to his brow theatrically.

"Oh come on, we've been lenient with you lately," Anna grinned. They had. In the five weeks of travel to get to KAM, the twins had kept their questions locked away and carefully not pestered Joe. "What are we doing in this kingdom? All Beau will say is 'business' and you've been hiding inside the wagon ever since we crossed the border. I have the idea it's more than just delivering information this time."

"I have the same feeling, so don't try and dodge," put in Nehemiah. The wagon arched up as they slid over another green grassy hill, and he grabbed his seat to keep from toppling backward. "Are we listening for something? Or did you hear something that's brought us here? Does it have something to do with the FFs? Come on, please let us in on it!"

"More like something we saw," Joe signed with a little smile. "It has to do with the FFs but don't ask any more, please. I won't answer. We have to go through several little towns before we get to Freedom so just relax."

"Freedom?" both twins asked.

"The capital city of KAM," Joe signed, and looked at them with interest. "This is one of the major kingdoms. Gaia, Prophet's Peace, KAM, The People's Kingdom, the Sojourners, there aren't many major kingdoms in this world. You haven't heard of its capital before?"

"Oh, our parents taught us all about it," Anna said with an airy wave of her hand, "but Nehi and I were very bored with geography and never paid any attention, especially to the names. Which means we don't know much, in case you hadn't noticed."

"I had noticed. It's refreshing to meet someone who admits they don't know everything," Joe signed back with a wink. They topped the hill and Beau hit the brakes, the wagon slewing as it slowed. The three friends spun toward the front to see why. Pristine grassland, rising here and there into lovely round hills, stretched out to make up the kingdom. In the distance buildings rose and dotted the landscape, showing a town. But a host of hoverers covered the short-cropped grass in front of them, and more whooshed up at every moment, filling the air with their hot steam clouds and hisses.

"Goodness, that's a lot of people," Anna said.

"Why are they all headed the same way?" Nehemiah asked.

"Going into that little town up there, it looks like, but why I wonder?" Anna answered and asked in one breath. Joe slapped his forehead to show what a dunce he had been. He looked behind them, saw they were being hemmed in by more of the snazzy hoverers, and even a few bigger vehicles tied to the road by their wheels, and made a face.

"__ Day, of course, I forgot. We should have taken another route." he signed. "Oh well, we'll do a concert. We could use the practice."

"What day?" both the twins asked. Joe began to spell it out, but Cobeau interrupted.

"Joe, people are looking at you," he almost whimpered. Anna and Nehemiah looked at Beau in surprise. They had never heard that tone come from the cheerful, fierce chimera. Joe dropped his hands into his lap and winked at the twins, nodding toward the town. "You'll find out," the look said. He hopped off, motioning to Beau, and the two Ravens quickly clicked the wheels in place and shut off the steam. The wagon settled into a gentle rocking motion and the VKs traveled slowly into the stream of vehicles. Beau concentrated on keeping Prissy from nibbling curiously on the people and hoverers around them in the press of traffic as they moved steadily over the grassy plain towards the little town. Joe dropped to his seat beside the chimera. His hands strayed to his leather jacket's collar, making sure it was up for the hundredth time that day. He leaned against the wood, listening to the twins talk, his eyes darting around the crowd.

It took an hour to get into the small town, even after the local traffic police unit flashed up the temporary holographic lanes and signs, sorting the mass of vehicles into an organized stream. But everyone seemed remarkably cheery despite the backed up traffic. As they finally rolled off the grass into the asphalt streets of the town, the twins decided it was trim, well-kept, and pretty. Elegant shops and big houses were scattered here and there, looking modern and comfortable. The crowd around them was boisterous, happy, and so normal Anna and Nehemiah felt their muscles and nerves relaxing more than they had allowed themselves in ages. Streamers depicting atoms and DNA helixes in pretty pastel colors flew from the light posts.

"What are the rounded hats for? Do people always wear those here?" Anna asked, pointing to a mother and father and two little boys walking past, all with poofy round circles on their heads and around their wrists. Joe motioned to the family, his "Ask them, not me" look on.

"Excuse me!" Nehemiah said quickly, dropping off the crawling wagon and walking beside one of the little boys. "We're strangers here and were wondering about your magnificent hat. Are you–"

"I'm a mole cool!" the little boy shouted, beaming at Nehi. His brother bapped him on the poofy hat.

"He means molecule, mister," the older boy spoke up. "It's Bloodstream Day in town. We drove all the way from Freedom to come!"

"Yes dear, and we'll miss the best seats for the Blood Cell Count if we don't get there soon," his mother said as she took her boys' hands. She gave Nehemiah a stressed smile as she moved off. "I hope you have fun!"

"They celebrate bloodstreams?" Anna asked, looking at the Ravens. Cobeau was busy trying to maneuver Prissy out of the crowd and Joe seemed too busy grinning at the efforts of his large friend and the escapades of the pig to reply.

"Sounds fun. How about we go check it out?" Nehemiah asked. Joe sobered suddenly and looked at the twins uncertainly. He motioned them to follow and dropped back inside the wagon. When they landed in the Day Room, Joe began signing swiftly. Anna and Nehemiah had to concentrate to follow his words.

"Go ahead, but be careful. It's a fun time, I've heard. But don't forget this isn't Sojourner's Kingdom and start quoting Bible verses or something. Strangers are safe enough in KAM just so long as you don't show you're a part of the Way. Got it? No showing you're a member of the Way."

"Yes sir," Anna said, saluting smartly. "But aren't you and Beau coming?" Joe shook his head and gave a shiver, half serious and half silly.

"No thanks. I've been in enough crowds here and I think Glue has too. Besides, I need to help him with Prissy before one of them ends up with a broken neck."

"You sure you don't need us? We would be fine sticking around," Nehemiah offered. A nagging fear crept underneath his friend's carefree attitude here, Nehi saw it in the way he kept fussing with his collar and only signed inside the wagon. But Joe shrugged and grinned, and Nehemiah knew it meant he wasn't going to explain.

"Go check it out. It's a strange, fun time I hear. Oh, but I bet we can pick up some good business, come find us in the empty lot on 10th Street around four this afternoon. We'll do a concert for the __." He grinned at them, leapt for the skylight, and pulled himself up onto the wagon in one fluid motion.

"What do you think that last sign was?" Anna asked. "Revelers? Partiers? Partying people?"

"Something to do with that. Shall we go?" Nehemiah said, pulling open the door for Anna.

"Thank you, yes. I want to go see what this Blood Cell Count is!" Anna responded as she hopped out of the rocking wagon to join the crowd outside. The brother and sister waved to Joe and Beau as the Ravens stood, each holding part of Prissy's harness trying to get her to go where they wanted and not eat straw hats. The pig's piercing whistle followed the twins as they tagged after the crowd toward the center of town.

The White Blood Cell Count turned out to be a sort of half parade, half charade. Crowds lined the streets and watched as people dressed as white blood cells fought off the people dressed as the evil bacteria. Anna and Nehemiah caught on fast and booed the bacteria and cheered the white blood cells as loudly as the citizens around them, laughing at the melodramatic antics of the actors. The parade ended with a narrator walking behind the battle, explaining in a booming voice that happy functioning of the body was restored.

Anna and Nehemiah hopped off the metal bleachers and wandered among the crowds, listening to the conversations. Most of them were so normal and homey, the twins found themselves grinning as they strolled. This place felt...free. It felt almost right. Almost. Joe's warning hung in their minds, playing against the normalcy and telling them there was a strand somewhere that was off. Nehi began to guess a little of it as he walked and listened. He filed the facts away, reminding himself to ask Joe about it later, and pulled Anna toward a scent of hot cherries and sugar.

A booth stacked with cherry pies came into view, people laughing and milling around it, a banner over the top declaiming it a pie eating contest. Nehemiah gave a happy skip and shoved his way through to sign up. Twelve minutes later he found himself opposite a very portly middle-aged man, a stack of pies at his elbow, and more contestants ranged among the folding chairs. The timer dinged. He grabbed for a pie and dug in, cherries oozing between his fingers. He heard Anna laughing and groaning behind him.

Four pies and five minutes later, the timer dinged again. The man in front of him leapt to his feet, red fists balled in triumph, his belly jiggling as he shouted. Nehemiah slumped back with a happy, sticky sigh and reached for the pack of towelettes provided. There wasn't much he could do for his shirt front, but he was fine with that.

"You were only a quarter of a pie behind!" Anna wailed, laughter lacing it.

"I was?" Nehemiah said. "I mean, of course I was. Of course I was trying to win and it wasn't all about the pie. You need to provide more opportunities for me to practice this sort of thing," he grinned at his sister as they wandered away into the crowds again.

"Um, no, I am not spending a whole day baking something only to watch it be spread all over you in five minutes. I hear music, this way!"

The twins found a concert where several young men and women screamed about various bloodstream activities while they hit drums and played guitars too loudly. They didn't care much for it and wandered off again. They joined in the games held on a lawn in the center of town. In their favorite, they had to form a particular molecule and hold the form as they tried to beat the other teams across the lawn. Anna and Nehemiah joined the water molecules and beat the other teams three times before falling over one another and deciding it was enough.

Three hours later, their arms full of cotton candy and little trinkets won in booths, the twins wandered into the empty lot, as directed; happy, smelling of cherries, and more relaxed than they could remember feeling since home had disintegrated. The Ravens were already set up, and after a quick smile from their cohorts, Anna slipped into her concert coat. The twins leapt into their places and turned to watch Joe. The mute tucked a violin under his chin, closed his eyes, and focused.

The first soaring note on Joe's violin brought crowds surging around the wagon. Excited faces turned toward them, more joining with every musical phrase. At the end of that first song the cheering went wild. Anna saw Nehemiah laughing out of pure enjoyment, and found a happy, thankful prayer surging toward heaven's King.

It felt good to be alive today.

"Maybe I shouldn't have played that fifth round of 'Molecule Battles,'" Anna groaned. She stretched her legs sideways on the wagon top trying to get the kinks out, and leaned back against Nehi's brawny side. The wagon whizzed on, over grasslands, up and down hills, skirting past sprawling farmhouses and little towns. The stars twinkled down at them from the rich black sky. Nehemiah pulled his eyes away from the landscape with an effort. Without trees obscuring the view, there seemed to be so much sky here. He caught a flash of movement and glanced down. Joe's white fingers tugged at his jacket collar, for the eighth-hundredth time today.

"Joe, do they worship science all over this kingdom?" Nehemiah asked. His little friend needed a distraction.

"Yes," Joe answered simply.

"That's a strange thing to worship," Nehemiah said. "They don't talk about it like that and would probably get offended to hear us say it. But they put faith in it like a god. Even their hope, did you notice, Anna? It was all about how the race will evolve to better things."

"I did notice it," Anna answered. "It was pitiful. The race isn't evolving to better things, it's degenerating under the curse–"

"I know, everyone who puts their hope in that is going to be very disappointed," Nehemiah said. "Actually, I guess discovering there *is* a real God will be enough to forget a minor disappointment like their errant ideas of 'advancement of the race.'"

"It's true," Anna said. "But having just traveled through Prophet's Peace, I think, on the whole, I prefer this god if they're going to serve a false one."

"It does seem a little more supportive of freedom and less cruel," Nehemiah agreed.

"But what a fairytale to believe, evolution!" Anna suddenly giggled.

"What's funny about it?" Joe asked.

"Can you imagine really believing you came from an ape?"

"How about from a rock?" Nehi answered with a grin. "Or an unknown, rather–"

"That's right, they never get to the end, do they?" Anna cut in. "A science that can't be explained, that takes some faith."

"I know, and everyone we heard today was all about facts," Nehemiah said with a chuckle. "It's like they can't see past their own noses to see their 'facts' begin and end in faith."

"It is a little funny, isn't it?" Anna grinned. Joe turned his face away and glowered at the grasslands. Anna noticed it, and her mind ran back over her words. Oops. She leaned over and dropped a hand on Joe's shoulder. He jumped at the touch, pulling toward Cobeau.

"I'm sorry," Anna apologized. "We shouldn't have ridiculed it like that. Especially without knowing what you think."

"Oh, it's not true," Joe signed, his hands cutting through the air in sharp arcs, embarrassment covering him. The twins waited, and he grimaced at them. But he answered, reluctantly. "I know it's not true, it's just I've...it's not funny either, not with what it allows people to do. Science can be just as hard as Allah as a master, you just have to dig a little deeper to find the cruelty and despair. But it's here." His hands dropped to his lap, his face a blank slate. Beau threw an arm around his shoulders and Joe huddled gratefully into his big friend.

"So, you've hinted something about the FFs being why we're here," Nehemiah said abruptly. "What are we looking for?"

"Information," Joe signed. Nehemiah's heart stopped beating for an instant, and then rushed on to make up for it. He turned and grinned at his sister at getting an answer from Joe.

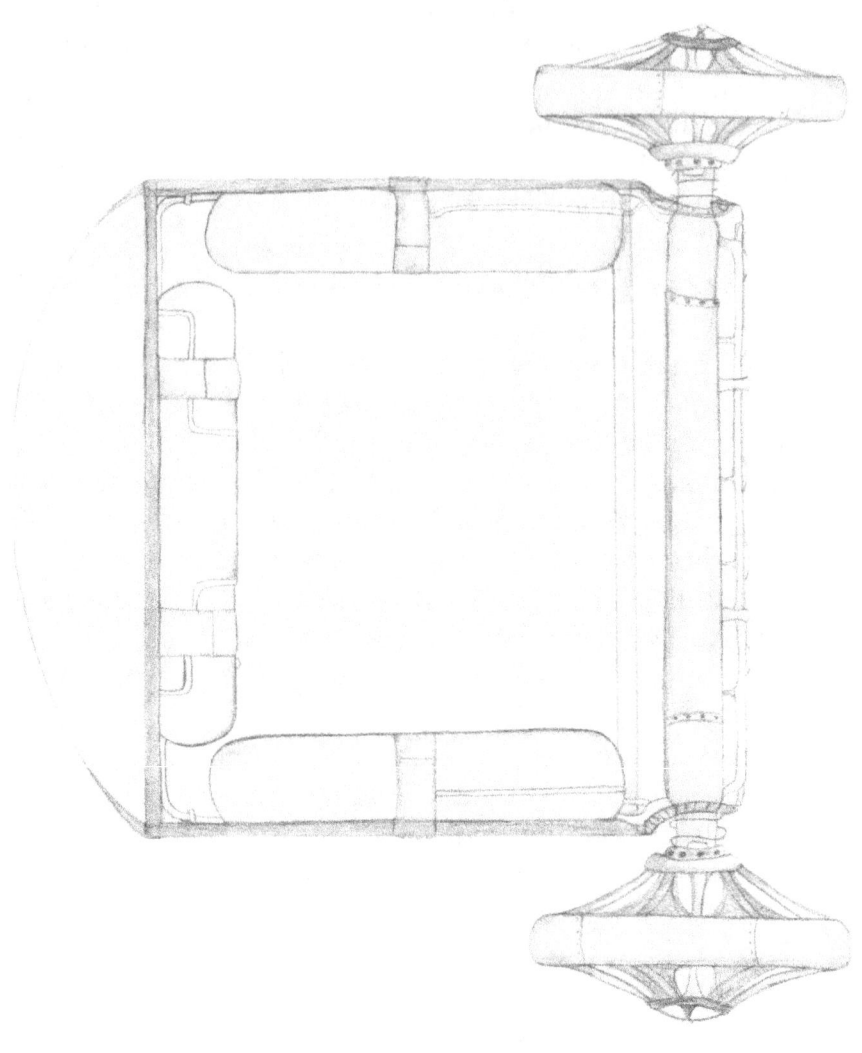

Cutaway to show water tanks

Her dancing eyes reflected his same excitement.

"That's not very helpful as an explanation," Anna said. Joe smiled at her and added more, Cobeau translating so the mute could speed.

"Okay then, information about someone who lives here, a Quintus Leeman. He's an inventor."

"Why are we looking for an inventor?" Nehemiah asked.

"To keep up with the FFs," Joe answered.

"Keep up?" Anna said doubtfully.

"I would think it was a good idea to stay away from people like Simmons," Nehemiah said. Joe's eyes darted away and he hunched into himself, seeming suddenly smaller. Anna decided it was the mention of that name.

"I think our concert went well," she said. It worked. Joe spun off on an analysis of their playing, and the twins let the conversation turn to music. A few minutes of it and Joe was relaxed again, leaning comfortably against Beau, smiling and laughing over Nehi's mistake with the drums earlier today. Nehemiah didn't mind the laughter.

Late that night, Nehi's eyes flew open and he stared around him. The Raven wagon lay camped between two little hills beside the road to Freedom. His dew protector hadn't sensed liquid and inflated, and it felt great to wake up under the clear skies instead of the rubber covering. The scent of green grass and cool, wet air hung around Nehemiah as he lay on his blanket blinking at the gentle green hill, which was just high enough to block out any other view to his right. This soft grass made a night outside feel like a feather mattress to the young vagabond, and he was deliciously comfortable and content. The stars sent their surreal light cascading into the thin valley around him, making his mind turn to what might lie behind them. It was pleasant. He yawned. But he was too tired to enjoy it well. Why was he awake?

Boney knuckles slammed into his cheekbone and he jerked up, rubbing the spot. Joe tossed back and forth beside him, writhing in his dreams. His sharp face twisted with terror or pain (Nehemiah couldn't decide which), his mouth stretched in a silent scream. Nehi grabbed the mute's shoulder and shook him.

"Joe? Come on, wake up," Nehemiah said, just to let him hear a friendly voice as he came out of a dream like that. Joe's eyes shot open. They shone with fright, fastening on the hill across from him. He lay still, his breath coming in short, labored bursts and his eyes wide and staring. Nehemiah moved so that he was beside Joe's rigid, thin shoulders, so there would be no doubt a friend was near. He pointed up at the stars and forced a gentle smile. This was the first constellation party they had held in Joe's honor.

"The lion is beautiful tonight," Nehemiah said. "He's looking down on us with all the great steadiness of the constellation's Maker. Just like the Lion of Judah's watching over us. And there's the donkey, too. You remember, the one that miraculously spoke to Balaam?" Joe's breath caught, and his eyes filled with tears. He curled on the ground, shaking and sobbing violently, his superb self-control lost. Nehemiah sat still, stunned. He had seen many people cry in his time, but never over a talking donkey in the stars. This was more than just waking up from a nightmare. Nehemiah laid his hand on his friend's quaking shoulder.

"What's wrong?" he asked awkwardly. Joe sobbed in a breath that shook his whole body, pushed himself up, and slumped against the nearest thing; Nehemiah's broad side. Nehi could feel the small body trembling, and shaking with sobs. Nehemiah tossed his blanket over the thin, slumped shoulders and waited. After a moment Joe swiveled to face him so Nehi could see the mute's hands, and started to sign.

"What's the verse you and Beauty quote back and forth, Knee-High?" They quoted many verses back and forth, but Nehemiah guessed the one he was asking about.

"'For I am persuaded, that neither death, nor life, nor angels, nor principalities, nor powers, nor things present, nor things to come, nor height, nor depth, nor any other creature, shall be able to separate us from the love of God, which is in Christ Jesus our Lord,'[6]" he recited.

"Is it true?" Joe signed, not bothering to wipe away the tears. His violent shaking was calming to an occasional tremble, and Nehemiah answered quickly.

"Of course it is! I may have had my doubts sometimes, but that doesn't change what's true. Once Jesus claims us, nothing can take His love from us, any more than anything could keep Him dead." Nehemiah's certainty went a long way to stopping even the trembles. Joe sat quiet for a few minutes considering. A breeze stirred the wet air, and the starlight went on unchanged. Nehemiah listened to Beau snore and the occasional chirruping cricket, wondering if he should press Joe into signing more or let him be.

"Knee-High," Joe finally burst out, his hands moving in exaggerated patterns in his emotion and the tears beginning to course down his cheeks again, "am I just another animal, like Prissy? No, am I less than that? Even she has the ability to voice her thoughts to her fellow pigs! Me? I can't. I don't have the most basic human right, I can't even scream for mercy, Knee-High, or beg for food, or say 'I love you,' or..." Joe's hands dropped gently to his lap as if he was too tired to go on. He sat still, his shoulders slumped forward and his head bowed so low his tears fell straight onto his hands. So that's what was bothering him.

"You're voicing your thoughts to me right now, Joe. And even if you couldn't explain a word, you would still be one of God's crowning creations."

"It says so somewhere in the Bible, right?" Joe signed. His tears stopped, but were replaced by such a sense of weary sorrow and searching, it was worse than any passing tears.

---

[6] Romans 8:38-39

Joe's mask had slipped further away tonight. Nehemiah could see this question delved deeper than a single nightmare. The lost sorrow Joe was allowing to be seen was so furrowed in his sharp face...it was a part of the mute, not just a passing mood. Nehemiah looked up at the stars and prayed for the right words.

"Have you ever heard Psalm 8?" he asked. Joe shook his head and Nehemiah began to quote. "'When I consider Thy heavens, the work of Thy fingers, the moon and the stars, which Thou hast ordained; what is man that Thou are mindful of him? And the son of man that Thou visitest him? For Thou has made him a little lower than the angels, and hast crowned him with glory and honor. Thou madest him to have dominion over the works of Thy hands; Thou hast put all things under his feet. All sheep and oxen, yea, and the beasts of the field; the fowl of the air, the fish of the sea, and whatsoever passeth through the paths of the sea. Oh Lord our Lord, how excellent is Thy name in all the earth!' You're pictured here, Joe. Only a little lower than the angels, crowned with glory and honor, ruler over all the beasts. There's no stipulation about speech. Or whether you're fat, or purple, or old, or even nice. God made man. 'After His own image created He them; male and female created He them.[7]' You are God's image bearer. Not only that, you're one of His chosen ones, His child. You are one of God's vessels made for honor. God loves you, Joe. He picked you as His child, and made you special for Himself, because He loves you just like you are. Never think of yourself as anything less."

Joe didn't move perceptibly, but something in the pull of his shoulders let Nehemiah know his words had helped. The two sat on, Cobeau's snores, the chirruping cricket, and the occasional hiss of the passing hoverer on the road to their left the only interruptions to the quiet night. Joe was thinking, turning over the truths he had just been given, and Nehemiah didn't interrupt.

---

[7] Genesis 1:27

"I wish I had a copy of the Bible," Joe signed suddenly. The idea of owning a Bible had never occurred to Nehemiah. It was his turn to ponder.

"Yes, that would be nice," he said. "No, that would be astoundingly wonderful and life-altering! Wow, that would be amazing. To have it always there, to be able to study it deeper, or just to browse the pages and find truths whenever... Wow. But we have to get it back from whoever has it before we can think about a move like that. Could we really copy it? We don't know how to do that...and do you think people would let us come up with a way?"

"Probably not," signed Joe, though in answer to what question he didn't specify. "How do you know it hasn't been destroyed?"

"Because Jesus said it wouldn't be, He said heaven and earth would pass away before His word would be lost.[8]"

"Really?" the mute asked, lifting his head to look up at Nehi. Nehemiah nodded, and Joe went on signing. "That's a relief. I still wish we had it here."

"Well, until we do, how about having a talking Bible from the bits my parents taught me?" Nehi asked. Joe smiled at him, and it almost reached his sad eyes.

"How about one on the stars?"

"'The LORD doth build up Jerusalem: He gathereth together the outcasts of Israel. He healeth the broken in heart, and bindeth up their wounds. He telleth the number of the stars; He calleth them all by their names...'[9]" Nehemiah quoted, and Joe gave a real smile. He slid the blanket comfortably around him, leaned against the wagon, and asked for one on birds next. Nehemiah obliged. Then came another, and another, on into the night. The stars began to fade and morning came. It found the two boys fast asleep on the smooth valley floor, peaceful and content in the dawn's light.

---

[8] Matthew 24:35; Mark 13:31; Luke 16:17
[9] Psalm 147:2-5

Bloodstream Day
Genesis 2:7

Chapter Twelve: The Advancers

"For the invisible things of Him from the creation of the world are clearly seen, being understood by the things that are made, even His eternal power and Godhead; so that they are without excuse." Romans 1:20

The town of Freedom sprawled on a wide plain, with rolling grasslands rippling into hills, and lakes glittering in the sunshine. It was a beautiful city, the twins granted it that. Clean asphalt streets, landscaped with bright flowers and trees, the buildings modern and mostly in excellent condition (though the outskirts held some that could only be called slums). As they drew into the city proper, well-kept houses lined the street, pretty, and very large. Some were nearly as large as the office buildings and factories they passed. A host of windows gleamed from the houses, storefronts, and office buildings. The panes acted like mirrors on the side facing the streets, the VK's own reflections stared back at them as the group traveled.

Nehemiah turned away from the windows, glowering at the street. He knew what few people learned. Stare at your own reflection long enough and it becomes a punishment, not a pleasure. Cobeau headed the wagon toward the center of town where Nehemiah and Anna could see tall buildings reaching up into the sky, those strange windowpanes glinting in the sunlight. As they got closer, Nehemiah craned his neck back and still couldn't spot the tops of the skyscrapers. His neck started to ache.

"'And they said,'" Nehemiah murmured, "'Go to, let us build us a city and a tower, whose top may reach unto heaven; and let us make us a name, lest we be scattered abroad upon the face of the earth. [10]'" Joe looked up at him from the wagon's seat and frowned. Nehi stopped quoting the passage and the

---

[10] Genesis 11:4-5

twins grimaced. They were tired of lands where Bible verses were frowned on. Cobeau passed Prissy's stick to Joe and stood up on the top of the wagon.

"Men! Women! All who hear me in freedom, let your wills guide your senses to a feast of sound and sight you have never experienced before!" he boomed, repeating it with slight variations as they went. Anna and Nehemiah started a recorder duet on top of the wagon and watched with interest as the habitual crowd began to gather behind them. They looked eclectic and affluent, with the exception of the random bum. The crowd grew quickly, and the twins were surprised when Joe pulled Prissy to a stop in the midst of a small park. Cobeau introduced the troupe as the others set up their show. A flash of red hair caught Anna's eye from a window in a white stone apartment building, and she glanced up. Fredrick, the fat smiler, stared down at her. He waved as he saw her looking. Anna waved back, not quite pleased to see him, and turned toward Joe, a vague unease playing through her. Joe signed their first song.

"'The Choice of the Baker,'" he prodded. Anna's mind rushed off, trying to remember all the words; she forgot to mention Fredrick.

Nehemiah and Anna began the humorous ballad to the accompaniment of Joe's whistles. They sang back and forth, answering each other in clever quips and lines, and laughter rippled through the crowd. They ended with a duet, for the baker won his lady. As the last note died, Joe burst into his rhythm dance. Anna smiled as every jaw dropped and every eye opened wider. Nehemiah slipped his guitar strap over his shoulder, Joe readied his whistles again as he kicked and spun, and Anna began to sing a reel. Apart from the hymns she loved so much, this was her favorite song. The words were only da's and do's and it was such fun to mix them and make them chase each other and not let her tongue get twisted as she did it. The crowd seemed to enjoy it too, and it began to grow.

An hour later, Nehi, Anna, and Joe joined hands and took

their third bow, applause and cheers almost deafening them. The crowd stood packed so tightly some people couldn't even move, and it spilled into the streets surrounding the park. Anna dropped the boys' hands and turned to gather things, but her eyes stayed on the crowd; it was going to take a long time to unpack itself and move away. She turned to ask Joe if she should clean his whistles, spotted the Ravens, and suddenly wondered if that was just what Joe and Co had planned. She caught a glimpse of Joe's blond hair disappearing into the stairwell leading to a basement of the skyscraper behind the wagon. Beau lumbered behind him, melting into the shadows as if he could become a part of them.

Anna studied the recess of concrete stairs, leading down into something unknown. She was the one counseling waiting, to let the Ravens have their own way. But...she was more than curious this time. She liked Joe and Beau, and there was something worrying them in this country. And it had to do with those disturbing FFs Nehemiah and Joe were both terrified about, which meant she and Nehi were definitely involved. Maybe if they could find out just a little of what was happening they could help. Anna grabbed Nehemiah's arm and pulled him after their friends. The bright sunshine was swallowed by the musty, stinking dimness of the stairwell, concrete sides rising over them to form almost a tunnel.

"What are we doing?" Nehemiah whispered.

A black painted door below them crashed open, slamming into the concrete with a bang. Nehi's hand landed on Hope, tucked away in her hidden pocket. Beau stood framed in light spilling from the doorway, staring up the stairs, his face rippling with a snarl. Then he caught sight of the twins and his features dropped into a delighted smile. He stepped aside and politely held the door open.

Anna and Nehemiah slipped in and found themselves in an enormous room that must take up the whole of the base of the skyscraper above them. The walls were covered in white boards and papers with mathematical figures and formulas scrawled over them. Counters and tables stood everywhere, with test tubes, burners, instrument panels, notebooks, and things Anna and Nehemiah couldn't even name. A pleasant-faced, sandy-haired man somewhere in his early thirties leaned against one of the counters, a white lab coat draped over his lanky form. He stared at them in surprise. Joe stood next to him, green eyes twinkling and mouth twitching in a smile. His laughing expression made the twins feel as if they were children again, barging into a grown up's conversation. But at least he wasn't angry. Anna smiled at the stranger.

"Excuse us for bursting in on you, we were just curious what our friends were doing in the basement."

"And it turns out it's a lab," Nehemiah said, studying a test tube with yellow liquid bubbling juicily in it. The man looked at Joe and the mute nodded, admitting them as friends. Joe pointed a thumb at the sandy-haired man.

"The branch leader for the IDP in KAM," he signed as an introduction. The man smiled and held out his hand to Nehemiah, who was closest to him.

"Paul Sireton, a pleasure to have you here. Any friend of Joe and Co, as the saying sort of goes," Nehemiah took his hand and smiled back, liking this stranger.

"Nehemiah," he answered the unspoken question. "And the one toying with the Bunsen burner is Anna, my sister." Anna stuck her hands behind her back, spinning around guiltily. Paul laughed. He had a nice laugh, easy and smart.

"A pleasure to meet you, Anna," he said. Then he turned back to Joe. "Now, you don't come here just for social calls, I know you that well, anyway. What do you need from me?" Joe gave his little whistle asking for Cobeau's translation services.

"I was hoping to talk to Quintus Leeman," the Ravens said together.

"My old partner? Oh, he's long gone by now," Paul said. Joe's face fell.

"Gone where?" he said through Cobeau. "How long?"

"About a year ago, he got a very good offer from the People's Kingdom."

"And he accepted, and went *there*?" they asked incredu-
lously, even Beau sounding shocked.

"I know, it's not exactly the place I would want to go. But
Quintus went for a sort of test trial and when he came back he
said most of what we hear about them is false. He was convinced it was a good place to live, and he was enjoying his
work immensely. Though he wouldn't tell me what it was.
Maybe he's right, I've never actually been there." Joe snorted
and Cobeau looked as if he had just swallowed something very
nasty.

"Don't believe it, it's worse than the tales tell. Is Q still
there?"

"He was last I heard, about three months ago," Paul said, a
worried frown on his face. "His call didn't sound as happy as
I'd expected, I confess."

"Paul, how old is Quintus?"

"What?" Paul blinked, taken aback. "Um, I guess he's in his
sixties now."

"Not getting too frail or anything?" Joe and Cobeau asked.

"No, not anymore than—"

The door crashed open, rebounding into the wall. People in
white lab coats flooded in, spreading out in a practiced formation. Eight dart rifles leveled at the little group. Nehi just
caught a glimpse of Joe's face, color drained, eyes staring,
muscles pulled tight in terror, when a bestial roar tore
through the room.

Cobeau arched over the table.

His hairy face rippled with fury and he aimed for the center of the white-coated people, at two who came in behind the
others, a series of leather straps dangling over their shoulders.

A soft pop, Beau jerked, went limp, and thudded into the
concrete in a heap. Anna gasped and jerked forward as Nehemiah's hand went to Hope's hidden pocket on his thigh. Paul
grabbed their wrists, jerking them back. He didn't grab Joe.
The mute shot forward, reaching Beau's side in a single

bound.

"It's the Advancers, there will be more up top, lots more," Paul hissed in the twin's ears. Three dart guns twinkled in the glaring artificial light, never wavering as they pointed at the group. The other five swiveled, leveling at Joe as he gripped Beau's shoulder and dragged him to his side. The mute slipped a hand over the chimera's heart to see if it was still beating. "We can't do anything." The words seared into Nehemiah, burning in his twisting stomach.

One of the men stepped forward and dug a dart gun under Joe's chin, driving his head up. The mute went rigid, his hands carefully held in plain sight. His eyes were dim and downcast, his face a set blank; only his quick, labored breathing showed any emotion. One with the leather straps stepped towards him, a business-like woman, her blond hair pulled back in a neat ponytail. She slid a finger onto Joe's collar and pushed it down as another finger brushed his hair away. Two long, long seconds ticked by as she stared at his neck.

"He's the one, Freddy was right," the woman said. A burly man slid the straps off his shoulder and shook them out. The leather fell into the shape of a harness. The woman gripped the back of the collar and pulled Joe's bulky jacket off. The mute's arms went limp, letting her do it. Offering no help, no hindrance. The man crossed the mute's arms on his chest and began to fasten the harness around Joe's torso. He pulled the intricate leather straps through a series of S hooks as the woman clicked a copper stick to the back of the harness, at the middle of Joe's spine. They were quick and efficient; only twenty seconds had passed since the door crashed open. Nehemiah's hand tightened on Hope's stock. Paul could feel his muscles bunching and his fingers bit into the young man's arm.

"Don't!" Paul hissed. "I'm telling you, there's nothing we can do here! You act and we all go down."

If they were all taken, there would be no one to help Joe. Nehemiah's fingers loosened. The man took the copper stick and levered Joe to his feet. The control was obvious as he swung the mute around and pushed him toward the stairs. Joe's gaze shot from the floor and locked onto Anna. His eyes darted to Cobeau lying still on the ground and then up to her again. She nodded.

"I'll take care of him," she murmured, her voice choked. The man pushed the stick, and Joe was shoved firmly out the door. The competent woman turned to the group, flashing them a business-like smile. Anna thought she probably practiced it in her mirror at home.

"Sorry to have troubled you. Just collecting a GI," she said. Then a frown crossed her face, tight and annoyed. "We really should fine you for this, you know you're supposed to contact the Advancers about stray GIs!" Her blond ponytail whipped behind her head as she spun and headed toward the door. She paused, a speculative frown on her face as she looked at Beau, lying limp and still. "I'd get rid of that chimera immediately, he seemed pretty fierce."

"Thanks for the thought," Paul managed weakly. The door closed behind her. A van's engine roared to life in the street above, and the quiet bubbling of the lab took over. In the sudden silence the twins felt paralyzed. Beau twitched and began to move. He gave a low groan and pushed against the floor, his arms shaking and weak. Anna ran forward and knelt beside him, dropping her hand on his thick shoulder and trying to think of something to say. Cobeau sat up slowly, his eyes cloudy.

"Joe," he muttered. His voice was barely audible. He pulled his knees up to his chest, laid his hairy face on them, and began to weep. They were quiet tears, not the wild wailing the twins had always heard from the chimera. The change frightened them.

"He's in Jesus' hands, Beau," Anna murmured.

"We should go," Paul spoke up, changing his white lab coat for a knitted sweater. "They might be back to make sure we took care of Cobeau."

"Who are 'they'?" Nehemiah asked. He walked numbly across the lab and picked up Joe's jacket, laying it gently over his arm.

"And why did they take Joe?" Anna asked, her voice tight and a little wet.

"You two aren't from here, are you?" Paul asked as he began to clear up his work from the day. Images of their gentle, free country sparked through their mind, and homesickness settled like a burning rock in their chests.

"No, we're not," Nehemiah murmured.

"We need to go," Paul repeated. Nehemiah nodded and knelt by the weeping chimera.

"Beau, we have to go," he said. There was no response. Nehi looked at Anna. She laid a hand on his big shaggy head and stroked it.

"You know Joe wants you to take care of yourself," she told him.

"Joe!" Beau wailed and began to rock back and forth, his sobbing growing louder.

"How are you going to help him if you don't help yourself?" Anna persisted.

"No help," Cobeau sobbed. "No help. Joe!"

"What do you mean no help, Cobeau?" Paul said, his voice soothing. "It's only his third time. They'll mark him, and send him out, just like before."

"Before?" Anna cried.

"Third time?" Nehemiah gaped.

"No. Fourth," Cobeau whispered. He began to rock harder and his sobs grew. "Fourth! Fourth, fourth, fourth, fourth!" he wailed. Paul stared at Beau, his eyes wide and mouth set in a tight line. He knelt beside the big man and began to speak slowly and distinctly so the chimera would understand.

"Cobeau, do you mean this is Joe's fourth time in the Institute?" Cobeau nodded through his sobs and Paul sat back, gnawing his lip, his face lined and eyes troubled.

"We have no idea what you're talking about!" Anna burst

out.

"And we need to go," Nehemiah reminded them. He circled Cobeau's waist with his arm and Anna did the same on the other side. Beau leaned heavily on them, but walked where they led. Paul collected his wits and leapt up, following the group up to the street and over to the wagon. Anna took charge of Cobeau as they got close and led him inside; he would be no help right now. Paul hopped up beside Nehemiah on the bench as the young man pushed the primer down and listened to the swift flow of the water heating and beginning to fill the coils. It felt surreal and horribly sad as Nehemiah's hand rested on the steam button and pressed the wagon into life. Joe always did this job. The wagon rose, the pig squeaked, and he steered Prissy into the streets.

Paul began to guide him through the town to where he could safely park the wagon. The mirrored windows stared back at them as they traveled, seeming to mock Joe's empty seat. They aimed for a little wood just outside of town. The lighting grew green and mottled as it was filtered down through the trees, but Nehi wasn't comforted. The two men hopped onto the leaf covered ground, quickly got Prissy settled, and ducked into the wagon.

Cobeau slumped in a chair, half lying on the table in the day room, his hand resting on the painting of the raven with the green eyes. His sobbing had quieted. But his face was distant. He didn't stir as the door opened. Anna stood next to him, her lips pursed and her eyes troubled. She spun to Nehemiah as he stepped in.

"All he'll say is 'Joe' and 'fourth,' I can't get anything else out of him. He's so crushed I'm afraid for him, Nehi, he won't even eat!" Anna cried. She spun to Paul, her dark eyes pleading. "What is this all about?" Paul sighed and dropped onto a chair. He thought for a moment, trying to decide where to start.

"I can tell you two were shocked at the treatment Joe got in my lab," Paul began. "That means you're from a much gentler country than this one. At least much gentler to GIs. This is the country that named them, you know. Incomplete. Not a complete human. Still lower down on the evolutionary track. Not entitled to the same rights as a real human."

"Wait, so if you're an incomplete, you're just another animal here?" Nehemiah interrupted. His conversation with Joe last night suddenly made horrible sense. Paul nodded. He stirred uncomfortably but went on.

"There's a reason they're treated like that. Our book, the *Humanist Manifestos*, protect human rights, and freedom in general. But they also promote human advancement, especially in the area of science. And it's an evolutionary science, that the human race is rising to new and better things and we can help them get there."

"And if you're not perfect, you won't help it rise," Nehemiah said, beginning to understand. Anna was by Cobeau again, murmuring gently to him and trying to get him to respond.

"Exactly," Paul answered. "There are differences, even among the incompletes. Some become incomplete by accident. Those aren't worried about in the least, there's nothing wrong there. It's the ones who are GIs from birth, genetically so by their parents' genes. These incompletes–"

"Stop calling them that!" Nehemiah snapped. Joe's tossing form last night haunted him, and the mute's uncontrolled sobs at the thought of even a donkey that could talk. Nehi suddenly found he couldn't stand the word. "There is no incomplete with God, He forms and fashions and creates each one just as He wants them to be. There's a beauty in learning to speak with those who can't speak, and learning to see with those who can't see, and...just stop using that word. Please." Paul nodded and went on.

"The people who took Joe are part of the Advancers of Science, a government funded program that's committed to (like it sounds) the advancement of science. Especially to the human race's advancement. Part of what they do is try and keep the race from being polluted or held back. In their estimation the Joes of this world hold us back. Once someone comes into this world and is...not perfect, the Advancers are called in. They run tests, and if it's a genetic problem, the baby is marked. Do you have a pencil and paper somewhere around here? I'll show you what I mean." Anna pulled her notebook out of her pocket and handed it to Paul. He flipped it open, put a piece of paper on the hard white pad, wielded the pencil, and turned it around for the twins to see.

GI

"They put this mark on their necks to show that they are a Genetic Incomplete," Paul explained. "I'm sorry to use the word again, Nehemiah, but I'll have to for you to understand what comes next. These people retard the human race and so need to be dealt with, but they can't be if they are under human laws. So they solve the problem by declaring GIs aren't really humans, that there's something missing in them the rest of us have, their evolution is incomplete. Once they're marked as a GI, they're put up for adoption, allowed to go out to other kingdoms. Like a stray cat from a shelter. It's the same type of policies, actually. The ones who aren't taken... Well, they call it putting them to sleep. The GI's that are taken, it's not usually for nice reasons. At least, it wasn't. Now the IDP is aware of the situation and so we've been doing our best to take them in."

"Why now?" Anna asked quietly, already pretty sure she knew the answer.

"Joe," rumbled Cobeau, still stroking the little raven with the bright green eyes.

"Yes," Paul nodded. "Joe brought the need of those children to our attention, when he came into our midst about six years ago. We didn't know about it before that. We should have. But to get on. Now quite a few of the GIs are taken in by IDPs in other kingdoms. But of course most of our adopters were Sojourners, and now that there is no kingdom... Sorry, that's another problem, right now you're still wondering about Joe. If a

GI comes back, if they show up here in KAM again, the advancers run the tests to make sure of the mark (they're very thorough, whatever else they are). Another mark is tattooed on their necks, then they're sent out again." Paul wrote on the paper and turned it around.

"A circle is added after the second time. Here's where it gets bad for Joe, according to Cobeau. This is what I thought Joe had on his neck, a second time around mark, just a beginning troublemaker, if you will. I thought now, this would only be his third time in the Institute."

"Wait, how do you know he was taken a second time?" Nehemiah asked.

"Ah, well, that puts us into KAM's policy about us Christians. We are humans not incompletes – oops, sorry, grown up with it. We are entitled to all human rights. But, it's still illegal to be a Christian. The thought of a transcendent God, an immortal soul, right morals, creation, and various other matters contained in the Way are deterrents to human advancement, according to the *Humanist Manifestos*. If they find us out they try to re-educate us. They have a center up in the mountains, and Christians are sent there for re-education. The trouble is when you come back (unless you're declared "uncooperative" in which case you're deported instead), you're not allowed to have anything from your old life back. This means all family ties, everything is gone. And you're watched like a hawk for the rest of your existence practically, bringing anyone into danger who tries to come to you.

"Soon after Joe first came here, there was a situation with a mother of three who was tagged for her Christianity. She was taken to the Darwinian Institute for the Advancement of Science and Knowledge, to the Advancers. (That's where they're always taken at first.) The father had just died and the children were devastated to be losing their mother too. Joe volunteered to be an 'inside man' since the moment he stepped into the light he would be taken straight to the Institute. He duly stepped, and with Joe's help we managed to get her out, and send her and her children on to the Sojourners. I heard she had married again, but who knows what's happened to them now. Anyway, Joe was marked and put on the 'adoption lists,' the IDP of Gaia caught him, and we were all very happy that it worked out so well." Paul drew again and flipped it around.

"It's not much of a change, but if Cobeau's right and this is what Joe has on his neck–"

"It is," the twins said, the words roiling in their insides till they felt sick. Paul sighed and his freckled face seemed to sag as his eyes dropped.

"Then that time he helped us in our rescue was his third time in the Darwinian Institute. He must be a very brave young man indeed to have gone in there voluntarily." Nehemiah's mind flew to Joe's nightmarish terror and heavy sorrow. And he knew he had still only seen the surface of Joe's troubled heart last night.

"You have no idea how brave," Nehi murmured.

"So since today, now that this is his fourth time there..." Anna prodded, determined to hear the end.

"He's a confirmed trouble maker, like a bear that's tagged and won't leave the area. Joe will be humanely killed," Paul answered. Cobeau trembled as if the word pierced him with a thousand needles. He began to sob again.

Chapter Thirteen: The Institute

"Withold not good from them to whom it is due, when it is in the power of thine hand to do it." Proverbs 3:27

Silence claimed the wagon. A heavy silence, brooding on despair and grief. Cobeau shattered it, murmuring Joe's name over and over to himself in a broken rumble as he petted the raven. Anna moved to a chair across from him and took his hand. He gave no response to show he noticed her. She looked over at the painting of the ravens, their life-like feathers rippling in a gentle breeze, and the little raven's bright green eyes. Those pretty, bright green eyes. Joe had been so kind to them, from the very beginning, when they needed kindness most and were entirely vulnerable! Oh sweet, secretive Joe!

Nehemiah looked at his sister, crying over a painting, and Cobeau's shattered form. He glanced away but found himself staring at that little raven in the oak tree again. Oh Joe. With his exasperating secrecy, tyrant rulings over music, his silly fear of all things sticky, his hurtful nasty moods when pressed... And his gentle, selfless spirit that would stay up all night with a trembling stranger, and voluntarily put himself back into one of his worst nightmares for a fellow Christian. Nehi's throat tightened, and he felt his stomach tighten with it. But he knew what his role had to be.

"Beau, we're going to get him out," Nehemiah said, dropping a hand on the chimera's shoulder. "We aren't going to let him die in their hands. If God wills it and we yet live,[11] we will get Joe back." A light spread over Cobeau's face (what could be seen of it through all his black hair). His spine straightened and he stared at Nehemiah, searching for something. Tears left as his expression turned eager and determined, his shoulders lifting.

---

[11] A rephrasing of James 4:15

"Yes. You will do it. You can do it! Let me help?" he cried, suddenly jumping up, tense and fierce, the wagon rocking under his swift change. "I can do many things, but I can't plan. You plan, and I'll do."

"Of course you'll help, but you have to wait till I tell you," Nehemiah told him. Cobeau nodded and sat down again, but all the despair had flown from him. Now he sat and fidgeted, watching Nehi with bright eyes.

"Nehemiah, do you know what you're saying?" Paul said, his voice quiet, hesitant. "The institute is probably the most important building in this kingdom and it's guarded like it. Once someone goes in, they don't come out unless the Advancers say so."

"You rescued someone out of there, didn't you?" Anna asked, her voice low and thoughtful.

"Well, yes, but we had Joe on the inside–"

"He's on the inside now," Nehemiah pointed out.

"That's the problem," Anna also pointed out.

"–and we had a faultless plan from the leader of the IDP himself," Paul continued doggedly. "The person at the very top of the International Discipleship Program, the one who coordinates all of us branch leaders. He's brilliant, he has to be to keep all of our underground branches safe. The IDP is the only thing in the world that stretches under every kingdom, no one else has achieved that. Our leader's plans are (to put it in a sardonic understatement) pretty good. And it sort of helps when you have a good plan."

"So we make one," Nehemiah said, his face set and determined. Paul sighed; Nehemiah looked so young.

"Do you know what happens to you if you'rc caught trying to rescue a deterrent to human advancement? Cobeau's a chimera, even lower on the evolutionary track than a GI. He would automatically be executed. And he would probably be better off than you and your sister. You and Anna would be sent to the center, Nehemiah, and they would do everything they could to make you give up your Christianity. Sometimes, if they're especially determined, they even try their hand at brainwashing."

"I'm pretty sure the center would be better than the place Joe and Co rescued me from," Nehemiah said evenly. Paul looked at him again and paused. Nasty scars snaked out from Nehi's three-quarter sleeve jacket, and something in his demeanor and a thoughtful wisdom in his face told of a man equipped to deal with more than his years should qualify. "But I agree with you about Anna–"

"No!" she cried, leaping to her feet and facing her brother. "Three are stronger than two, and you might need a woman's head, we think about things differently. And different means we might be able to overcome obstacles better."

"Anna, I don't want to put you in danger–" Nehemiah began, but Anna interrupted him.

"Protecting women is good and true, Nehi, but this is a world filled with danger, and if I'm with you at least we can help each other get out. I'm coming along." Nehemiah looked at her for a moment, his lips pursed. He nodded and turned back to Paul.

"If this leader is such a brilliant planner, can we get him to think about it? How much time does Joe have?" Nehi asked. Paul looked at the three.

"You're sure about this? I mean Joe is a..." He stopped himself and nodded. "Okay. And you're four, not three. At least. If you need more people, I'm sure we can get volunteers from our group. The IDP leader won't be able to help, it takes time to contact him. No one even knows what his name is or if he is a 'he,' actually. Joe has about twenty-four hours. Probably. He's already been in for two."

"Right," Nehemiah said, trying to sound as if he had some idea of what to do next. "Beau, do you have a map of the Institute in that cubby hole of yours?" Cobeau leapt up and darted around the partition, the others trailing him. He shoved his thumb down on an aspen branch, a click rang in the room, and a small door swung open. Maps spilled out onto the floor, and

Nehi and Anna blinked at it. That cubby hole opened from inside the wagon? They had lived in these two rooms for over half a year, and never known that. How many other little cubby holes and drawers were in this wagon that they had no idea about?

Ten minutes later Anna gave a shout and held up a blue and white paper. Everyone waded through the papers littering the room to crowd around her and stare at a detailed blueprint of the Darwinian Institute. It had everything they needed; the frequency of the security radios, hours the guards patrolled, details of the personnel's uniforms, a numbered grid naming each room, the map held it all. The date at the top read from four months ago. Paul's mouth dropped open as he stared at it. His mind began to ache as he tried to figure how a chimera and a GI managed to get hold of such a thing. Nehemiah leaned over Anna's shoulder and the two studied it in silence. Nehi pointed and Anna nodded slowly.

"That's our way," Nehemiah muttered, and turned to Paul. "Thank you for your offer of a fourth, I think we'll take you up on it. We'll need somewhere to go when we come out. The hunt is going to be strong, do you think you can handle it?"

"We can handle it," Paul grinned. "The KAM IDP has a few little tricks."

"Thanks," Nehemiah said, vastly relieved someone else was handling that part of the problem. "Is there somewhere you can safely watch for us..." He studied the blueprint, and pointed. "Here. Here's where we'll come out. At one o'clock this morning, hopefully without a problem, but be prepared for us to have the whole town on our heels."

"We'll be watching, and we'll be ready for you," Paul said, standing up and grabbing his sweater off the back of his chair. He shook hands all around and left to prepare. As the latch to the wagon door clicked home behind the branch leader, Cobeau spun around and slipped his hand under the bottom bunk. A wooden board flew up, sending the mattress flying into the back wall.

A cavity yawned up at the twins, encompassing the whole space below the lowest bunk. Anna and Nehemiah gaped at it. Inside lay a regular arsenal and burglary store, everything they could wish for a venture like they were going on tonight. Some of the gadgets were so advanced Anna and Nehemiah had no idea what they were. Cobeau reached to the back and pulled out an armful of black garments, perfect for shrouding two people. It could easily be stretched to cover all four of the VKs.

"Okay Beau, the guards are on the other side of the building. Let's go," Nehemiah muttered. The big man shot forward, Anna and Nehemiah tagging along like extra shadows. Inky blackness spread over the world, and they thanked God for the cloudy sky. If the moon had been out they would have been reflected in the hundreds of glass panes of the Institute. It towered twenty-three stories over them, and seemed to be made out of the peculiar windowpanes. The building reached up and up, ending in a beautiful, cruel pinnacle, hundreds of feet over the trio's heads. The city roared around them, near enough to be heard but set back enough from this magnificent building to only be heard. The nearest city building stood ten yards away from the vast, painted concrete fence stretching around the tower. It was ten yards that seemed to stretch forever to the twins as they bolted over it.

Nehemiah's back slammed into the wall, and he pressed himself against it, hardly daring to breathe. No outcry rang through the night, no sound except their own panting. And the whine of the lethal power coursing through the wire on top of the fence. He prayed Joe bought good quality gadgets, and the little mute had labeled them right. Beau lifted Anna to the top of the fifteen-foot fence. Anna slid two rubber balls on the wire, about two feet from each other, and clipped them closed. She tossed a leaf onto the wire suspended between the two, holding her breath as she watched. The leaf hit the wire, tee-tered there for a moment, then tumbled to the ground, not electrified into ash. Anna let her breath out and pulled herself quickly over. She dropped silently on the ground inside the fence, her legs burning with the force of the fall. Nehemiah came next. Beau climbed over last, quickly, deftly, taking the two rubber gadgets with him as he flipped soundlessly past.

The three ran forward, hunched close to the ground and staying in the deeper shadows of the south wall. They grouped around a small vent in the side of the building. You couldn't see it from the road, but it had been on the Ravens' map. Ne-hemiah knelt down and sprayed a dense cloud of green gas over it. The label on the bottle said it was guaranteed to deac-tivate any alarm system, and Nehemiah hoped it was right as he stuck his screwdriver on the corner screw and spun it. The screws twisted out, he pulled the vent cover off in less than a minute, and no alarm sounded. A rectangular metal air duct yawned out at them. Musty darkness seemed to pour out of it.

Nehi scrambled inside, his teeth clenched. The walls pressed close as he crawled forward, careful not to make a noise on the metal surrounding him. It was so dark. And so cramped. What if something collapsed in here, what if it was a trap, what if Simmons waited – Nehemiah clamped his lips tight and forced himself to breathe, pushing the panic far in-side. He switched on his little penlight even though he knew it was a risk. *Just nasty memories of the dark in Abid's Box and Simmons' rooms, that's all,* he told himself over and over. It was all right. Anna and Beau moved behind him, God watched above, and he was free.

With a prayer on his lips and cold sweat swiftly soaking him, Nehemiah moved farther up the ventilation tunnel, forc-ing himself to breathe the close, dirty air. Cobeau squeezed in, and Anna came last, pulling the vent cover back over the opening as she heard the guards returning on their patrols. The three crawled forward, making as little sound as possible as they shuffled higher and higher into the building. Nehemiah

paused on the fourth story, at a vent reaching into a room filled with dark. It should be the home of brooms, cleaners, and uniforms. He motioned Anna forward. He couldn't hear anything moving behind him and turned the penlight that way. She grinned and pointed at Cobeau.

"I can't get around him," she signed clumsily in Joe's language. Nehemiah crawled forward obediently, and Cobeau shuffled after him, lying on his belly and pulling himself with his elbows, allowing Anna access to the vent. She waved a cheery hand at the two farther up and dropped out of the reach of Nehi's light into the room below them.

Anna picked a uniform to wear over her clothes and slid out of the closet into the glaring light of the security section of the Darwinian Institute. Her heart pounded but there was an element of fun to this. They were fooling everyone, and doing God's work as they helped a brother. She wore the uniform of a security guard and decided its smart black and gray wasn't actually ugly as she marched to her station, four hallways away.

Anna shivered as she moved, though she recognized the temperature was normal. With a few scented candles and a couple of paintings on the whitewashed walls, it could be a stylish place. Instead, the vague smell of cleaners pervaded, with no relief from the sharp, modern architecture of lines of white making up the ceiling, floor, and walls. Everything was so white. It surrounded her, even spilling from the lighting. It made her eyes ache, and somehow got into her heart and depressed her. How could something so bright be so cold?

Anna shivered again and wondered how Joe was doing in a cheerless place like this. She prayed God would grant him hope and joy, and then realized she was praying it for herself too. A sharp frown cut into her face as she marched down the last hallway, her eye searching for the proper door. All their fascinating travels, Nehemiah getting strong again, Joe and Beau becoming such good friends, it was all a marvelous blessing. But she still desperately missed the life she no longer had. Simple things she had taken for granted, like going to church on Sundays and smiling at her friends in the pews, especially her sweet, sweet parents...all gone.

Anna lifted her chin and told herself to stop being melancholy. What a horrible place, that sucked joy from a person like a nurse taking blood, leaving despair and gloom coagulating in the soul! And Joe had been in here for hours? They had to get him out, quickly.

She spun around a sharp white corner and saw it. A simple white metal door, with a pearly colored "11" on the front in reflective paint that caught the bright white light and twinkled in the still hallway. She stood alone in the empty hall. That made things easier. Much, much easier.

A vent cover rattled in a small hallway of the floor for Testing of Lower Creatures. It swung away with a little ping of metal and hung on one screw, a black cavity yawning in the ceiling where it had been. Two black forms dropped through it onto the tiled floor. Nehemiah flipped the safety off Hope and padded down the hall, every sense heightened in his adrenaline rush, tingling with the expectation of seeing a guard around any corner. But they had picked their time well, and no one was out on the twelfth floor. Cobeau followed him, his big feet silent as they stole along the white passageway. The smell of chemicals tickled Nehemiah's throat. He blinked as he padded forward.

Everything was so white. It almost blinded him. The whitewashed walls, tiled floors, smooth ceiling, florescent light spilling from the overhead lamps, everything bleached. There was no relief to the stiff corners and hard, ticklish chemical scent. It reminded Nehemiah of a pile of white bones, all dried and useless, lifeless, and cold. He shivered as he spun cautiously around a corner, Hope sweeping the area. A cruel whiteness, that sapped all homey warmth, gave headaches, stole– Nehemiah jumped as Cobeau touched his shoulder. The chimera's black-gloved finger pointed and Nehemiah followed it. A white steel door stared back at him. "Incompletes" stood out in pearly letters.

"I'll watch," Beau signed. "Get him, Knee-High." The chimera melted through a door marked "Chimpanzees," leaving it cracked so he could see the hallway. Nehemiah pushed open the door, his hand on Hope. More whiteness flooded his vision. That cold, wearying brightness that sapped all rest, all peace, and joy. Kennels lined the room, five feet by six feet, he guessed. All the ones he could see were empty. The whole room looked empty. He moved forward, not daring to call out to Joe in that dead silence. He darted a look to his left, and his heart skipped.

A water bottle sat in one of the kennels, a cold metal bowl filled with some sort of brown paste in one corner, a small toilet in the back, and a white pallet near the gate. Joe lay on the pallet, wrapped in only a white robe, too big for his scarred form. He curled in a fetal position. An arm snaked around his stomach as if it hurt. He lay deathly still, his face a set blank, so pale it looked nearly as white as the robe. His eyes scrunched closed, not in sleep, but trying to shut out his surroundings. One finger curled around a link on the kennel, a hopeless, desperate longing for life outside that place. Nehemiah fumbled out the metal wire that had been marked "lockpick" in Joe's cubby hole and shoved it in the lock. Metal scraped against metal. Joe pulled into himself at the noise, fear shot over his face, and his eyes screwed tighter. Nehemiah poked his friend's finger. The mute jerked his hand back, his arm curling against his chest, his eyes still screwed shut. Nehi rolled his eyes and risked a whisper, even though Anna was only supposed to deal with the viewers and leave the sound monitors alone.

"Joe," Nehemiah whispered. The mute didn't open his eyes. "Joe!" he hissed. Joe's eyes shot open and met Nehemiah's. His lids rose till his green eyes shone. Shock, hope, disbelief, and joy all flitted over his white face, ending in a look of total astonishment.

"We're getting you out," Nehemiah signed, his fingers feeling clumsy and fat as he formed the words. "Beauty, Glue, and me." He pointed at the lockpick and then took it in his hand again. A shrill squeal sounded from the lock. Joe stuck his hand through the kennel links, shoved Nehemiah's away, and took hold of the lockpick. The door swung open, and Nehemiah fell back in surprise. He fell back farther as Joe collided into his arms, squeezing him so tight he couldn't breathe. When the mute pulled away his eyes were wet, but his pale face was radiant as he leaned against the side of the kennel. He looked as if he needed its strength just to stand. Nehemiah quickly handed Joe a pair of black cargo pants, his habitual black shirt and leather high-collared jacket, and what had been left of the "burglary clothes," as Anna called them. That white skin and blond hair of his would never do out in the dark streets.

Joe shed the white robe like it burnt his skin, and quickly began to don the clothes. Nehemiah winced as he saw Joe's bloated stomach and bruised throat, but he just helped him slide the jacket on instead of commenting. The mute's lithe fingers flew down the line of dull smoky buttons on the jacket's side as Nehi grabbed the soft black wrappings left-over from the burglary clothes and started to wind them over Joe's head. Another moment and only his green eyes showed through the gap. Nehemiah gave his friend a cheery grin and leapt toward the door. Joe started to move beside him. He staggered, a retching gag pulled from him, and his hands splayed on the wall as he doubled over. He pulled the black leather from his face and vomited, coughing so violently his whole form shook. His hand began to slip down the wall as his knees buckled. Nehemiah shot an arm around the mute's

 *200*

chest and held him up. It took a moment before Joe's stomach stopped heaving. He leaned on Nehemiah, his breath coming in harsh wheezes.

"Sorry, pain killers," he signed weakly, and one arm wrapped almost involuntarily around his stomach again. Nehemiah kept an arm around him and moved to the door. He got one foot into the hall and Beau's shadow loomed over him. Joe's weight left his side as Beau swept up his master, cradling him like a child. Joe slumped, everything going limp. One arm wrapped around the thick, hairy neck, and he lay still, eyes closed to slits, content to let Nehemiah lead the way out. Nehi glanced at his watch and his face tightened. That had taken longer than it was supposed to; the next round of security checks was on its way. He took off at a run, his boots pounding down two more hallways to a door marked "Stairs."

Nehemiah skidded to a halt and shoved the lockpick into the keyhole. The lock squeaked like an arthritic dying rat. Cobeau reached out, gave the pick a quick, silent twist and the door swung open. *Apparently I need practice on those,* Nehemiah thought wryly as he locked the door behind them and began to run down the stairs. The eight flights down seemed interminable. *Please, please let us be on time!* he prayed over and over as he bounded recklessly down, taking it three and four stairs at a time. He stared through gaps between the metal stairs as he ran, and caught a glimpse of black hair, shining in the bright artificial light. He spun another corner, pounded down another flight, and there she stood.

Anna waited for them on the fourth floor landing, back to her old worn leather dress, zipped down to create her pants suit. Only four flights left. Nehemiah grabbed Anna's hand and ran harder down the stairs. She glanced back and Joe signed "Hello" from Cobeau's arms. Anna waved back with a grin, and then concentrated on running down the flights. Level Three. Two.

The building erupted in a cacophony of sound.

Bells and whistles and alarms blared everywhere. Nehemiah hit the ground floor at a sprint, still holding onto Anna as he bolted for their door. Speed was their only hope now. He and Anna flung open the back door, leapt over the few stairs, and ran with all their might for the only way out, leaving the guard gaping at the door. This seemed familiar, Nehemiah reflected grimly. It felt painfully like their escape from their own country, nearly eight months ago. But at the same second he strong-armed the door open and fresh air rolled over them, two things happened.

A thrill of terror ran down Nehemiah's spine as he realized something that wasn't like that escape; he had made a fatal error. Bored soldiers at the front of a building they cared nothing about, like in front of the Judge's house, was one thing. Trained security guards at a building they held in supreme importance were another.

But as he realized it, a familiar weight lifted from his thigh as Hope disappeared. He twisted to see Joe pointing the Compton laser over Cobeau's shoulder, covering for Nehi's mistake as they raced on. A van barreled through the gate, filled with security guards and personnel, a siren wailing from it. Joe swung around and tossed the laser back to Nehi. Nehemiah spun Hope toward the gates.

The van careened to a shrieking stop as its two front tires exploded. It slammed into the gate, holding it open. A flame spurted up from the car's engine. Nehemiah tightened his grip on his laser and ran harder. A huge spout of flame shot from the car, and Nehi threw up his hand to shield his eyes as he plunged into the chaos at the gate. They met the screaming crowd head on, barreled through it, and crashed out onto the road, running hard. Whining laser shots fried the road behind them. A patch of melted burning asphalt landed on the back of his calf and burnt through his pants. Nehemiah hissed, trying to rub away the asphalt burning his skin with his other boot as he kept running, his eyes darting wildly around the streets. Where was Paul?

A hand shot out of an alleyway. It clamped onto his arm

and pulled Nehemiah into darkness. Nehi jerked Anna after him, and she just managed to grab onto Cobeau before they plunged into a narrow alley. And then, somehow, the alley became an echoing tunnel. They couldn't see anything, darkness pressed around them.

"Who–" Nehi tried to ask. A sharp, "Hush!" cut him off, echoing eerily around them. Nehemiah clamped his jaw shut and prayed they were following a friend. They stumbled on, twisting back and forth and going down, always down. The ground leveled suddenly and Nehemiah stumbled and nearly lost their guide's hand. The stranger tightened their grip and pulled him up. They kept running. The sound of their footsteps echoed hollowly and the air lay close and still around them. Nehi heard Joe coughing again behind him. Anna took a firmer grip on Nehemiah and Cobeau, her memory carrying her to the cellars where she had spent so much time; there didn't seem to be enough air to breathe down here. She closed her eyes, forcing herself to pray and not hyperventilate.

A few more turns, several stairs down, and their guide began to slow. Whoever he was, his breathing came in sharp pants now. Nehemiah suddenly realized how far and how fast they had run, and how easy it had been physically. He silently cheered for Joe's rhythm makers and stopped as their guide stopped. The tinkling of metal striking little metal, of someone pulling out keys, drifted through the darkness. Nehemiah took the opportunity to unwind the fabric from around his face, slip his goggles back into Hope's pocket, and take off his hot gloves. The scrape of a metal key turning in an iron lock sounded, and light flooded the little group. They all threw up their hands, their annoyed groans echoing in the tunnel.

"Sorry about that," the guide said in the unmistakable accent of a Northern Sojourner, mixed with a twang from the Southern half of the kingdom. Nehemiah caught his breath in surprise and looked up quickly.

"Peter!" Nehi yelled. He leapt forward, his arms shooting around their guide in a brawny bear hug. A dry sob sounded in Nehi's ear as the ex-guard's arm grabbed him, squeezing hard. Peter's hands landed on Nehi's shoulders, driving him back at arm's length.

"Nehemiah, we thought you were dead!" Peter gasped, looking him up and down, his freckled face shining in delighted astonishment. "We all did! And here you are, as tall as me, a man running raids on the Institute! We heard nothing about you after the disintegration, and then Anna was caught–" Anna stepped forward and curtsied pertly, her dress back to a dress again. Peter's jaw dropped open and his soft eyes grew bright.

"You're alive!" he shouted as he scooped her up and swung her around.

"I take it you've already met Anna and Nehemiah," Paul commented from the room. Peter plunked a breathless Anna down so fast she stumbled. But his grin stretched his face in two as he led the way into the light. Nehemiah stepped out of the tunnel into a spacious, comfortable living room. Floofy, mismatched chairs and couches, an old leather recliner where Paul Sireton sat, wooden paneling, family pictures on the walls, a cinnamon candle burning... Anna and Nehemiah gave a simultaneous sigh and their tight shoulders relaxed. Peter closed the door behind them and the click made the twins turn around. They could see no trace of the door in the paneling of the wall.

"Isn't it great?" Peter beamed. "You are now in the basement of Paul Sireton's home, and no one saw you come in, and no one will see you leave. We have passageways like this all over town, all over the kingdom!"

"I'm impressed," Nehemiah nodded. He turned around to see what Anna thought of it, and found her with Cobeau, helping settle Joe on a red couch by the wall. Nehemiah quickly crossed to them. Joe grinned at him, his face white and radiant.

"Thank you," he signed simply to the trio. Nehemiah and Anna grinned back. Cobeau's smile was too happy to be classified as a grin.

"Just be still, Joe," Anna ordered. "I'll go get you a cup of tea. I see a little kitchen over there, if Mr. Sireton doesn't mind?" Paul waved his hand at the kitchen as he sorted his long legs into position to get out of the chair. Anna darted into it, pushing a strand of her black hair back into her ponytail. Weariness flooded Nehemiah. He dropped down on the floor next to Joe's couch and blew out a sigh. They had done it. Cobeau already sat on the floor, his head drooped on the couch, one hand next to Joe, the other under his flappy ear. A gentle snore lifted from the chimera, a look of happy peace on his simple face.

"I'm glad to see you back, Joe," Paul said. His handshake and smile showed he meant it, but that his mind was occupied elsewhere. "This is Peter Lovine, a Sojourner refugee, and a very good friend of our family. Peter, Nehemiah... I don't want to seem like I'm prying, but when you two knew each other, I just put the pieces together. Nehemiah, are you and your sister Hillsons, the Judge's children?" Nehemiah hesitated. Samuel's warning crossed his mind, and then that mysterious FF group looking for them... But he was among friends here. And the FFs already knew who they were.

"Yes, we're the youngest Hillsons," he answered. "Why do you ask?" Paul crouched on the floor next to Nehemiah and paused the same way he had in the wagon, trying to decide where to start.

"About a year ago," he began, "I was kidnapped and put through a pretty bad time by someone. I still don't know who or why. They wanted to know about the Judges. I was rescued by two people in black who called themselves the Black Raiders, sort of ultra-ninja types who dumped me back at home. My wife found this note on me. I assumed it was from my rescuers." He pulled one of the battered coffee table drawers open, reached in and picked up a dirty scrap of paper, and handed it to Nehi.

Tell the IDP: Watch out for the Judge.

Nehemiah recognized the writing immediately.
Only Joe had that distinctive scrawl.

Chapter Fourteen: The Black Raider

"Hast thou not known? Hast thou not heard, that the everlasting God, the LORD, the Creator of the end of the earth, fainteth not, neither is weary? There is no searching of His understanding." Isaiah 40:28

Nehemiah lowered the paper to his lap and looked at Joe, anger and curiosity fighting inside him.

"Well," Paul said, his voice bright, "Peter and I have to go make sure no one recognized you tonight, or managed to follow us. But, Nehemiah?" Nehi looked up at him, and Paul smiled, laughter lines crinkling his green eyes. "We've been watching for the Judge ever since I got this note. We are very honored to have you and Anna here, Mr. Hillson. Whatever you may need, we'll help."

"When we get back, you're filling me in on the last year," Peter broke in with a grin. "You've obviously got stories to tell!"

"My wife Mary is upstairs keeping an eye on things there," Paul took over again, "if you need anything tonight give her a shout. We should be back before sunrise." He beamed at Nehi, nodded to Joe, and slid out the hidden door with Peter on his heels. Nehi blinked at the door, wondering if he had seen that nod right... Paul's reaction to Joe had seemed, respectful but almost...hesitant. Not the friendly, open way he had been to Nehi.

Joe coughed beside him. And in an instant, Nehi's blood rose again, rushing to his head, as all the frustration at his little friend's secrets collided with waning adrenaline and weariness. He spun on the mute.

"A year ago?! You were telling people my dad was evil and needed watching a year ago?"

"I didn't say he was evil," Joe signed. His eyes darted to the note and a grimace crossed his face. He gave his "awkward!"

click, but it was drowned by Nehi, as all his frustrations poured out in a tirade. Anna walked out of the kitchen carrying a clay mug and a damp compress. Her eyebrow rose as she looked at the ranting Nehi. Joe looked up at her.

"Knee-High lectures almost as well as you do, Beauty," he signed. "All it's missing is Glue saying, 'Are you listening?' every three seconds." Joe mimicked Cobeau's expression so well that Anna laughed. Nehemiah was too hot to notice, and he didn't slow down his one-sided argument. Anna laid the compress gently on Joe's forehead and handed him his cup of tea. He signed a heartfelt thank you, leaned back against the couch arm again. Anna dropped cross-legged beside her ranting brother, and reached for the note in his hands.

"What did I miss?" she asked.

"Paul was kidnapped and rescued by 'ultra-ninja Black Raiders' who gave him that note! I guess I don't have to tell you who wrote it."

"I haven't practiced forgery enough to be good at it," Joe signed. Anna noticed two spots of color on his white face, and his expression... he was a little ashamed maybe?

"Joe, I'm losing it, in case you hadn't noticed," Nehi growled. "I don't want to hear about your failed forays into forgery! Instead why don't you try telling us what we need to hear, for once! What do you really do? Who *are* you really? Why are you going around telling the IDP our dad is evil?"

"I didn't say he was evil," Joe signed again, more emphatically.

"And the way you just happened to be there to snatch Anna and I up when we had no other choice, and were so, so quick to suggest we stay! What have you been planning for us? Is this whole thing an elaborate scheme to hand us to someone for reward money?"

"I don't deserve that one," Joe signed, a frown flashing over his face. His eyes leapt to Anna's, his green ones pleading. "I don't, do I?"

"No, you don't," Anna said easily, talking over Nehi as he

kept ranting. "But you barely missed deserving it; scraped by within an inch, I would say." She punched Nehi's arm. "Shut up for a minute. Joe, listen. Even I want to know about this one. For some reason you're a fourth GI instead of a third, you've been running around rescuing people as an ultra-ninja, and you know something odd about our dad. Please explain."

"Joe doesn't explain things, Anna, remember?" Nehi almost hissed. His eyes were bloodshot as he climbed to his feet. "Come on, I think it's time we get a little distance from the Ravens."

Joe sat up, determined to get his side of the story out. His face twisted, his mouth opening in a gasp. He shoved his mug into Nehemiah's hand and doubled over, coughing and gagging uncontrollably. One arm stole around his stomach. Cobeau woke up, laid a big hand on his Joe's shoulder, and pushed him flat on the couch. Joe curled up, still coughing so violently he could hardly breathe.

"Master, no getting excited," Cobeau rumbled. He turned and glared at Nehemiah, shaking a big finger under Nehi's nose, his words almost a growl. "Don't excite him! He acts fine, but he's not. No exciting!" Nehemiah nodded, his anger gone as quickly as it had come.

"Don't you think he needs something?" Anna said, anxiously watching Joe's twisted face.

"He mentioned pain pills back at the Institute. Paul said his wife was upstairs–" Nehemiah said, turning toward the staircase. Joe's hand shot out and his shaking fingers wrapped around Nehi's wrist, holding him back. The mute darted a look at Beau.

"Joe doesn't take pain pills," the chimera rumbled, his face sagging and lined.

"You need something," Anna objected quietly, gently. "A headache's one thing but you need something now." Joe stopped coughing and lay still, concentrating on breathing. Another instant and he had himself under control enough to be able to sign.

"Thank you, no," his eyes turned to Cobeau again as he saw the twins about to object. The chimera looked miserable, but answered for him.

"Can't," Cobeau said. "Can't take them. Allergic to most, addicted to the others."

"Past," Joe signed weakly from the couch.

"Was addicted," Beau amended. "Needed them too much. Deals with pain without them now. Safer."

"Problem now from the pain pills," Joe signed shakily. He closed his eyes to fight off a cough, then picked it up again. "A-d-v-a-n-c-e-r-s don't exactly give an option, and I'm allergic to the large dose they force after their tests are run. Overdose for me, I'm too small. Hurts. No more." Nehemiah reluctantly slumped back to the floor beside Anna. Joe's breathing rattled out of him in a wheeze, but it began to grow more even. After a few moments he was able to relax. Nehi handed back his cup.

"I'm sorry I blew up at you," Nehemiah said, his voice tired.

"I deserved it," Joe signed back, and Nehi's eyebrows rose. "Look, I didn't say your dad was evil. I'm a...maybe I should try explaining this from the beginning."

"Are you sure you're up to it?" Anna asked. Nehi elbowed her in the ribs and darted her a look; *He's finally willing to explain something, don't give him an out!* She made a face at him, wrinkling her nose and sticking out her tongue. Joe's breathing turned to soft huffs as he laughed at them. The mute's tight muscles relaxed under the humor. His eyes stayed shut, but a smile hovered on his face as he began to sign.

"I'll tell it chronologically, if you don't mind. My second time in the Institute came when I was six or seven, don't know which," Joe signed, quickly fingerspelled "Advancers," made his sign for it, and sped off. "The slavers had sold me to a family as a pet, but they had gotten bored with me, my owner then was greedy, and the Advancers were offering money for a GI of that age for testing. Our bodies are 'remarkably similar' to 'regular humanity,' according to them."

"Wait, a pet?"

"You were a guinea pig or lab rat in that horrible, white institute? For how long?" the twins interrupted, appalled. Joe shrugged.

"Months. Years. A lifetime. It's hard to tell time in some places. A bit less than a year, I think. I can go faster at this if Glue translates?" Cobeau's sing-song rumble filled the quiet as Joe went on. "When the Advancers sent me out again I was bought by a traveling musician who moonlighted as a cat burglar. It wasn't a nice life. At all."

"That bad?" Nehemiah asked, nausea playing through him at this glimpse of Joe's past.

"I can't think of one even decent memory from that time, it was all pretty horrible," Joe signed evenly, and swept on. "He called himself The Music Maker, and I was his secret tool. He wanted someone with good rhythm for his music and a small size for his burglary, and as I was good at both he held onto me pretty tightly. I learned a lot from him, and barely survived his method of teaching. But God kept me alive somehow, and I finally successfully ran from him about two years later."

"It took two years to get out?" Nehi muttered. Joe shrugged again.

"Took him that long to die. After that was about a year of surviving on my own, then I was caught by a Producer in Kallipolis. Not a nice life there either, but it didn't last long. A young man came by one day and paid a ridiculously extravagant price for me, packed me into his sleek hoverer, and sped off. I was pretty scared, not knowing who had me or why. But it didn't take long to realize I was better off than I had ever been. The man's name was Joshua Noble, I called him Diamond."

"That's a different name," Anna said. "Why did you call him that?" Joe paused, his lips pressed tight and his eyes fastened on the wall across from him.

"When most people talk about love, they mean a sort of weak fuzzy feeling that makes them happy about being with someone," he started to sign falteringly, and Cobeau rumbled in his monotone. "That's not love. Love...real, honest, God-fearing love is hard, set, firm, and the most beautiful thing you'll ever see. It doesn't change even when it hurts like anything to hold onto. And it's not comfortable to hold onto, because it means you have to constantly kill your will, yourself, to love others, as you place their needs at the same level of importance as your own. It's like a diamond, I've always thought. Crystal clear and heart-breakingly beautiful, but harder and firmer than nearly anything else, made beautiful by going through the great pressure forced on it. J-o-s-h had that love, diamond love. No, he *was* diamond love, it defined him. You saw it just looking at him; his love for his God and each fellow human was firm and deep, and as unchanging as the stars."

"That's all quite poetic," Anna said, staring at him in surprise. "You've never opened up enough to show your poetical side." Joe looked a little embarrassed and went on quickly.

"Anyway, that's Diamond." He stopped and a smile flashed over his white face. "I don't usually name people like that, where it takes ages to explain, but nothing else fit Diamond. He was a man with vision, the most dedicated and fiery follower of the Way I have ever met. He walked into a room and everyone stopped what they were doing and thought about if it was worth it in Heaven's estimation."

"Sounds like a good man," Nehemiah said.

"He was. He was the best man I've ever met." Joe looked away, swallowed, and went on. "Diamond took me in, gave me love and a home, and pointed me to Jesus. I took him under my wing too, he didn't know much about the world then. That was a good life." The happy, wistful smile that crossed Joe's pale face as he signed that said volumes beautifully. Anna found she was mentally heaping blessings on this Joshua Noble for noticing a hurting outcast. "We settled in Story Land officially, but were off in Diamond's little hoverer most times, driving through the world. He explored and dove into every kingdom we came to, with me as his unofficial guide. Soon we had a working understanding of all of them. And a pretty complete knowledge of the little pockets of Christians scattered around inside the kingdoms.

"One night, about a year after he had taken me in, we were sitting in his hoverer. Just sitting. Then suddenly he starts up, telling me he saw all the little pockets connected underneath the countries, and all these connected Christians working together to make Christ known in the lost world. I told him he was crazy. But it was a beautiful crazy. Diamond was a crazy kind of guy, and he saw it done, and founded the IDP. I helped where I could. Diamond was amazingly good at connecting with people, getting them 'activated,' as he put it, in Christ's work. I'm not very good with people. But I am good at finding out the logistics of the matter, what the policy on members of the Way is in a kingdom, and how to help the IDP live with it. So, we parted ways a little."

A coughing fit, milder then the last but still painful, broke the conversation. Beau shifted his chosen master to a more comfortable position. Joe controlled himself quickly, his green eyes on his gigantic friend. He laid a hand gently on the big chimera's shaggy head and Cobeau beamed at him. "The first time I went out on my own, I ran across Glue. He's been my guardian angel ever since we joined up."

"Joined up, Master?" Cobeau interjected. "You rescued me when I was-" The big man stopped and started, as if a long forgotten memory resurfaced in his mind. His face wrinkled, horror beginning to shake him, water gathering in his eyes. Joe slapped him on the cheek and shook his hand under his nose. Cobeau's horror melted, his shoulders slumped, and he smiled.

"I mean Joe," he said.

"As I was signing," Joe signed and Cobeau said, "ever since that day five years ago when Diamond went one way and I went another and got stuck on Glue, we've been working to keep the IDP functional in a world that hates Christians. That's what I do. To earn money I'm an informant, as I've already told you. But the real reason I'm a traveling musician is because it's my cover for being the IDP troubleshooter. I'm the sea wall between the IDP and the world trying to break in. I'm there to try and keep the various IDP pockets safe, as best I can in this haphazard, dangerous world."

"That's quite a job," Nehi commented, studying Joe with new respect. Anna didn't speak her main thought; *A sea wall takes a lot of pounding.* Nehi's lips tightened into an exasperated frown. "You know, if you had mentioned this earlier I might have been able to help." Anna jabbed him in the ribs. "We might have been able to help," he amended. Joe shrank back against the couch, two spots of color coming into his white cheeks as he dropped his gaze. The twins looked at each other in astonishment; he was embarrassed!

"Yes, well, I thought... I haven't had many people in my life I could trust, okay, and running from kingdom to kingdom playing spy doesn't make that likely to change. There are people even in the IDP who are enemies, you know, who pretend they're of the way but who aren't."

"'Beware of false prophets, which come to you in sheep's clothing, but inwardly they are ravening wolves,[12]'" Anna murmured, quoting it automatically.

"Sheep and wolves?" Joe signed, his forehead wrinkling.

"Same thing you were saying," Nehemiah explained. "Sheep are Christians, wolves are the enemy pretending to be Christians."

"Oh. That's surprisingly appropriate. Well, to put it that way, there are wolves among the IDP flock."

"You thought we might be wolves?" Nehi asked, his frown on strong. His eyes darted to the paper and Joe followed the look.

"So that note..." Joe started, and paused as if he couldn't decide how to go on. He sighed, sat up and sped off at a furious rate. "This is going to be a lot of information to take in all at

---

[12] Matthew 7:15

once, so pay attention. The IDP isn't the only group who runs underneath the kingdoms. There's also the UPC, the United Peoples Commission; it's sort of the antithesis to the IDP, a group of picked agents and diplomats who are trying to make the world into what they think it should be. What they tend to think the world should be, is a place without Christians. They don't like the ideas held by the Way, and they don't like the fact that their people tend to flock to Christianity if it manages to get inside their kingdoms. All people long for real freedom, and only the Way offers that, the philosophy given to us by the God of liberty. The UPC is afraid of Christianity getting a hold on their people. So they go after us whenever they find us."

"'Go after,' how do you mean?" Nehi asked. Joe glanced down, his face suddenly blank.

"I mean find ways to kill off. They found Diamond two years ago. He went charging into one of the wolves. I kept telling him he needed to keep his distance, but Diamond...he never kept distances. A person was someone to dive into and find out where their soul stood so he could help them on their walk with God, he..." Joe sighed, a heavy, tired sound. "His best friend (asides from Doctor, Glue, and I) turned out to be UPC."

"I'm sorry," Anna murmured, her parents' faces in her mind bringing true empathy; she hoped he could see she meant it. He looked up at her. A little thankful smile flitted over his worn face, and she knew he did understand.

"I hadn't actually meant to get into that. But that's the UPC. They have wolves scattered through the IDP unfortunately, and I'm always trying to weed them out. Then," Joe leaned forward, his hand motions becoming smaller, in what would have been a whisper in a voice, "there's the FFs. Glue, stop translating please." The chimera's head dropped onto the couch and he began to snore. Nehemiah tried not to squirm, in his desire for Joe to go on. The mute took a long drink of his tea, leaned back against the couch, and started to sign.

The siren lights spun and blinked, dyeing the night florescent blues and reds. Peter and Paul spun into the deserted bakery. The darkness closed in again as the police hoverer moved slowly past. Paul bent over, his hands on his knees, gasping in air. Peter slumped against the wall, panting, his eyes bright as he stared through the broken blinds.

"That was close," he murmured.

"Much too close," Paul panted. "Next time I decide it's a good idea to sneak into an empty police hoverer to listen to the radio chatter, tell me I'm an idiot." A chuckle came from Peter as he swiveled to get a better view up the street.

"It was a fine idea. We just need to find one that's a little emptier next time."

"When that hobo in the back sat up and shouted at me, I thought sure I was going to die from cardiac arrest on the spot."

"We should make sure no one got a good look at us," Peter said. Paul dropped to sit on the dusty floor, still panting heavily. He waved vaguely at the door.

"My old bones aren't up to it. Go finish it, Peter. Meet me back at my house."

The light shifted as Peter slid out the door and up the street, trailing the small crowd of vagrants and people of the night, curious over the business on the streets at such a late hour. You could learn almost all you needed from a good crowd, if you found the right people to listen to.

Paul slumped back and panted some more, waiting till he caught his breath. His hand slid into his jacket pocket. When it came back into the dim light seeping through the door of the ruined bakery (dust motes dancing and choking the air) a hologram disc lay on his palm. Paul slid the disc onto the floor and tapped his jaw to activate his bone plant. A slight vibration in his jaw told him it was ready.

"Quintus Leeman."

A blue glow invaded the dim light. The disc hummed gently

as it projected the name in a clear blue script, rotating it as it waited for the other end of the call to connect. The letters faded, taken over by a round, wrinkled face, mutton chop whiskers white and fluffy on cheeks that were sunken and worn. But the blue light that formed his mouth turned up in a joyful smile as he saw his caller.

"Paul!" Quintus Leeman said, delight lacing it as he stared at the annalist.

"I don't have much time, Quin," Paul told the projection, "but I wanted to check in. How's it going? You still enjoying the work?" The delight left the inventor's face. His eyes turned worried, and he looked back over his shoulder before answering.

"The people who hired me, who bought the patent, they aren't nice people, Paul. I..." He swallowed and looked over his shoulder again. "I can't say more. But I... I shouldn't have come here. And I've gotten hints that I'm not coming back to KAM. Once you immigrate, the state here is...exacting." A deep sigh slid from him, his face sagging. "Stick close to your family, Paul. When life grows close to the end, it is a terrible thing to be alone."

"What about–"

A sharp intake of air came from the old inventor, cutting Paul off. The hologram shut down, dropping the room back into the dark, dust-filled world of KAM.

"Quin old man, what are you up to?" Paul murmured. "What do you know?"

"The FFs are book thieves."

Anna and Nehemiah's jaws dropped open and they stared at Joe. Two books had been stolen, they knew but...these people actually made a business out of something as precious as books?

"They pick kingdoms that can pay heaps of money, steal

their book, and let the kingdom buy it back. If they can't buy it back, or they miss the deadline the FF gives them, the FFs let the news leak out that the book is gone. And disintegration comes. Their book stealing wreaks havoc with the countries (naturally), and when countries are stressed, they go after the little problems they can deal with. That means cracking down on the IDP and, as its official troubleshooter, that gets me involved. No one's ever gone after the FF because the only ones that know about them are the countries that have been targeted. And they're either destroyed or too scared to admit they lost their book even for a little while. That means I'm practically the only thorn in their well-moneyed sides. As you've noticed, the FF gets around and packs a good deal of power. If they ever found out whom it was that's annoying them (that's about all Glue and I can do on our own) we wouldn't annoy any longer. So we took to wearing the black costumes to help us stay unknown, and were dubbed the Black Raider. We've been able to do some good at least in that character."

"Like stealing Paul Sireton away," Anna said.

"Who had him?" Nehemiah asked.

"S-i-m-m-o-n-s," Joe fingerspelled, wrinkling his nose in disgust. He leaned back again, his eyes closing. "Evil, I call him."

"Where did you meet him?" Nehi broke in quietly, needing to know for some reason he didn't try to explain to himself.

"Evil was a friend of my cat burglar-musician owner." Nehemiah's stomach churned at the time-frame he was just handed. But Joe swept on, apparently unconcerned. "But since Music Maker moved around a lot, Evil wasn't around often and I survived to get out two years later."

"Two years!" Nehemiah choked.

"Took him that long to die, despite how hard I tried to make it happen earlier," Joe shrugged, his eyes still closed; he missed Anna's shocked horror at the comment, and Nehi found he was glad for it. "But all this is a ___ from my point."

"A what?" Nehi broke in, poking Anna. She blinked and got her face back in order before Joe's eyes flew open. Nehi tried to make the sign he didn't know.

"D-i-g-r-e-s-s-i-o-n," Joe spelled. The mute's natural humor, all his gentler features, disappeared. The lines on his white face melded with his scars, falling into a calculating, sharp, sorrow that seemed ingrained. "Here's what you need to know. You're going to get pulled into the IDP in the next few days. That's a good thing, but please remember, we have wolves loose. One wolf in particular, for you two to worry about. The founder and leader of the FFs is a member of our flock."

"What?!" both the twins burst out.

"Truth." Joe crossed his heart. "I told you I used to lie. I didn't trust even myself then. I will do everything in my power to never lie again. So watch. That same wolf is also in the UPC. I have to catch that wolf and do it well, and it's going to be harder than any hunt-in-the-shadows I've been involved in yet. A brilliant enemy, unfortunately, a genius in the chosen field. And that wolf is after you two."

"Oh come on!" Nehemiah almost wailed, throwing his hands out in exasperation.

"It's about that treasure, isn't it," Anna said, her nose wrinkling. "We don't know anything, we don't even own anything anymore!"

"I may know that, and you may know that, but the wolf doesn't believe it," Joe signed. "Please watch what you say and who you trust! Don't repeat anything I'm telling you tonight. P-a-u-l and the other IPD members only know me as a traveling musician who carries messages for them occasionally, a GI nonetheless; they don't know what else I do. And they don't know anything but the initials of the UPC, and to dread them. I don't think any of them have even heard of the FFs. Don't tell anyone what you know."

"Do we really know anything?" Anna asked.

"We know the FFs have the Sojourner's book," Nehi said,

his face grim as he thought it out. "And that they caused disintegration. Because...because they wanted to bring it, not as a by-product of another operation; disintegration didn't bring them any closer to getting the money for our book."

"That's what I've thought too," Joe nodded.

"Why are you suddenly telling us all this?" Anna broke in. "What changed?"

Joe's expression altered. The brilliant delight Nehemiah saw when he opened the kennel door earlier that night flashed onto his face. It radiated from him, his eyes bright and his expression so happy it beamed.

"Only if you two were what you say you are would you have risked yourselves and gone into the Institute after a GI. Now I know."

"So we're actually trusted by the Ravens now?" Nehi asked, hardly daring to believe it. Joe nodded emphatically a grin plastered over his shining face. A cough shook him, overshadowing some of the delight with a sharp pain. He slumped onto the pillow, letting his head drop onto the couch arm. Anna noticed his hands shaking before he laid them on the couch.

"Joe, you need to sleep," she said reluctantly. His eyes flew to hers and an impish smile twisted his lips.

"But..." he prodded.

"All right, know it all, since you could guess what I was thinking," she said with a playful pout. But then she dropped the play and grew serious. "We're trusted by the Ravens, you say. But you still haven't told us what that note is about. Or who this dangerous wolf is. Are you sure you're being truthful about our new status?"

"I trust you two as much as I do Glue, and that's saying something!" Joe signed quickly, his hands flashing and his face earnest. "That note really isn't about your father. My contacts fed me some information earlier this year, and I decided to drop that warning with the IDP while I had the chance. But now I know it wasn't even about your dad. Look, I'm really tired. Is that enough about it for now?"

"What about the wolf, don't we need a name, or description, or something?" Nehi pushed. Joe frowned and looked away uncomfortably. He signed slowly, reluctantly.

"I trust you, I really do. But you're both rotten actors."

"What's that got to do with anything?" Anna demanded. She didn't bother to argue it.

"If a sheep acts towards a wolf in a way that lets the wolf know they're found out, the wolf gets the sheep slaughtered. And probably slaughters a lot of others along the way. To overload you with initials, this GI member of the VK isn't going to tell you who I suspect the wolves from the UPC or FF are in this KAM branch of the IDP. I really don't want you to get slaughtered. Selfish of me, I know. But there it is."

Nehemiah's lips tightened, his eyes troubled. But he didn't argue it either. His voice when it came was thoughtful and intense.

"Joe, I...you're doing good work. And it's really hard work, and you shouldn't have to do it alone. I would like to help."

Another smile twisted Joe's lips. His eyes closed as he leaned back and signed, his movements small and shaky.

"Maybe you already are."

Nehemiah's mouth opened then snapped shut on whatever he had been about to say. He sat still, his gaze on the cream-colored carpet, but his focus very far away. What did that mean? It was so close to what Joe had said in the wagon when they first agreed to join up with the Ravens... Joe meant something by those words. But what?

"I'm sorry your man wasn't here, after all the danger you went through to get to him," Nehi commented. Fishing for something. What he didn't know. Joe's eyes flew open and fastened on the ceiling. His face was stony, showing nothing. "Why were you looking for this Quintus Leeman, anyway?"

"The FFs have something... Evil has something..." Joe signed. He was having trouble forming the words, his hands shaking. "We need to know more about it. We need–" A cough wracked him, and merged into harder coughs, driving him to his side as he tried to breathe. Anna caught the cup as it tumbled off the couch, and her other hand flew to Joe's thick blond hair. It was an automatic response, a thing her mother had done for her and Nehi whenever they were ill; her hand ran over his hair as she gently pressed him back to the pillow.

"Shh, be still, Joe," she murmured, helping him settle comfortably again. His coughing evened out. His breathing still came in wheezes, and he didn't lift his eyes. But as he slumped back to the pillow and Anna darted off to poke into closets looking for blankets, Nehi noticed the mute's smile had changed. It hovered like a breakable, fragile thing as he wheezed and shook, his messy hair spilling over his eyes; a look of hope, of the dawning of a suspicion that happiness might be nearby, though only part of him believed it. Nehemiah blinked and shook himself. That was silly, you couldn't really read that much in a single smile. He needed sleep, he was getting fanciful.

Anna swept back up, her arms full of linens. She dropped a folded blanket on Nehemiah's head and pointed behind her at a fluffy loveseat, shook out a second blanket and draped it over the snoring Cobeau, his hand still on his master's knee. Then she shook out the third blanket and laid it over Joe. His eyes were still closed, and his breathing was evening out into the slow, smooth way of sleep. His face changed as sleep took him. All his carefully trained expressions melted away. Sorrow fell into the natural lines of his face, meeting with fresh ones from pain, and complimented by a little nervousness as if he worried about who might be near while he slept. He looked ageless. His life had put him in a category by himself, old in experience while still young in years. She leaned forward and gently tucked the blanket around him, wondering if anyone had ever tucked him into bed before, as her parents had so often done.

Anna straightened and her spine complained at her. Oh, it had been a long day. She turned and flopped on the loveseat beside Nehi, drawing her feet up onto the seat so she could lay her head on her knees. The two sat, watching the Ravens sleeping.

"How could anyone say he isn't human?" Anna burst out, her voice wet. "All he's been through, it's all because some idiot decided just because he couldn't talk he couldn't be human! How could they make themselves believe it?"

"I think you just answered it," Nehi said quietly. "They make themselves believe it. Because it fits the way they want the world to be. They don't want the Joe's of this world, so they find a neat, simple way to explain why they can just get rid of them." A sniffle came from Anna. Silence drifted into the room, punctuated by Beau's impressive snores.

"We need that book back, Ann," Nehemiah said suddenly. "Joe and Beau, and the thousands of others like them, need the Sojourner's Kingdom!"

"They're hunted," Anna nodded, "as chimera, GI, and Christian. A triple threat. The Sojourners must have been the only place they could really be themselves and still be safe."

"We know who has our book now."

"And also that the same group is hunting for us," Anna grimaced. "I'm not sure how much good that knowledge does us."

"It's something. Every bit of knowledge helps. Sooner or later if we can get enough of it we should be able to piece together an idea that will work. We have to. We need the Sojourners back. They need the Sojourners Kingdom," he added, nodding toward the sleeping Ravens.

"Joe knows more than he's told us–"

"That's the truth! And he hasn't told us what he needs us for, I'm sure of it!"

"But he says we're helping," Anna finished. Nehi's jaw snapped closed again and he stared bleary-eyed at Joe. Anna spoke again, quietly. "It's all right, Nehi. We don't have to know it all. We just have to be there to help him, like tonight. I don't think Joe's going to ask for us. But I do know he needs us, and that if anyone can get our book back, it's the Ravens."

Nehemiah nodded slowly. And found his head didn't want to come back up again. He slumped over on the loveseat's arm and let his heavy eyelids close. Beside him he heard Anna yawn, a long, deep sound, and smiled to himself. He knew she would be asleep before the sound died. He wondered idly what position the stars were in, somewhere high above this basement room. Somewhere up there, the Lion constellation looked down at them. And high above that God watched over His children. No. Not just high above them, He was here. In the midst of their weariness, their anxiety, their frustrations and sorrows... Nehemiah shifted and started to pray, pouring his insecurities out to the God who held and helped, and knew all things.

Somehow they would find their book, and reset the light on the hill. And he would help Joe despite his little friend's determined independence. Nehemiah slumped farther on the couch and smothered a yawn. Boy he needed sleep. But tomorrow? Tomorrow he would start wolf hunting with Joe.

A bead of sweat trickled slowly down Simmons' neck. He resisted the urge to reach up and rub it. The hologram projector spilled blue light around him, but no picture formed in the blue lines. He could see nothing of the boss, only hear that cold deadly voice. But he knew the Wolf could see him.

"It's been eight months. That is unacceptable."

"We've almost had the Hillson kids several times since they slipped out of the kingdom, it's not our fault their luck has kept them ahead of us!" Simmons' words came out fast and high. He swallowed and forced his panic down; he knew what had happened to the last man the Wolf had declared "unacceptable." He had to stay on top of this situation and panicking wouldn't help. "We know that they're in KAM, still traveling with the mute musician and his doggy pal. We'll have them delivered to you any day."

"You will, but clearly not if you keep acting on your own ideas," the voice from the projector sneered. The bone plant embedded in Simmon's mandible vibrated and lightning darted through him. Simmons grunted, his face paling. "I've sent you instructions. We have a few projects to take care of, let the Hillsons drop out of sight for a month or two. Take what I just sent to Freddy and tell him to contact the person I've named, and to wait for my call. I'll give more specific instructions on our next heists during that meeting, we have a lot to accomplish. And tell him I'm tired of waiting for him and his FFs to get this Hillson situation under control, I'm going to finish it. It won't take me long. Now go."

Simmons' hand went to his jaw, searching for his instructions as he almost ran from the room. Sweat spilled down spine, soaking his shirt. When the Wolf finished something, it was a very bad day for someone.

Keep reading in

RAVENS RETURN

APPENDICES

903

March 234: *Born in KAM, marked as GI, "adopted" by the Incomplete Keepers of the People's Kingdom.*
April 238: *Successfully ran from the IK Station.*

The boy staggered as he broke from the forest into the sandy wasteland. His small frame seemed more bone than skin. Torn, bleeding, stomach bloated from hunger.

He turned to the east, green eyes searching the horizon, scanning for something. A desperate hope twisted his face. It should have been a young face. He hadn't seen more than four years.

A vast machine crawled over the edge of the horizon into his sight. Rectangular, three-stories tall, metal treads crunching the earth with each grinding foot it moved over the land. The boy's dull eyes brightened, hope sparking over his bloodied, wasted face. He began to run, staggering, lurching, his little legs too short to give him much speed. His arms waved desperately over his head, and even in that moment a part of him cringed; you never drew attention to yourself. It was the quickest way to die.

But he was dying already.

He wouldn't live another day, not out here. Not alone.

His leg buckled under him. The boy stumbled, falling face first onto the hard ground. He pushed himself back up, arms shaking, all of him shaking, and lurched forward. The machine crawled across the horizon, moving steadily, the noise of the engines thrumming through the air. It drowned out the rustling of the black pine needles and even the steady bubbling of the bogs. To the boy those thrumming engines (old, rusted, grating) sounded beautiful. It sounded like hope. Like life.

He knew it was a slaver's caravan. Out combing the area for runners, ready to add whoever might have freed themselves from the stations to their own stock of merchandise. But he didn't care. They would have food. They would have safety from the animals. Medicine for the sickness from the bogs. They had life.

His leg buckled again and he hit the ground. His little arms pushed into the ground, fingers biting into the dry dirt. But he didn't have the strength to raise himself. Not anymore.

A screech came from over his head. Another joined it. Then ten more, merging into a ceaseless cawing shriek. The birds were out hunting again.

The boy curled on the ground. Slowly, painfully, his arm wrapped around his bloated stomach. His face creased with despair, tears washing the dirt and blood from his cheeks. His green eyes closed.

He didn't see the hoverer drop from the belly of the machine. His consciousness had drifted off into dark, painful nightmares of past days. He had experienced so few days in his young life; but every one held a nightmare.

A strafing laser hit the flock of birds. Ten of them tumbled to the ground, feathers smoking, meat fried. The hoverer rushed on, as the flock flew off, cawing its way deeper into the pine woods of the People's Kingdom. The oval wooshed to a stop, and a guard in tactical gear stepped out, laser still at the ready. Her black boots raised small spurts of dust as she strode to the tiny, curled figure and knelt by the boy.

"Is it alive?" the driver asked. The guard ran a black gloved hand over the curled form.

"'He,'" she said, her voice quiet. Not many things still touched her with pity. But something about the little torn form, desperate to flag down even a slavers caravan... "It's a he. Yes, he's still alive." She scooped him into her arms and strode back to the hoverer. "Let's get him back to the caravan while he still has some hope."

August 238: *Picked up by Geego Thomle's slaver caravan.*
January 239: *Sold to Bart Meilson as a pet for his ninth birthday present.*
February 240: *Acquired by the Advancers of KAM for testing.*
March 241: *Bought by Jarl Furt, the Music Maker, traveling musician and cat burglar.*
April 243: *Upon the death of Furt, able to slip off into the street of Hurn in the Kingdom of the Wise.*

June 244: *Captured by Gretta Netters, Purveyor of Inferior Peoples.*

September 244: *Sold to Valus, pawn shop owner in Kallipolis, for odd-jobbing, renting out, and venting anger.*

February 245: *Freedom purchased and home established by Joshua Noble.*

October 246: *Rescued the chimera Cobeau in the People's Kingdom.*

November 248: *Joshua Noble betrayed and slaughtered in the arena of the Battle Kingdom.*

December 250: *Met Nehemiah and Anna Hillson.*

CURRENCY

Currency after the Collapse returned to precious metals. During the Book Base Age no paper currency existed. Each kingdom minted their own coinage. The type and rarity of metal, as well as the weight of the coin, defined its worth. Though sizes, shapes, names, and designs varied from kingdom to kingdom, any coinage was accepted so long as the weight and metals were true to the price to be paid. For example:

The 1 oz Golden Marx from the People's Kingdom is rarely seen in the streets of Freedom and most citizens go their whole life without laying eyes on one. A single such coin could buy a cartload of goods in the People's Kingdom. If that Golden Marx is taken to the Kingdom of Gaia, it will purchase only a barrel load, if you will, because gold is more plentiful and prosperity more general in Gaia. But because 1 oz gold is 1 oz gold no matter where you go, it will be accepted as payment. Though it will likely be sliced into first to ascertain it is pure gold, as most merchants are skeptical of Golden Marxes. Once the merchant in Gaia has enough of the Golden Marxes and other pieces of pure gold to make it worth his copper, he takes them to the Stampers. For a fee the Stampers weigh the precious metal, melt it down, and restamp it into whatever coinage the merchant chooses. A merchant will have it restamped in his kingdom's currency as it is a mark of professionalism and business curtesy to barter in your own country's coinage. A Gaia merchant will likely choose to stamp most of it in the half flower ounce (the "three petal" as it is commonly known), as that is the more common payment form. But he will likely have a few full Gaia flower two ounces (the popular name being the "six petal") made for larger purchases and his own banking ease.

Golden Marxes

CHIMERAS – BREED 49

Year 133 BB

SOLVING
THE
GUARD
CRISIS

Karl Kitchenbur

Chimera Breeder 351

In Review

Ten years ago, it came to my attention that we had a shortage of guards to patrol our CK and IK stations. The numbers of those successfully running from the stations had climbed to nearly 30% annually. (By "success" I mean the runners are not returned to the stations: the majority of those cases who ran ended in death from the elements or wild beasts.) I proposed a simple solution: allow me to breed guards. I chose from my stock DNA samples 720, labeled "Rottweiler," and mixed it with the embryo batch 639. Combined with a regime of training and control I predicted powerful returns for our stations. Now, ten years later, I am in a position to report the results.

Report

Report: Litter 1 – 3 of chimeras labeled "guardogs" have successfully reached a useful age. I would submit the experiment is more than successful, even perhaps brilliant. Allow me to detail this:

Each litter has been honed and sharpened through rigorous training as they grow. Now, at only year ten, each chimera has the strength of a normal guard, as well as intense skill at arms and hand to hand combat. I am confident enough in their training, I would pit any one of my guardogs against any mere human guard, and easily see mine win out. I have begun training a select few in more clandestine arts, as I have noticed they have the ability to move silently despite their bulk. As hunters they have no parallel in the human world.

Being chimeras, they are easily controlled. Each litter has been split into packs, and each pack assigned a human handler. The control collars created by our sister Georgina Smyt has proven the perfect pairing with the guardogs. Once the handlers have the controls to the collars, no challenge is possible, and each chimera falls in line, obeying orders with perfection.

Already the number of runners from the IK and CK stations have dropped to a mere 2% success. Almost all that have attempted to leave have been hunted down and returned to be made an example. I predict the GIs and chimeras will stop trying to run very soon.

Guardogs are quick to learn, quick to obey. As an unexpected bonus, they are both expendable and unable to think for themselves. If sent on foreign missions, success would be highly likely with no chance of the pack taking what they were sent to retrieve and defecting. (A problem, forgive me for noticing, I have seen happen too often in our human guards.) In the event of a pack being caught, they would not be capable of pointing out those who sent them on the mission, or giving any information of use to our enemies in other kingdoms. As I mentioned above, I have begun honing several of the packs for use in this specialized field. If I might make so bold, the ettorts of a certain Hertz and his team might be very easily turned to success by one of my packs.

In closing, I reiterate that these successes by the guardogs come while they are merely age ten. I await their future stories with great interest.

Comparative Skills

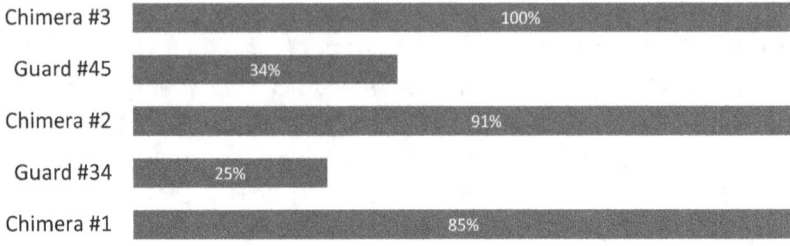

Chimera #3	100%
Guard #45	34%
Chimera #2	91%
Guard #34	25%
Chimera #1	85%

Report: Chimera Litter 308

Begun in the Year 220, BB

Month 1: DNA 720, "Rottweiler," successfully integrated into human embryos 1298-1308.

Month 6: Litter growing at excellent rates. The ones called by the dam "Calla," "Hemsfer," and "Cobeau," especially strong and virile. Hemsfer showing distinct signs of leadership; during a contention over the food bowls two mornings ago he broke the female Callber's arm in two places. A promising beginning for a guardog chimera.

Month 12: Litter graduated from nursery, all running with the packs in the young yard. We have allowed the dam to stay with the litter until further notice. Hemsfer, the alpha male, undecided whether to challenge others in the yard. He seems to be settling for aggression within his own pack for now.

Month 18: An interesting development, Calla and Cobeau together challenged Hemsfer for the pack leadership. It began when Hemsfer again

tackled the female Callber; her arm healed sufficiently, but her spirit has always been of a cowering alpha Z since the food contention. Hemsfer took her down with ease. But then with no visible discussion beforehand, the two large males Calla and Cobeau charged Hemsfer, knocking him four feet with the initial confrontation. In the ensuing scuffle, Hemsfer was forced to retreat to the other end of the yard, where he remained till dark.

Year 2: The litter progresses with training. The female Callber and a male, Oro, did not survive the exposure test. The other eight remain virile, growing daily in strength and hardihood. The three males Hemsfer, Calla, and Cobeau remain the most promising as guardogs. They are more promising than any previous DNA 720 I have bred.

Year 3: The litter is down to six, one a fatality to a fall during obstacle training, one losing to the alligator during combat. Hemsfer ripped the head from the alligator and attempted to devour it whole. Calla is the strongest of the litter, and I matched him with the most seasoned of the alligators. It threw him, and attached to his leg. I checked the male's name off the list, regretting his loss; but I was premature. Cobeau broke the rope keeping him in line with the others, scaled the enclosure wall, leapt onto the alligator, and broke its spine before the reptile could move in for the kill. Cobeau's punishment for entering the enclosure unallowed was severe, yet the two seem only to have grown deeper in each other's affections.

Year 4: I have introduced the control collars, and after some initial difficulty with Hemsfer, the pack has fallen in line. The dam has been removed. I subsequently shifted them into the adolescent yard. They swiftly became the rulers. Hemsfer attacks any who do not cater to him. But not in the presence of Calla and Cobeau. Those two are never separate unless forced apart.

Year 5: Five left in the original litter, but exceptional progress in those who remain.

Year 6: I have begun pairing the litter with older teams, sending them into combat to complete their training with hands on experiences. Calla disobeyed, accompanying Cobeau's team when ordered otherwise, and did so again even after severe punishments. Then Cobeau slipped off to Calla's team. Upon reports of their superb skills I relented and have allowed them to hunt together.

Year 7: Hemsfer has fought his way to second in command of his team. It is the most feared of the yard. If runners hear they are the object of Hemsfer's hunt, the result is often suicide. He is performing better than I could have imagined. Lost one more in the bogs.

Year 8: During Operation Dark Dog[13] Calla and Cobeau lost all of their pack, and only survived by assisting each other. I have chosen to allow them to form their own pack.

Year 9: Hemsfer is the leader of a masterly band of hunters. His littermate Heala has joined his band. Calla and Cobeau remain joint leaders of a quickly progressing band of stealth agents.

Year 10: The remaining littermates have settled into their places. Hemsfer has accepted Heala as his second in command, though the other pack members fluctuate due to a high mortality rate. It is his band most often sent in advance in a hunt after runners. I find myself relying more and more on Calla and Cobeau's pack for stealth operations. They have yet to lose a pack member. The other guardogs have named their pack the Shadow Fangs.

Year 15: The Shadow Fangs have become revered in their skills. Their successful completion of Dark Horse alone earned them a right to the highest recommendations by the brotherhood. When not in combat I keep them in rigorous training and patrolling the fences. Between their skills and the fear of Hemsfer's BloodLusts, the amount of runners has dropped by almost twenty percent this year alone. I trust I am justified in my original assessment of this litter. It has proven my worth as a trainer.

.

---

13 An attempted raid on the Kingdom of the Wise's treasury, gone disastrously wrong and subsequently denied by the People's Kingdom and wiped from their records.

LASERS

The word "laser" started as an acronym, not a word by itself. It stands for Light Amplification by the Stimulated Emission of Radiation. Energy is poured into a lasing medium (a liquid, solid, or gas whose atoms emit light when excited) in order to produce a laser. At its most basic, a laser is a beam of light. But it is light concentrated along narrow, very similar wavelengths. A laser's light has a high concentration of energy. It is able to focus that energy with extreme precision, at the speed of light. (In case you were curious, a phaser is more scientifically accurate than a blaster; the human eye cannot follow the speed of a laser beam, we see it only when it strikes.) If the energy reaches high enough levels, it becomes an effective weapon.

In the early days of research, the main problems with using lasers as a weapon were the source of energy and the heat emitted by the process. It takes so much power to create a weaponized laser, the apparatus used to excite the atoms was too heavy for even a tank to carry, and handheld weapons were out of the question. Also, most of a laser's energy burns off as heat, before the laser light becomes strong enough to be useful. One more problem with the practicality of lasers was atmospheric interference. A high concentration of dust or water in the air might tamper with a laser's accuracy, bending the beam, or causing it to reflect off the atmospheric conditions.

The first two problems were finally solved by the Pylum battery. A man named Ralph Pylum, in the year 20 of the Book Base Age, discovered a battery powered by heat. It is the perfect solution for a laser weapon energy source. The Pylum battery requires an initial charge, which it uses to start the lasing process in a weapon. The laser passes through its chosen medium and begins to bounce between a complicated series of mirrors, increasing the atoms' excitement and thus the power of the laser. This is called priming. Some take more time than others to reach a weaponized level of energy, it depends on many factors including the size of the battery and the medium chosen. But as it primes, the laser is giving off wave after wave of heat. The Pylum battery absorbs it and uses the energy. This creates a weapon which basically powers itself. If allowed to sit unused for some time the battery loses its charge and needs a "jump start" of external heat to start the lasing process. But if kept in proper order, a Pylum battery laser will provide its own energy indefinitely.

Atmospheric conditions are still an issue with some lasers, throwing off the accuracy. The lens of a laser (what the beam is finally sent through, after the energy has climbed to useful levels) as well as the lasing medium affect the accuracy. It is possible for the beams to be reflected back, or even scattered. This kind of reflection would be too weak to cause much damage, unless they landed in a person's fragile eyes. Because of this danger lasers are never to be fired without safety-dyed goggles.

Compton

A revolutionary weapon, the Compton laser is the first to utilize dark energy and matter as an energy source. Two balls of carefully fashioned Z shielding are bound next to each other in a copper fitting. Inside one is a ball of dark matter, inside the other dark energy; they are small enough as to be almost trace amounts. But when activated, a "window" is cracked between the two. Dark matter and dark energy excite each other when combined, and create what science currently sees as an inexhaustible source of energy. The gun then utilizes Compton scattering between the two balls to harvest gamma rays. The rays are fired through a diamond lens fashioned after the Krackmens' excellent design. Gamma rays are invisible to the human eye, and so most Compton guns are sold with specially dyed goggles to allow the shooter to see where his rays land. Currently thought inexhaustible, nearly unbreakable, and as small as a Ruby laser (though considerably heavier), a Compton is viewed as the best weapons breakthrough since the Pylum battery.

Priming: 0 seconds
Holds Charge: Unknown
Weight: 9.4 pounds
Accuracy: Very Exceptional

Krackmens

The Krackmen is a prepossessing weapon with its intricately crafted red carbon stock. It is a dye laser utilizing rhodamine. The lens is a carefully shaped diamond and the accuracy is legendary, making this a popular weapon with many. The priming time is a serious drawback to the weapon.

Priming: 7 seconds
Holds Charge: 1 week
Weight: 15.9 pounds
Accuracy: Exceptional

Ruby

A mass market weapon, the Ruby is a solid-state laser found in most kingdoms during the Book Base Age. It employs a synthetic ruby rod as a medium and is prized for its small size. Because of the single-handed size, the battery is necessarily smaller, making the power less effective. It creates a lethal laser shot, but only at a range of up to six feet. A popular choice for personal defense, but not optimal as an army weapon.

Priming: 4 seconds
Holds Charge: 5 days
Weight: 6.3 pounds
Accuracy: Average

Tolen 43

Nevil Tolen went through 42 versions of this rifle, before he settled on the argon-fluoride as a medium. The combination of inert and reactive gas creates ultraviolet light wavelengths. It is a reliable weapon. But creating enough energy to weaponize the laser takes a large battery indeed, and also more time than many would like. Nevil Tolen fashioned the stock and barrel of the rifle from carbon, in an attempt to mitigate some of the weight from the battery. Those who want a laser that is steady, sturdy, and reliable often choose the Tolen 43.

Priming: 6 seconds
Holds Charge: 2 weeks
Weight: 22.3 pounds
Accuracy: Decent

KINGDOMS WORLDVIEWS

The Kingdom of Autonomous Man (KAM)

Book Base
Humanist Manifestos, I, II, and III
Copywrite by the American Humanist Association.

Government Structure

Humanists are concerned for the well being of all, are committed to diversity, and respect those of differing yet humane views. We work to uphold the equal enjoyment of human rights and civil liberties in an open, secular society and maintain it is a civic duty to participate in the democratic process and a planetary duty to protect nature's integrity, diversity, and beauty in a secure, sustainable manner. [Manifesto III]

The here and now is all that is. We, as the highest race, have the ability and responsibility to help each other and the world around us. Science and socialized government can achieve these goals.

These are at the core of how KAM functions.

The Kingdom of Autonomous Man exists as a haven of free thought and open hands. Provided newcomers do not strive to propagate a religion based on deities that cannot be proved scientifically. Or attempt to hoard or monopolize their commercial business. Or knowingly cause harm to other citizens. If these (and a few other reasonable limitations) are adhered to, there is little that is outlawed within the kingdom. Free expression is applauded.

The government consists of a body of two-hundred officials, elected by the citizenry of the kingdom. General elections are held every five years. After the general elections, a minutia election is held; four double officials are elected from within the body of the two-hundred. These four become overseers of the affairs of state. Out of those four, one is selected to be the highest official, affectionately (and unofficially) termed "the chairman." It is the duty of the chairman to be the tie breaker among the four double officials, and the chair is usually seen as the true leader of KAM.

The freedom for people to do what they like, the natural resources and industries, as well as the inclination to accent hard work and individual accountability, have compiled to make KAM a prosperous kingdom. The government requires heavy taxation from its people and distributes the accumulated funds to those people and institutions it deems necessary.

Religious humanism maintains that all associations and institutions exist for the fulfillment of human life. The intelligent evaluation, transformation, control, and direction of such associations and institutions with a view to the enhancement of human life is the purpose and program of humanism... A socialized and cooperative economic order must be established to the end that the equitable distribution of the means of life be possible. [Manifesto I]

Some have expostulated this has resulted in a large number of people who do not embrace the need to pour their work into the society to benefit the general mankind. In a word, panhandlers, who care only for a free handout and not for their neighbors. It is a verifiable fact that the outskirts of the larger cities have become rundown areas where rent is not charged and people who do not earn paychecks emerge to beg from those who do earn.

Others have noted (in political criticisms or letters of complaint to KAM's government) that the over taxation of the wealthier citizens causes migrations to other kingdoms. It is again, a verifiable fact that almost every person within the higher wealth bracket immigrate to some other large advanced kingdom.

Incompletes and Chimeras

FIRST: Religious humanists regard the universe as self-existing and not created. SECOND: Humanism believes that

*man is a part of nature and that he has emerged as a result
of a continuous process... [Manifesto I]*

*Humanists find that science is the best method for deter-
mining this knowledge as well as for solving problems and
developing beneficial technologies... Humanists ground
values in human welfare shaped by human circumstances,
interests, and concerns and extended to the global ecosystem and beyond. We are committed to treating each person
as having inherent worth and dignity, and to making informed choices in a context of freedom consonant with responsibility. [Manifesto III]*

KAM upholds the theory of evolutionary science. That mankind is evolving continuously to a higher state. The state funds a
great many scientific institutes and research labs, including the
prestigious Institute of Science and Advancement located in the
center of its capital. Individuals within the kingdom look forward
to their children becoming a part of the higher races that will develop as chance, nature, and scientific man mold them.

Those born without all the natural abilities are not fully
formed humans, in KAM's judgment. Those without fully developed intelligence, or without the power of speech or hearing,
those who are born genetically imperfect, are considered lower
down on the evolutionary tract. They have somehow missed a
step on the ladder, and are therefore not fully human; like an
ape, one of our long-time ancestors. They are Genetic Incompletes.

It is unacceptable for a GI to remain in KAM. The citizenry
have been known to be sentimental over the subject, and it is also possible a slipup might cause a whole strand of incompletes
to infect the human line. The citizens are not allowed to keep GIs,
they are only allowed for exportation to other kingdoms.

[Warning: Mildly Graphic Topic] The Advancers have instituted very similar policies about GIs as they use with stray animals
taken in KAM. When a GI reaches an age that their bodies develop from juvenile into a more mature adult (typically between 12
or 13), they are carefully sterilized to guard against polluting the
human race. Most GIs dealt with by the Advancers are newborns

from KAM's hospitals, and are not yet eligible for sterilization. But occasionally stray GIs are taken within the kingdom, or those who return again for reasons unknown. If a GI returns for the fourth time, after the usual tests have been processed (typically a period of twenty-four hours), the GI is marked as an "uncooperative troublemaker" and administered a lethal dose of pentobarbital. In such cases, it is considered an unnecessary expenditure to also apply the sterilization.

Sometimes, in the quest for knowledge and further medical advancement a GI is acquired for testing purposes. But KAM is very careful to provide good care and has a policy of never keeping a single test subject for over eighteen months. They make a point of being a humanitarian kingdom.

Chimeras are several rungs lower down the evolutionary ladder than GIs. They are interesting animals, and if properly kept in check, are allowed to be owned as workers inside the kingdom. The state has instituted a restriction on the numbers, however, and closely monitors the chimeras within KAM. There is a moratorium within the kingdom against creating more chimeras. As one prestigious KAM professor put it, "We know now no higher race will come from a mix of animal and human genes. It is a step backward on the evolutionary track, not forward."

Art and Music

Humanists find that science is the best method for determining this knowledge as well as for solving problems and developing beneficial technologies. We also recognize the value of new departures in thought, the arts, and inner experience—each subject to analysis by critical intelligence. [Manifesto III]

This is a continuation of the same quote used in the discussion of incompletes and chimeras. In order to gain a full understanding of KAM's books, it should be recognized that while science is held in high importance, the benefit of mankind is held even higher. Art and music fall under the category of bringing value to humanity, and so are prized. Free expression and individuality are carefully husbanded by the state and citizenry of

KAM. That, and a fairly high immigration rate and general prosperity, makes the arts within KAM a virile and eclectic community.

Science and Advancements

Science has sometimes brought evil as well as good... Using technology wisely, we can control our environment, conquer poverty, markedly reduce disease, extend our lifespan, significantly modify our behavior, alter the course of human evolution and cultural development, unlock vast new powers, and provide humankind with unparalleled opportunity for achieving an abundant and meaningful life. [Manifesto II]

Science is the trump card and the hope of KAM. With time and the proper breakthroughs, man should be able to conquer all problems through scientific advancements. The state funds numerous scientific studies and labs across the kingdom. Most national holidays are based on some portion of science.

Army

Humanists long for and strive toward a world of mutual care and concern, free of cruelty and its consequences, where differences are resolved cooperatively without resorting to violence. The joining of individuality with interdependence enriches our lives, encourages us to enrich the lives of others, and inspires hope of attaining peace, justice, and opportunity for all. [Manifesto III]

KAM is not a warlike kingdom. They do not strive to expand their territory at the expense of other kingdoms, or to exact vengeance on rivals. However, they are a practical people. Other kingdoms are warlike, and envy KAM's natural resources and prosperity. KAM found it necessary to have a standing army for defense.

KAM's army is outfitted with modern kit, and well trained. The other kingdoms tend to view it as a well-fed tiger resting in its lair. Nothing to worry about unless you tread on their toes;

but when roused, beware, they are very capable of finishing what you start.

Social Structure

Ethical values are derived from human need and interest as tested by experience...

Life's fulfillment emerges from individual participation in the service of humane ideals...

Working to benefit society maximizes individual happiness. Progressive cultures have worked to free humanity from the brutalities of mere survival and to reduce suffering, improve society, and develop global community. We seek to minimize the inequities of circumstance and ability, and we support a just distribution of nature's resources and the fruits of human effort so that as many as possible can enjoy a good life. [Manifesto III]

The here and now is all that is. We, as the highest race, have the ability and responsibility to help each other and the world around us. Science and socialization of the Kingdom's wealth can achieve both goals.

How do these play out in reality in the kingdom? Mostly in education, taxation, and hard work. Everyone has a job. Most see their worth through how well they can help society through what they do, and how good a paycheck they achieve. Social status (how big my house, how fancy my vehicle) is a large factor inside KAM, as it is very difficult to measure *"inherent worth and dignity" (Manifesto III)* without anything to go on except hopefully being evolved enough to be part of the higher race. How much you earn is one measuring tool. It would be quite inaccurate to say it is the only one, however. Many find their worth in training the next generation, or creating beneficial scientific breakthroughs, counseling the needy, any number of things to help their fellow man.

The new generation is the hope of the kingdom, and they are treated as such. Parents receive substantial stipends from the government for each child. Large families (more than four children in a home) are frowned on, however, as it poses a greater possibility of poor conditioning during the formative years, and also risks overpopulating the world. Enrollment in the government schools is required, and teachers are kept strictly to curriculum developed to form proper adherents to KAM's philosophy.

Anyone is welcomed within the borders of KAM. If someone holds ideas different from theirs, they are mostly shrugged off and tolerated. However, if someone insists that ideas different from the Manifestos are the *only* correct ones, and insists that KAM's philosophy is false, that begins to pose a problem. Young people might listen to the agitators, and it could cause unrest in the social system. If an agitator continues to hold onto their own subversive ideas, they will find themselves arrested, and sent to a center in the mountains. The Center is run by the Advancers, and it employs a great number of phycologists and brain specialists, as well as a few philosophers and experimental doctors. It is believed that such cases are victims of their upbringing or an inherent lack within themselves. Those interned in the Center are treated more as insane and sick then as law-breakers.

If, after a period of two years, no progress has been made on an agitator and they still insist on holding to their subversive ideas, they are deported to other kingdoms. If they are deemed "cooperative" they are allowed back in KAM, but surveillance is required to be certain they do not relapse into former thinking.

The Kingdom of the Prophet's Peace

Book Base
The Koran
Rodwell, J.M. translator, *The Koran*. Everyman, 1909. Phoenix Paperback, division of Orion Publishing Group, 2001.

Government Structure
> *Your God is one God: there is no God but He, the Compassionate, the Merciful. [2:158]*

And SAY: Praise be to God who hath not begotten a son, who hath no partner in the Kingdom, nor any protector on account of weakness. [17:111]

The faithful of both sexes are mutual friends: they enjoin what is just, and forbid what is evil; they observe prayer, and pay the legal impost, and they obey God and His Apostle. On these will God have mercy: verily, God is Mighty, Wise.

To the faithful, both men and women, God promiseth gardens 'neath which the rivers flow, in which they shall abide, and goodly mansions in the gardens of Eden. But best of all will be God's good pleasure in them. This will be the great bliss.

O Prophet! contend against the infidels and the hypocrites and be rigorous with them: Hell shall be their dwelling place! Wretched the journey thither! [9:3-6]

Allah is the Almighty, Wise ruler, and all must be done in submission to his rules. Paradise waits for the believer who submits and obeys. The Muslims do not see themselves as simply a kingdom based off a book. They are the only faithful ones, the kingdom of Allah's chosen people and he is their ruler.

A Muslim would say the Kingdom of the Prophet's Peace is a theocracy, with Allah appointing the Caliph. The rest of the world looks at their Caliph and says it is a dictatorship; the Caliph's word is supreme.

A Muslim believes all men start out as a blank slate, and must choose to be believers. Those who do not become believers, are infidels who resist the truth of the Koran. Their book has a great deal to say about how Allah despises the infidels, and of their miseries in Hell in the next life. Believers are expected to follow all that Allah prescribes, and he is precise in his orders. An oft quoted line, in one form or another in the book, is *"they enjoin what is just, and forbid what is evil; they observe prayer, and pay the legal impost, and they obey God and His Apostle." [9:3]* For fear of their soul and eternal fire, each Muslim is careful to obey the law, and watches jealously over justice. They strive to be fair and generous amongst themselves.

The Caliph oversees the laws, passing them to local courts and law-enforcement officers. The kingdom's prestigious and numerous army are always available for backing up local officers if needed. The punishments are harsh for disobeying. It creates a safe haven for any believer, as well as making it very difficult for an infidel to remain secret within the border of the Prophet's Peace.

There are seven main things all citizens of the Prophet's Peace must do in order to be a good Muslim (and not be arrested under suspicion of being an infidel). The first is to make a sincere profession of faith. Second, purity, in mind and soul, and (according to some definitions of the Koran) in rituals of cleanliness. Third, to pray: five times daily, at prescribed moments, and toward where they believe the ancient city of Mecca used to exist. Fourth, alms-giving to the less fortunate than themselves among the believers. Fifth, fasting during Ramadan the holy month. Sixth, once in their lifetime to make a pilgrimage to Mecca. This sixth decree of Islam has distressed the Muslims of the Book Age, especially those of the earliest days; in a world devastated and rearranged by nuclear fallout and natural disasters, where *is* Mecca? After two generations of intensive study, archeological data scans, and studying the Koran, they finally settled upon the likeliest place. The Prophet's Peace moved in a body three hundred miles across the wild lands (overtaking two smaller kingdoms on their route and swallowing them whole). Now, it is believed Mecca lies at the heart of the kingdom. Most citizens make the religious journey there yearly.

The seventh decree is to struggle, or contend; it has two main interpretations, and how the Caliph interprets this commandment changes the policies of the nation.

One definition all Muslims agree on, is that they should struggle in their own lives to be wholly obedient and submissive to Allah and his ways. That, as it were, goes without saying in their religion. The second interpretation is to physically make holy war upon the infidels. All Muslims agree this is needed sometimes (for a few select passages from their Koran see "Army"). In the earlier days of the Book Age the majority of Caliphs saw it more as a command to self-defense, and to purge their own kingdom of infidels. But as time went on, the kingdom became more settled and prosperous, and the army continued to be strong and large, more and more Caliphs turned their eyes outside their borders. The Koranic scholars agree waging physical war on those who refuse to convert to the Koran is a legitimate interpretation of the book's meaning. The debate lies in whether the *main* meaning of the texts is in physical war or inner-personal war.

The Kingdom of the Prophet's Peace often ventures outside their borders and attacks various kingdoms. They are well-trained, large, well-kitted, and wise about it. Most often it is the smaller kingdoms they make war on, overwhelming them by numbers and superior weaponry. Once overwhelmed, the kingdoms become offshoots of the Prophet's Peace, with local governors appointed by the Caliph and directly responsible to him.

The people inside conquered kingdoms are required to convert to Islam. In the earlier days of the Prophet's Peace, Caliphs experimented with allowing conquered people to have their ruler make a perfunctory confession of faith. The rest of the kingdom would then be subjected to a high tax rate, as "allies" somewhere between infidels and true believers. But as the years progressed, prosperity took firmer hold within the kingdom, and Caliphs watched several of their offshoots revolt and regain their independence, policy changed. During the year 156 of the Book Age, Caliph Mohammad Al-Mufta made a blanket law that all within the dominion of the Prophet's Peace, including offshoots, are required to make a valid confession and live as a true Muslim, or else be subject to enslavement or death. That is still the official policy.

Incompletes and Chimeras

If good fortune betide them, they say, 'This is from God;' and if evil betide them, they say, 'This is from thee.' SAY: All is from God: [4:80]

And let those be afraid to wrong the orphans, who, should they leave behind them weakly offspring, would be solicitous on their account. Let them, therefore, fear God, and let them propose what is right. [4:10]

And entrust not to the incapable the substance which God hath placed with you for their support; but maintain them therewith, and clothe them, and speak to them with kindly speech. [4:4]

Allah is truly sovereign, and therefore those who are born not perfect, it is by his will. So long as they are true believers among the faithful, they are to be treated with kind words and not oppressed. In the philosophy of the Prophet's Peace, there are no incompletes.

In the Koran [4:118], we see Satan talking to Allah; *"'A portion of thy servants will I surely take, and will lead them astray...and I will command them and they will alter the creation of God.'"* Chimeras are considered a corruption of Allah's creation. Creating new chimeras is outlawed within the Prophet's Peace. Existing chimeras are treated with pity, and (so long as they are considered as among the faithful) are often the objects of alms-giving.

Art and Music

Yet have they adopted gods beside Him which have created nothing, but were themselves created: [25:3]

There are no direct injunctions about art or music in the Koran. The above quoted text (Sura 25:3), however, has been taken by Koranic scholars to mean the act of creation itself is frowned upon. At the beginning of the Book Age, there was a nagging memory of art being forbidden by other texts than the Koran, texts that are no longer available. But mankind has an innate desire to create, and art will be formed in any culture. With further meditation on the text, it was decided it is an injunction against creating images of living things: Allah is the creator of life, and the faithful are not. Mosaics, tapestries, patterns, many beautiful things are created within the Kingdom of the Prophet's Peace.

There is no direct text on music. It is only commanded that the faithful abstain from any type of music or lyric that is impure.

Science and Advancements

Assuredly in the creation of the Heavens and of the Earth; and in the alternation of the night and day; and in the ships which pass through the sea with what is useful to man; and in the rain which God sendeth down from Heaven, giving life by it to the earth after its death, and by scattering over it all kinds of cattle; and the change of the winds, and in the clouds that are made to do service between the Heaven and the Earth; - are signs for those who understand. [2:159]

The Koran has various statements about creation and how it works, and about the importance of gaining understanding. The sciences are researched and enjoyed within the Prophet's Peace, and great breakthroughs have been made historically within the kingdom's borders. However, greater even than a love of science is a fear of overstepping Allah's laws. That fear runs underneath every Muslim's actions; it tends to trump most scientific studies and keep them studying things that are known absolutely to be allowed by the Koran.

Army

And when the sacred months are passed, kill those who join other gods with God wherever ye shall find them; and seize them, besiege them, and lay wait for them with every kind of ambush: but if they shall convert, and observe prayer, and pay the obligatory alms, then let them go their way, for God is Gracious, Merciful. [9:5]

Make war upon such of those to whom the Scriptures have been given as believe not in God, or in the last day, and who forbid not that which God and His Apostle have forbidden, and who profess not the profession of the truth, until they pay tribute out of hand, and they be humbled. [9:29]

They desire that ye should be infidels as they are infidels, and that ye should be alike. Take therefore none of them for friends, till they have fled their homes for the cause of God. If they turn back, then seize them, and slay them wherever ye find them; but take none of them as friends or helpers,

Except those who shall seek and asylum among your allies, and those who come over to you... But if they depart from you, and make not war against you and offer you peace, then God alloweth you no occasion against them. [4:91]

O believers! when ye go forth to the fight for the cause of God, be discerning, and say not to every one who meetheth you with a greeting, 'Thou art not a believer' in your greed after the chance good things of this present life!... Those believers who sit at home free from trouble, and those who do valiantly in the cause of God with their substance and their person shall not be treated alike. God hath assigned to those who contend earnestly with their persons and with their substance, a rank above those who sit still at home, [4:96-97]

Let those then fight on the path of God, who barter this present life for that which is to come; for whoever fighteth on God's path, whether he be slain or conquer, we will in the end give him a great reward. [4:76]

Verily, of the faithful hath God bought their person and their substance, on condition of Paradise for them in return: on the path of God shall they fight, and slay, and be slain: a promise of this is pledged in the Law, and in the Evangel, and in the Koran – and who more faithful to his engagement than God? Rejoice, therefore, in the contract that ye have contracted: for this shall be the great bliss. [9:112]

The last passage quoted (Sura 9:112) Koranic scholars unanimously interpret one way; if you give everything in Allah's war against the infidels, you are assured of paradise. In a religion where everything points to the next world, and yet offers no assurance of gaining paradise except this, the injunction becomes very compelling. Being the only sure way to paradise, combined with passages such as Sura 4:97 stating Allah gives greater reward to those who war than those who cry for peace or sit still at home, insure the Prophet's Peace a large voluntary force of fighters.

The Kingdom of the Prophet's Peace has a massive army. Partially because of the largeness of the army, they often work within the kingdom to assist law-enforcement. But most join in order to wage war on the infidel, not keep believers in line; for the sake of moral as well as the commandments of the Koran, the army looks past their borders as much as possible. Every one of their soldiers is willing to give their body and soul to the cause. They favor attacking at night, when the enemy is unprepared, and as such have chosen to uniform their soldiers in black. The rest of the world has termed them, the Black Forces.

They are religiously trained and extensively kitted with the latest and best in weaponry. It is rare that a kingdom can withstand their onslaughts. It has been stated (by a Gaia diplomat), "The only reason the world isn't already overrun by the Black Forces is the miles of wild lands filled with roaming, giant, carnivorous hunters lying between kingdoms." It is a verifiable fact that the distance between kingdoms is extremely difficult to march armies across. When tried, a tactician allots a third of their force to die before ever reaching their goal; that is generally an understatement. It is not unheard of for whole armies to perish in the wild lands as they try to navigate to enemy kingdoms. Large forces signal large amounts of meat to hunters.

Social Structure

There is no piety in turning your faces towards the east or the west, but he is pious who beleiveth in God, and the last day, and the angels, and the Scriptures, and the prophets; who for the love of God disburseth his wealth to his kindred, and to the orphans, and the needy, and the wayfarer, and those who ask, and for ransoming; who observeth prayer, and payeth the legal alms, and who is of those who are faithful to their engagements when they have engaged in them, and patient under ills and hardships, and in times of trouble: these are they who are just, and these are they who fear the Lord. [2:173]

And if ye are apprehensive that ye shall not deal fairly with orphans, then, of other women who seem good in your eyes, marry but two, or three, or four; and if ye still fear that ye shall not act equitably, then one only; or the slaves whom ye have acquired: this will make justice on your part easier. Give women their dowry freely; but if of themselves they give up aught thereof to you, then enjoy it as convenient, and profitable: [4:3]

With regard to your children, God commandeth you to give the male the portion of two females; [4:12]

The men shall have a portion according to their deserts, and the women a portion according to their desert. Of God, therefore, as his gifts. [4:36]

O Prophet! speak to thy wives and to thy daughters, and to the wives of the Faithful, that they let their veils fall low. Thus will they more easily be known, and they will not be affronted. God is Indulgent, Merciful! [33:59]

Men are superior to women on account of the qualities with which God hath gifted the one above the other, and on account of the outlay they make from their substance for them. Virtuous women are obedient, careful, during the husband's absence, because God hath of them been careful. But chide those for whose refractoriness ye have cause to fear; remove them into beds apart, and scourge them: but if they are obedient to you, then seek not occasion against them: verily, God is High, Great! [4:38]

Men are very firmly in charge in Islamic society. They are called by the Koran to be kind to their wives. But there are also commandments to scourge the disobedient wife, and provisions are made for divorcement once past childbearing age, or if a wife no longer gives pleasure to a man (Sura 65). Much of the treatment of women in Islamic society comes down to the personality and choices of individual husbands and fathers. There are those who are harsh and cruel, and who marry many wives and indulge in collecting slaves to supplement. There are others who are careful and gentle, choose only one wife, and love her and care for her well.

Women are not allowed to join the army. Therefore, in a society where wars is not only a normal occurrence but a commendable action, there are not always enough men to go around. This is another practical reason you find one man with many wives within the country. Parents are not averse to marrying their daughters young, if the match is good.

Women wear loose, long clothing in public, along with veils over their faces.

Slavery is allowed, especially of the infidels and those taken in battle.

It is a prosperous kingdom, where the faithful are free to do what they like and live as they choose; so long as they adhere to the Koran in all things. It is easy to appeal to the law, and justice according to their book is freely and quickly administered. Praying five times a day has the effect of keeping everyone firmly focused on their religion, and remembering Allah and the next life. Because it is a religion where the only way to Paradise is through good deeds to please Allah, and if you fail you get Hell fires (very vividly and often described in the Koran), it creates a kingdom of law-abiding citizens. A whole kingdom of mostly law-abiding citizens creates an outward aura of peace within the borders of the Prophet's Peace.

The Kingdom of Gaia

Book Base
New Age and Neopagan Religions in America
Rodwell, Sarah M., *New Age and Neopagan Religions in America*. Columbia University Press, 2004.

Government Structure

For them the path of personal spiritual progress is central to life and is the best way to effect changes in the world around them. But it is hard to say that anything is typical of the New Age and Neopagan movements, which have been from the start diverse and individualistic. (Pg. 14)

For New Agers, self-growth techniques and physical healing practices are based on the assumption that positive thinking most effectively produces change. They believe that salvation comes through the discovery and cultivation of a divine inner self with the help of techniques that can be learned from books and workshops as well as spiritual teachers. In addition to positive thinking, they emphasize the idea that negative experiences are illusory and that it is within human ability to change them to positive ones. (Pg. 23)

Seth, and entity channeled by trance medium Jane Roberts during the 1960s, told Roberts that he had experienced many lifetimes and eventually became "an energy personality essence no longer focused in physical reality"... "Seth," for example, says that the purpose of his communication to humans is to provide "a means by which people can understand themselves better, reevaluate their reality, and change it." (Pg. 28)

Their goal is to create an alternate society that will eventually replace the one we live in. (Pg. 23)

It is difficult to reduce the Kingdom of Gaia to a single definition. Individual ideas and ways of living are prized above everything; their book is the only thing held in common by all living within its borders. We will deal here with "mosts."

Most citizens are polytheistic. Most of the Neopagans have made their home in the north of the kingdom, and there the horned god and the goddess of plenty are most widely recognized and worshiped. But within the majority of the kingdom, pantheism runs riot with polytheism. You are just as likely to find people with shrines to the horned god and also outside trying to speak to the divinity of the carrots to learn how to help their crop grow. In the majority of the kingdom, it is believed that all things are a part of the divine.

Everything makes up the great energy flow that is the divineness of the universe. Once an individual reaches a proper state of enlightenment, they too will become absorbed into the great life flow of the universe. Most call this life flow the Gaia.

Because all solid things will one day be dissolved into the energy flow, spiritualism and internal choices and wellbeing rank very high above the mundane solidity of what we can see, taste, and feel. Government is one of those solid things that are, while not scorned (everything has an effect on everything else and is therefore important), not as vital. The government of the Gaia wasn't voted in, or organized in any particular fashion. It formed like water flowing into an empty space in a sink. There was a hole, it needed filled, and those with leadership qualities flowed in and filled it. They created the Coalition. It has no set number of seats. To become a member one has only to fill out a few forms. Throughout the kingdom's history, the largest Coalition has been two-hundred and twenty seats. Not many within the kingdom have a desire to be involved in the sordid details of running a kingdom.

Once the Coalition formed, they took a page from KAM and elected people within their number to create committees for the oversight of various matters. There is one for the Recyclers (see Army), another for roads and transportation, one for the penal system (see social structure), for internal markets, for outside trade, etc. The Coalition does not have a central leader. But they do have an Ambassador, who acts as the figurehead of Gaia to the rest of the kingdoms. The Ambassador doesn't have particular power to make changes within the kingdom, no more than anyone else in the Coalition. But they keep themselves well versed in the doings outside their borders, and are quick to spot infringements to their kingdom's safety, and the more subtle influences that might upset the spiritual climb of Gaia's citizens.

Almost everyone and anything is welcomed with open arms and smiles into the kingdom. After all, if the Gaia is a part of all things, then all things are a part of us, and are to be drawn in and encouraged to understand where they fit within the universe. However, some things negatively influence people on their spiritual journey. There is a thriving culture of people and methods to help heal past scars (see Social Structure), but the Coalition decided it would be better still if one could stop the damage before it happened. The few laws within the border of the Gaia have to do with the affect on the economy (outright thievery for example), and attempts to keep negative influences away from their citizens.

The definition of "negative influences" changes depending on who is talking about it. But most definitions include those who teach opposing ideas to those central to the Gaia's book. The Prophet's Peace, for example, with their teachings that "There are no gods but Allah," and that everyone must submit wholly to Allah, would be considered a harmful teaching. Muslims are allowed within the border (no one is initially turned away), but those in the Coalition has individuals watched who might be trying to overthrow the kingdom from within. If a Muslim entered and began to try to propagate their book's teachings loudly and profusely, it would be considered a problem. It might cause doubts in the minds of the more vulnerable of their citizens, and retard them on the path to spirituality. Direct speech against Neopaganism and New Ageism is dealt with quickly and thoroughly from the Recyclers of the Coalition.

One of the reasons those within the Gaia are so concerned with helping each other along the right path, is found in the basic makeup of their philosophy. When enough people have reached the right level of spirituality, it will be enough to draw the rest of the world into the energy force of the Gaia. All will be absorbed into the Gaia, and a new age without any negative energy will begin.

They speak in terms of positive and negative energy versus good and evil. To those within the teachings of the Gaia, there is no real good and evil; all things, remember, are a part of the Gaia. In a confusing twist, however, there are better choices and worse choices, and good karma and bad karma. It is unlikely you will get a sense of logic-fulfilled within the Gaia.

Incompletes and Chimeras

Most of them believe in reincarnation (rebirth — the continuity of the soul through many lives) and karma (derived from the Hindu belief that the condition into which each soul is reborn is the result of good or bad actions performed in previous lives), and they look to past lives to help them understand the present. (Pg. 15)

Most in Gaia view incompletes as people suffering from a poor choice made in a past life. They are truly human. (Well, as much as anyone is when everything is a part of the divine; those in Gaia are perfectly comfortable with someone claiming they are actually a radish in their inner spirit. Radishes are also a part of the divine, therefore it might be true that their inner self is more radish-like than human-like.) Incompletes are welcome and treated with the same openness as anyone.

Chimeras are of course made what they are by outside influences, not their own choices. To those in Gaia, tampering with lives in such a fashion is very bad karma. It is considered an outrage within the Gaia, and no one within its borders would dare such damaging of nature's own. Chimeras are welcomed, pitied, and the healers do their best to reach the original child within and heal the damage.

Art and Music

Everything about New Ageism accents self-expression and exploration. Music and art are two of the greatest forms of outward expression. The arts run rampant within the Kingdom of Gaia. There are a plethora of styles and uses. Most of it suits the mood of spiritualism and absence of organization; airy, somewhat vague, always reaching for what can't quite be touched and handled.

Science and Advancements

According to McLean, "God is an indwelling presence, the core of what I am and what everything is." She regularly contacted the Carrot Deva, the Pea Deva, and other plant spirits with questions about how to care for the plants and came to understand that the devas were angelic figures and representations of "the life force." (Pg. 28)

...humans are a part of the web of life that includes trees and animals. Destruction of other living beings, they say, destroys us all. (Pg. 33)

While television increased exposure to new ideas, many young people believed that technological changes were destructive and preached about moving back to nature and simpler lifestyles... Space technology and weapons of mass destruction were in the background of protest against what American society had become because the counterculture rejected the "high gods" of science and technology. (Pg. 75)

Again we find ourselves reduced to speaking of "most" within the kingdom. There are always exceptions to be found in the Kingdom of Gaia. But most within its borders are skeptical about the sciences. The basis of science lies in the five senses, what we can experiment with, and manipulate, and use. With most inside the Kingdom of Gaia, a compound of algae is as much a part of the mother earth as a human, and using it should be done respectfully and carefully.

Science isn't outlawed or even particularly frowned upon, and various people within the kingdom enjoy very advanced systems of living. But as a whole, those within Gaia aren't as interested in gaining scientific knowledge as some of the other kingdoms.

Army
it is 1968
i am a magic realist
i see the adorers of che

i see the black man
forced to accept
violence

i see pacifists
despair

and accept violence

i see all all all
corrupted
by the vibrations

vibrations of violence of civilization
that are shattering
our only world

we want
to zap them
with holiness

we want
to levitate them
with joy

(Pg 76)

This is a portion of a poem by Julian Beck, included in the Gaia's book. Violence is frowned upon. The Kingdom of Gaia is not warlike. They do have an army, and it works hard to drive off the wild animals that would eat the citizens, and is ready to repulse outward attacks from those kingdoms that might try to overrun the Gaia. But necessary defense is the main description of their work.

Inside the kingdom, the military is adjunct to the Recyclers. This select branch of the Coalition is the kingdom's most effective law enforcement, and is also in charge of those who are deemed uncooperative. The ones who refuse to become a part of the social system of the Gaia, who cast off all healing offered to them. Most offenders are sent to specialized healing sanctuaries; there are no prisons, as such, within the Gaia. If the New Age and Neopagan healers fail in their efforts to reclaim the positive energy, and only negativity radiates from an individual, they are sent to the Recyclers. Within the Gaia, it should be remembered, most believe in reincarnation. In their philosophy, when someone dies they are not obliterated, or sent on to a heaven or hell.

They are sent to a different plane of existence, a different life somewhere else.

Killing someone isn't execution. It is recycling negative energy.

Because of this belief, for even minor offenses it can be considered humane to send someone to the Recyclers. If someone remains a petty thief or insists on holding to a hurtful creed, refusing to cooperate with the psychics, witches, and practitioners of the ancient healing arts, recycling them to the next life might give them better karma then they have now.

Officially the Recyclers is the name of the small, committee in the Coalition formed for dealing with such distasteful chores. But they apply to the army for most of the actual leg work. Unofficially, the army of the Gaia is called the Recyclers.

Social Structure

Because they begin with the assumption that the self is sacred or divine, they place the responsibility for change with each individual. (Pg. 37)

Holistic health reflects the basic values of the New Age and Neopagan movements, especially in its focus on interconnectedness and its view that the self mirrors society. (Pg. 95)

Because they believe in the interconnectedness and the unlimited potential of human consciousness, many New Agers think humans have a special responsibility to the rest of the planet. Sometimes this view is accompanied by an understanding of the earth as a living being (called the Gaia hypothesis) put forth by scientist James Lovelock and Lynn Margulis.... Their goal is to create an alternate society that will eventually replace the one we live in. (Pg. 23)

For many New Agers and Neopagans, what they can make a past and current crisis determines the extent of their healing and self-growth... Wounds and traumas almost become an expectation. Participants in healing workshops are encouraged to dig deep into their past, and if they do not find anything that needs healing they may be seen as self deluded. (Pg. 101)

Psychics to help connect with past lives, Neopagan herbal healers, acupuncturists, specialized yoga coaches, purveyors of crystals and incense, these and many other jobs considered healing arts are the highest trafficked sector of the Gaia's economy. Most New Agers spend their life trying to improve their karma, gain a better spiritualism, and so have a better life in the next to come. And as noted in the last quote from the Gaia's book (on page 101), there is such an accent on healing past traumas, it is abnormal to find an individual who considers themselves completely unscathed by their journey in life. Healing the past drives you farther on in your path.

Individualism is the highest prized thing in the kingdom. For most, all is spirit, and no one can see inside another person's spirit life. (Unless you are a psychic, but that is a different case and not to be debated here.) Therefore, what is best for a person, what they need or desire, is up to them. There are very few actual laws banning things. Most people there have the sense to stop debauchery where it hurts other people, especially if it is likely to hurt the next generation. But so long as it is between people who have reached majority and their choices don't destroy someone else, any lifestyle is not only accepted, but applauded.

The economy is fairly robust in the kingdom of Gaia. Part of the philosophy, while having a heavy accent on the individual, also very clearly has a connection to everything else. We are all a part of the same mother earth, the same energy, we are all connected. Helping others where possible is not only laudable, but draws the whole world that much closer to the new age of being swallowed into the Gaia. This means that getting up in the morning and going to work to serve those around you (every job ever made provides some sort of service for someone) is necessary, useful, and laudable. The economy reflects that.

If you mention the Kingdom of Gaia to someone from another kingdom, it almost always conjures up a smile. Most of the Gaia (especially to someone passing through) seems a very friendly, happy, prosperous, sort of vague place, that it is pleasant to visit.

Most travelers avoid the north section of the kingdom.

RECIPE

Quick Pancakes

Makes 1 dozen 4 inch pancakes, when you need a swift break-fast; or dinner.

1 cup flour
1/8 cup sugar
2 ½ tsp baking powder
1 cup milk
1 egg
1 Tbs oil
1 tsp vanilla
Butter

Mix the dry ingredients in a bowl. Add the rest of the ingredients and either whist or beat till it is smooth and there are no more lumps. Heat your skillet or griddle and run the butter over it liberally; you will know your griddle is hot enough when the butter bubbles up a bit. Pour a round of batter onto the griddle for each pancake. Let it cook till the top begins to form bubbles. Flip to the other side till it is golden brown, or cooked to your desired "perfect pancake state." (I personally like them barely cooked, still almost doughy.)

Sign Language Alphabet

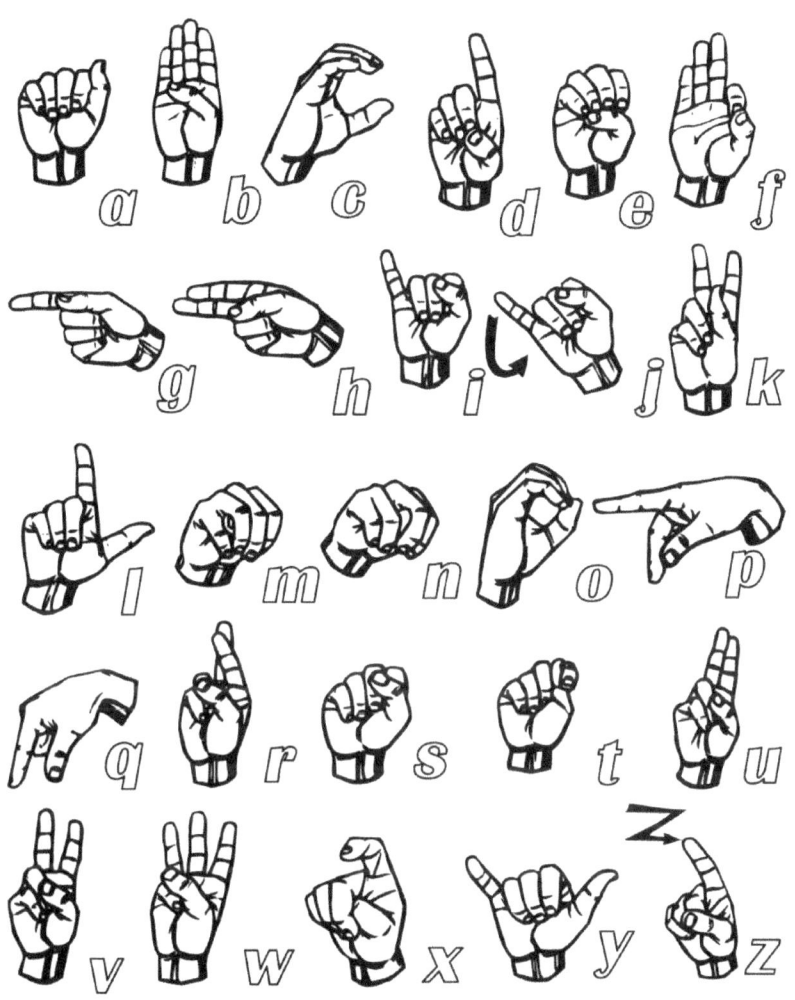

AUTHOR BIO

Catherine Gruben Smith lives in the middle of Texas, which she begrudgingly admits is probably better than a magical tower. She grew up mostly in a dusty town in the southern New Mexican desert and will always carry the quirks. (Yes, New Mexico is a part of the United States, and no, she was not a missionary, and yes, you can drink the water.) It is her delight and privilege to be a housewife, mother, and an Earl  Gray connoisseur. Another of her constant activities is trying to keep her dogs from terrorizing the house and neighborhood with their determination to be always underfoot and hungry. (The work of a dog lover is never done.) She has always been fascinated by the written word, philosophical reasoning, and good stories of bravery and honor. When not writing, reading, chasing children or dogs, Catherine can be found board-gaming, baking, hiking, or possibly broad sword fighting with her older brother. If you want a fuller explanation of Catherine, go and read Psalm 30. The heart and purpose of her life can be found there, especially in the last two verses.

Catherine prays reading her books will help her readers find the urge to get up off the couch and serve. The Lord of all life calls us to the battlefield, to mop up the enemy after He has won the war. Don't sit on the side-lines. We have the tools to fix this broken world.

Where to find more information, or contact Catherine:
catherinegrubensmith.com
catherinegrubensmith@gmail.com
posttenebrasluxbooks.com

Books by Catherine Gruben Smith

Parabaloni Series:
The Parabaloni
The Slingshot Effect
As the Eagle Flies
Solitaire
Adele Angst
Blind Leader

Dreaded King Saga:
A Son Rises
Reign Falls
Knight Duty
Heir Raising
Splitting Heirs

Faerytales of Deweot:
How to Unmake a Dragon
Faery Wings and Pirate Things

Sojourners:
Ravens Ruins
Ravens Rescue
Ravens Return
Ravens Refuge
Ravens Raid

www.ingramcontent.com/pod-product-compliance
Lightning Source LLC
Chambersburg PA
CBHW060537260626
47161CB00003B/935